FELICIA'S JOURNEY

'Extraordinary . . . you find yourself in the almost unbreakable hold of Trevor's narrative. The prose is crystalline, the artistry absolutely unerring; if there's a word out of place in *Felicia's Journey*, it's not to be detected with the human senses.' *The Financial Post*

'A subtle, plausible and infinitely pathetic portrait of a monster. Trevor shows just how wise and wry and funny and morally astute an observer of the human comedy he is. Frighteningly real . . .'
The New York Times Book Review

'A thriller with a psychological edge that lifts it well above normal whodunits.' *The Star Phoenix*, Saskatoon

'Trevor is a master of both language and storytelling, and in his hands the story ripples with irony and crawls with menace . . . This sinister, elegant, piercingly sad novel is surely one of the books of the year.' *Sunday Express*, London

'One of those rare pieces of literature that will awaken the sensibilities of almost any reader . . . A page-turner marked by brilliant psychological suspense.' *The Philadelphia Inquirer*

William Trevor was born in Mitchelstown, Co. Cork, in 1928 and spent his childhood in provincial Ireland. He attended a number of Irish schools and later Trinity College, Dublin. He is a member of the Irish Academy of Letters.

Among his books are *The Old Boys* (1964), winner of the Hawthornden Prize, *The Boarding-House* (1965), *The Love Department* (1966), *Mrs Eckdorf in O'Neill's Hotel* (1969), *Miss Gomez and the Brethren* (1971), *Elizabeth Alone* (1973), *The Children of Dynmouth* (1976), winner of the Whitbread Award, *Other People's Worlds* (1980), *Fools of Fortune* (1983), winner of the Whitbread Award, *A Writer's Ireland* (1984), *The Silence in the Garden* (1988), winner of the *Yorkshire Post* Book of the Year Award, and *Two Lives* (1991), which was shortlisted for the *Sunday Express* Book of the Year Award and includes the Booker-shortlisted novella *Reading Turgenev*. *Felicia's Journey* (1994), won both the Whitbread Book of the Year and the *Sunday Express* Book of the Year awards. A celebrated short-story writer, his seven volumes of previously published short stories, were brought together with four new stories as the *Collected Stories of William Trevor* (1992). Two further selections, *Ireland: Selected Stories* and *Outside Ireland: Selected Stories*, were published in 1995. A collection of his autobiographical essays entitled *Excursions in the Real World* appeared in 1993. He is also the editor of *The Oxford Book of Irish Short Stories* (1989) and has written plays for the stage and for radio and television. Several of his television plays have been based on his short stories. In 1976 William Trevor received the Allied Irish Banks' Prize and in 1977 was awarded an honorary CBE in recognition of his valuable services to literature. In 1992 he received the *Sunday Times* Award for Literary Excellence.

FELICIA'S JOURNEY

*   *   *

William Trevor

VINTAGE CANADA
A Division of Random House of Canada

VINTAGE CANADA EDITION, 1995

Canadian Cataloguing in Publication Data
Trevor, William, 1928-
Felicia's journey
ISBN 0-394-28123-3
I. Title
PR6070.R4F5 1995   823'.914   C95-931233-1

Printed and bound in the United States of America.

3 5 7 9 10 8 6 4 2

For Jane

I

She keeps being sick. A woman in the washroom says:

'You'd be better off in the fresh air. Wouldn't you go up on the deck?'

It's cold on the deck and the wind hurts her ears. When she has been sick over the rail she feels better and goes downstairs again, to where she was sitting before she went to the washroom. The clothes she picked out for her journey are in two green carrier bags; the money is in her handbag. She had to pay for the carrier bags in Chawke's, fifty pence each. They have Chawke's name on them, and a Celtic pattern round the edge. At the *bureau de change* she has been given English notes for her Irish ones.

Not many people are travelling. Shrieking and pretending to lose their balance, schoolchildren keep passing by where she is huddled. A family sits quietly in a corner, all of them with their eyes closed. Two elderly women and a priest are talking about English race-courses.

It is the evening ferry; she wasn't in time for the morning one. 'That's Ireland's Eye,' one of the children called out not long after the boat drew away from the quayside, and Felicia felt safe then. It seems a year ago since last night, when she crept with the carrier bags from the bedroom she shares with her great-grandmother to the backyard shed, to hide them behind a jumble of old floorboards her father intends to make a cold frame out of. In the morning, while the old woman was still sleeping, she waited in the shed until the light came on in the kitchen, an indication that her father was back from Heverin's with the *Irish Press*. Then she slipped out the back way to the Square, twenty-five minutes early for the 7.45 bus. All the time she was nervous in case her father or her brothers appeared, and when the bus started to move she squinted sideways out of the window, a hand held up to her face. She kept telling herself that they couldn't know about the money yet, that they wouldn't even have found the note she'd left, but none of that was a help.

For a while Felicia sleeps, and then goes to the washroom again. Two girls are putting on deodorant, passing the roll-on container to one another, the buttons of their shirts undone. 'Sorry,' Felicia says when she has been sick, but the girls say it doesn't matter. There can't be much left inside her, she thinks, because she hasn't had much to eat that day. 'Take a drink of water,' one of the girls advises. 'We'll be in in twenty minutes.' The other girl asks her if she is OK, and she says she is. She brushes her teeth and a woman beside her picks up the toothbrush when she puts it down on the edge of the basin. 'God, I'm sorry!' the woman apologizes when Felicia protests. 'I thought it was the ship's.'

Typical of her to go out somewhere at a peculiar time like this, her father would have said when she wasn't there to assist with the breakfast frying; typical of the way she is these days. He wouldn't have found the note until he went in with the old woman's breakfast. 'She's taken herself off,' he'd have told her brothers and there wouldn't have been time to talk about it before her brothers left for the quarries. She wonders if he went to the Guards; he mightn't have wanted to do that in spite of everything, you never knew with him. But he'd have had to call in next door to ask Mrs Quigly to keep an eye on the old woman during the day, to give her her cream crackers and half a tin of soup at twelve, the way Mrs Quigly always used to when Felicia was still working in the meat factory.

Announcements are made. There's a flutter of activity among the passengers, suitcases gathered up, obedient congregating in a designated area. A blast of cold air sweeps in when the doors are opened for disembarkation, and then the small throng moves forward on to the gangway. In the evening, when her father and her brothers had returned to the house, they'd have sat in the kitchen, with the note on the table, her father shaking his head slowly and mournfully, as if he in particular had been harshly treated: everything was always worst for her father. One of her brothers would have said he'd go down to McGrattan Street to tell Aidan, and whichever one it was would have called in at Myles Brady's bar on the way back. Her father would have cooked the old woman's supper and then their own, stony-faced at the stove.

Felicia's nervousness returns as she passes with the other passengers into a bleak, unfurnished building in which a security officer questions her. 'Have you means of identification?' he demands.

'Identification?'

'What's your name?'

Felicia tells him. He asks if she has a driver's licence.

'I can't drive actually.'

'Have you another form of identification?'

'I can't think that I have.'

'No letter? No documentation of any kind?'

She shakes her head. He asks if she is resident in the UK and she says no, in Ireland.

'You're here on a visit, are you, miss?'

'Yes.'

'And what's the purpose of this visit?'

'To see a friend.'

'And you're travelling on to where?'

'The Birmingham area. North of Birmingham.'

'May I look through your bags for a moment? Would you mind just stepping aside, miss?'

He pokes about among her clothes and the extra pair of shoes she has brought. She thinks he'll comment when he comes across the banknotes in her handbag, but he doesn't.

'I'll just jot down the address of your friend,' he says. 'Would you give me that, please?'

'I don't know it. I have to find him yet.'

'He's not expecting you?'

'He's not really.'

'You're sure you'll find him?'

'I will, through his place of work.'

Her interrogator nods. He is a man of about the same age as her

3

father, with a featureless face. He is wearing a black overcoat, open at the front.

'I'll just jot down your address in Ireland,' he says.

She says she is from Mountmellick, the first town that comes into her head. She gives an address she makes up: 23 St Mary's Terrace.

'Right,' the security man says.

No one stops her at the Customs. She asks where the trains go from, and is directed. When she makes further inquiries she is informed that the train for Birmingham isn't due to leave until a quarter past two. It is now just after midnight.

For a while, in the waiting-room, she sleeps. She dreams: that she is shopping for meat in Scaddan's, that Mr Scaddan thumps a huge cut of liver on to the weighing-scales and says he took it out of the bullock himself. This isn't true; in her dream she is aware that it isn't; Mr Scaddan is well known for his tall stories. One of the young Christian Brothers comes into the shop and Mr Scaddan says it is a disgrace, but she doesn't know what the butcher is talking about. 'I was out for a walk one night,' he says to the Christian Brother. 'Down by the old gasworks.' She knows then.

The train comes in, long before it's due to go out again. Felicia makes certain it is the right one, and when the journey begins she falls asleep again. Wakened by the ticket-collector, she is drowsily confused for a moment, not knowing where she is. The man is patient while she searches in her handbag for her ticket. Her mother's calm features are snagged in her consciousness, the residue of another dream.

'Thank you,' the man says, passing on.

The dream about her mother has gone; but although she cannot recall what it was about, it has stirred her memory. 'Hurry now, for Mrs Quigly,' her great-grandmother ordered her that day, ages ago. 'And tell Father Kilgallen he's wanted quickly.' The old woman was holding a cup of tea to her mother's lips and her mother's eyes were half closed; her cheeks were the colour of cement. 'Mrs Quigly! Mrs Quigly!' She was six that day, banging the letter-box of the house next door. Later she had to run to keep up with Father Kilgallen's urgent stride in Main Street and the

4

Square, and when they got to the house Mrs Quigly and the old woman helped her mother into the bedroom. Father Kilgallen whispered there, and then her brothers came in from the Christian Brothers' and Aidan went to get her father from the convent garden. It was her father who drew the sheet over her mother's face, a last few minutes he had with her while they waited in the kitchen and Aidan cried. The satchel with her schoolbooks in it was on the floor where she had dropped it, light-blue and shiny, Minnie Mouse with pink shoes on the flap. 'I'm sorry,' Mrs Quigly said, taking her apron off after she'd crossed herself, the flowers on it too garish now. 'Thank God,' Father Kilgallen said because he had arrived in time. 'I've outlived another one,' the old woman said.

The train judders on, rattling on the rails, slowing almost to a halt, gathering speed again. Felicia opens her eyes. A hazy dawn is distributing farmhouses and silos and humped barns in shadowy fields. Later, there are long lines of motor cars creeping slowly on nearby roads, and blank early-morning faces at railway stations. Pylons and aerials clutter a skyline, birds scavenge at a rubbish tip. There's never a stretch of empty countryside.

The train fills up. Newspapers are read in silence, eyes that meet by accident at once averted. Everything – people and houses and motorcars, pylons and aerials – are packed together as if there isn't quite enough room to accommodate them. Faces acquire an edginess when the train threatens to stop even though it isn't at a station.

Johnny will be going to work, too: Felicia imagines him, hurrying as everyone else is, but carefree, not worrying about it, because that is his way. For as long as she can she retains an image of his easy-going expression, then of his profile the afternoon he took the bus himself, the last time she saw him, when he didn't know she was still in the Square; as a faraway, whispering echo, there is the murmur of his voice.

2

Although he does not know it, Mr Hilditch weighs nineteen and a half stone, a total that has been steady for more than a dozen years, rarely increasing or decreasing by as much as a pound. Christened Joseph Ambrose fifty-four years ago, Mr Hilditch wears spectacles that have a pebbly look, keeps his pigeon-coloured hair short, dresses always in a suit with a waistcoat, ties his striped tie into a tight little knot, polishes his shoes twice a day, and is given to smiling pleasantly. Regularly, the fat that bulges about his features is rolled back and well-kept teeth appear, while a twinkle livens the blurred pupils behind his spectacles. His voice is faintly high-pitched.

Mr Hilditch's hands are small, seeming not to belong to the rest of him: deft, delicate fingers that can insert a battery into a watch or tidily truss a chicken, this latter a useful accomplishment, for of all things in the world Mr Hilditch enjoys eating. Often considering that he has not consumed sufficient during the course of a meal, he treats himself to a Bounty bar or a Mars or a packet of biscuits. The appreciation of food, he calls it privately.

Once an invoice clerk, Mr Hilditch is now, suitably, a catering manager. Fifteen years ago, when his predecessor in this position retired, he was summoned by the factory management and the notion of a change of occupation was put to him. As he well knew, the policy was that vacancies, where possible, should be filled from within, and his interest in meals and comestibles had not gone unnoticed; all that was necessary was that he should go on a brief catering course. For his part, he was aware that computers were increasingly taking their toll of office staff and when the offer was made he knew better than to hesitate: as a reward for long and satisfactory service, redundancy was being forestalled.

Mr Hilditch occupies on his own a detached house standing in shrubberies that run all around it, Number 3 Duke of Wellington Road. In 1979 his mother died in this house; he never knew his father. Left on his own at the time of the death, he committed to auction the furniture that had accumulated in his mother's lifetime and from then on made Number Three solely his. Visiting sale-rooms at weekends, he filled it with articles, large and small, all of them to his personal taste: huge mahogany cupboards and chests, ivory trinkets for his mantelpieces, secondhand Indian carpets, and elaborately framed portraits of strangers. Twenty mezzotints of South African military scenes decorate the staircase wall, an umbrella-stand in marble and mahogany vies for pride of place with a set of antlers in a spacious hallway. Number 3 Duke of Wellington Road is commodious enough to contain all Mr Hilditch has purchased: built in 1867 to the designs of a tea merchant, it spreads from this lofty entrance hall to kitchen and pantries at the back, and reception rooms of generous proportions to the left and right of the hall door. Upstairs, that generosity is repeated. Four bedrooms open off the first-floor landing, with a further four above them. Ceilings are rich in plasterwork mouldings and cornices. Ornate gas lamps, no longer in use, still protrude from the walls. Mr Hilditch regularly dusts them, an attention that over the years has resulted in a dull glow on the protuberances of the decoration. In spring and summer he attends to the shrubberies, keeping them clear of weeds, though not growing anything new. He sweeps up the fallen leaves in autumn and from time to time repairs the wooden boundary fences.

The private life of Mr Hilditch is on the one hand ordinary and expected, on the other secretive. To his colleagues at the factory he appears to be, in essence, as jovial and agreeable as his exterior intimates. His bulk suggests a man careless of his own longevity, his smiling presence indicates an extrovert philosophy. But Mr Hilditch, in his lone moments, is often brought closer to other, darker, aspects of the depths that lie within him. When a smile no longer matters he can be a melancholy man.

But on a Wednesday morning in February Mr Hilditch is aware of considerable elation: once a fortnight on Wednesdays the

7

factory lunch includes turkey pie, and a fortnight has passed since it was on the menu. He dwells upon this fact as he fries his breakfast eggs and sausages and bacon, and toasts pieces of thick-sliced Mother's Pride. It lingers in his thoughts while he eats in his shirtsleeves and waistcoat at the kitchen table, and while he washes up at the sink. Temporarily, at least, the anticipated lunchtime dish recedes then. He lowers the drying-rack from the ceiling, drapes the tea-cloth he has used over a rail and raises the rack again. He visits the lavatory with the *Daily Telegraph*, and soon afterwards lets himself out of his front door, double-locking it behind him. His small green car is waiting on the gravelled driveway. The shrubberies that shield the house from the street are dank and dripping on a misty morning.

Mr Hilditch drives slowly, as his habit is: he never drives fast, he sees no point in it. Being of the neighbourhood, born and bred in the town he now passes through, he has seen some changes. The most lasting, and fundamental, occurred in the decade of the 1950s when the town expanded and was to a considerable degree rebuilt in order to house and facilitate the employees of the factories that arrived in the area during that time. These factories are different from those that distinguished the town in the past, their manufacturing processes being of a lighter nature. Now, there is plain, similar architecture everywhere, shops and office blocks laid out in a grid of straight lines, intersections at right angles. Wide pedestrian walkways were planted in the 1950s with shrubs and flowers in long, raised central beds; and the new town's architects included burgeoning arcades, and hanging baskets on the street lights. Since then the soil has soured in the long raised beds; heathers have died there, leaving only browned strands behind, among which beer cans and discarded containers of instant food provide what splashes of colour there are. The flowered arcades are bare metal arches, the hanging baskets rusty. But paint-gun graffiti enliven the smooth brown concrete of a sculptured group – man, woman and child in stylized lumbering gait, *en route* from the post office to a multi-storey car park. Among low-slung office blocks an ersatz mosaic patterns the wall of a chain-store. Familiar logos – of shops and banks and building societies – snappily claim attention.

In Mr Hilditch's opinion the town is a city and should be known as such. It is the size of a city and has a city's population, but it does not possess a cathedral, which someone – his Uncle Wilf, as far as he can remember – once pointed out is the stipulation where urban status is concerned. Instead, there are six churches, four of different denominations, a synagogue and a mosque. There is a leisure centre, completed in 1981, which Mr Hilditch has never entered and considers a waste of public money.

He passes it now, then skirts the central area and patiently waits at the roundabout where traffic at this particular time of the morning invariably comes to a halt. After that the journey is easier, and within minutes he is driving through yellow factory gates. He parks where the registration number of his car is painted on the tarmac, and walks at an unhurried pace to his office – a partitioned corner of what was once a larger office – beyond the loading bays. As an invoice clerk in the old days, he worked there before all the partitioning went up, with seven other clerks in the same office space, each at a desk.

Just before midday on this Wednesday – a day that so far strikes Mr Hilditch as being in no way special apart from the promise of turkey pie – he makes his way to the kitchens in order to taste the lunchtime menu in full. Beginning with the pie, he passes from flaky crust to meat, then sips the gravy. An alternative dish is a casserole of beef diced with vegetables: dutifully, he samples this also – and potatoes, roasted and mashed, Brussels sprouts and parsnips. 'Splendid,' Mr Hilditch compliments his cooks. 'Good show.' He tries the raspberry-jam steamed pudding, the custard, and the apple crumble. He examines a costing print-out of each dish separately calculated, labour and electricity costs, ingredients as an individual total. His task is to avoid a loss – a task in which his predecessor was rarely successful – and over fifteen years he has done so, responsible for a transformation in the factory's catering accounts that has not gone unacknowledged.

'Good, that's very good,' he pronounces when he has glanced through the figures, the pleasant taste of raspberry jam still clinging to his palate. He smiles as he hands back the papers, reflecting that he will certainly go for the raspberry steamed pudding when he makes his choice of what to have after the turkey pie. He ambles about the huge, greasy kitchens for a few more moments, genially chatting to the cooking staff, who are part-time women mostly. Then, his appetite whetted, he makes his way to the canteen. It pleases him to be first in the canteen every day: he feels it emphasizes his position and draws attention to the fact that this hour of relaxation for all the factory workers, no matter what their status, is ordained by him. There is a dining-room for the managerial staff which he has a right to use but never does. The food is identical in both places.

At ten to one the shop-floor hooters sound, and soon after that the workers arrive, men and women, girls and apprentices. They queue up with trays at the long counter, shouting at one another, sharing jokes and mild obscenities. Mr Hilditch smiles at individuals as they pass close to where he sits, all of them in their working clothes, some with the *Sun* or the *Daily Mirror* under an arm. They trust him, he feels. They trust the food for which he is ultimately responsible because from experience they know they can, and that gives him pleasure. He can't imagine his existence now if he had remained an invoice clerk. Head of Invoices he would have become in time, but only his close associates would have known that such a title existed. There would have been no question of a place in the managerial dining-room, or the luxury of rejecting it.

'Damp one hour, cold the next,' a man going by grumbles. 'You don't know where you are with it, Mr Hilditch.'

'Shocking.' Mr Hilditch smiles back. 'But at least the days'll be getting longer.'

'Enjoy your meal, Mr Hilditch.' A woman with a tray nods pleasantly as she passes.

'And yourself, Iris.'

It is an expression they often use, 'enjoy your meal': picked up from the television, he supposes. Mr Hilditch doesn't have television himself. He hired a set once, but found he never turned it on. Sometimes, in reply to the good wishes about his meal, he says he enjoys all his meals, a little pleasantry that invariably causes amusement.

In the canteen the bustle has increased. He can no longer hear the greetings and comments from the queue by the counter. Dishes and knives and forks rattle on the trays, the trays themselves noisily deposited. In the smoking area cigarettes are lit; another queue forms for cups of tea or coffee; newspapers are spread out on table-tops.

Mr Hilditch likes to watch it all. Flirtations begin or continue in the canteen; girls, sometimes women, eye the young apprentices; men, known to Mr Hilditch to be married, chance their luck. Besides this kind of thing there are a couple of long-established liaisons. A man called Frank from the finishing shop, older by a few years than Mr Hilditch, sits every day with one of the Indian women; Annette from the paint shop keeps a place at the same corner table for young Kevin, to whom she could give fifteen years at least. You can't tell what is going on or if at other times, outside the factory, these companionships continue. Everyone knows, yet Mr Hilditch reckons that no one, meeting the legal partners of these people, would divulge a thing. The factory is another world; within it, so is his canteen.

He finishes his steamed pudding and queues for tea, exchanging further views on the weather with those on either side of him. He returns to the kitchens, stands for a moment in the doorway, then makes his way out of the building to his office beyond the loading bays.

As he progresses on the tarmacadamed surface, taking his time while digesting, he notices a solitary figure ahead of him. It is a girl in a red coat and a headscarf, carrying two plastic bags. He notices when he is closer to her that she is round-faced, wide-eyed, and has an air of being lost. He doesn't recognize her; she doesn't belong. *Chawke's* it says on the plastic bags, bold black letters on green. He has never heard the name before; it doesn't belong, either.

'I don't know am I in the right place,' the girl says as he is about to pass her by, and Mr Hilditch smiles in his usual way. Irish, he says to himself.

'What place are you looking for?'

'The lawn-mower factory. Someone said it could be here.'

'We don't make lawn-mowers, I'm afraid.'

'Then I've got it wrong.'

'I'm afraid you have.'

'D'you know the place I'm looking for?'

He shakes his head. Lawn-mowers are not manufactured anywhere near here, he says.

'Oh.'

She stands there awkwardly, her mouth depressed at the corners, her eyes worried. Escaping from the headscarf, wisps of fair hair blow about her face; a tiny cross, on a cheap silver-coloured chain, is just visible beneath her coat. Being curious by nature, Mr Hilditch wonders what her plastic bags contain.

'I have a friend works in the stores of a lawn-mower factory. The only thing is I'm not certain where it is.'

'There are definitely no lawn-mowers manufactured round here.'

The nearest to anything like that would be on the industrial estate half a mile away, where there are garden-supply showrooms. Pritchard's on the estate do grass-cutters – Mountfield, Flymo, Japanese.

'Haven't you got your friend's address?'

The girl shakes her head. She only has the name of this town, and the lawn-mower information.

'Pritchard's is retail, nothing manufactured there.'

'Maybe I got it wrong about a factory.'

'Try the estate anyway. It could be they'd put you in touch.'

Mr Hilditch, who is a careful man, doesn't wish to be seen with a girl on the factory premises. No one has observed their meeting, of that he is certain. No windows overlook the tarmacadam expanse; no one is, or has been, about. He has never been seen in the company of a girl on the factory premises, nor anywhere in the immediate neighbourhood. Nothing like that on your own doorstep is the rule he has.

'Walk out the yellow gates, the way you came in.' He hurries the directions, hardly waiting for the nods of acknowledgement they elicit. 'Turn right and keep on until you come to the dual carriageway. Turn left there. After that you'll see the sign to the estate. Blackbarrow Industrial Estate it says.'

Mr Hilditch nods to himself, an indication that the encounter has reached an end. Then abruptly he turns away from the girl and continues on his way.

3

Since she arrived in the town that morning Felicia has discovered that she cannot always understand what people say because they speak in an accent that is unfamiliar to her. Even when they repeat their statements there is a difficulty, and sometimes she has to give up. On the industrial estate she makes inquiries in a building that sells office requirements – filing-cabinets and revolving chairs as well as paper in bulk and supplies of envelopes and fasteners and transparent tape, everything stacked up higgledy-piggledy, not as in a shop. Half of what the girl says in reply escapes her, but she knows it doesn't matter because the girl keeps shaking her head, denying in this way all knowledge of a lawn-mower factory.

The industrial estate is an endless repetition of nondescript commercial buildings, each with a forecourt for parking. Trade names blazon: Toyota, Ford, Toys 'Я' Us, National Tyre and Autocare, Kwik-Fit, Zanussi, Renault Trucks, Pipewise, Ready-bag, Sony, Comet. Next to Britannia Scaffolding are Motorway Exhausts, then C & S Roofing, Deep Drilling Services and To-morrow's Cleaning Today. At an intersection a little further on, Allparts Vehicle Dismantlers share the corner with OK Blast & Spray Ltd.

The concrete roads of the estate are long and straight. Nobody casually walks them for the pleasure of doing so. No dogs meet other dogs. Business is in all directions, buying and selling, disposal and acquisition, discount for cash. It takes Felicia nearly two hours to find Pritchard's Garden Requisites and Patio Centre.

'A rotary you're thinking of, is it?' the salesman responds in answer to her query, and she asks if the place is a factory, if the lawn-mowers are made here.

'We have our workshops on the premises for after-care. The annual service we recommend, though it's entirely up to you. You'd be going for electric, would you?'

'I'm looking for a friend. He works in the stores of a lawn-mower factory.'

The man's manner changes. He can't help her, he states flatly, disappointment emptying his tone of expression.

'Someone I met said you might be able to tell me where a factory was.'

'Our machines are manufactured in works all over the country. I'm sorry. I believe someone else requires my attention.'

A couple are measuring garden furniture with a dressmaking tape. They're after something for their conservatory, they inform the salesman. Felicia goes away.

A man in a Volkswagen showroom is patient with her but doesn't know of a lawn-mower factory in the vicinity. Then an afterthought strikes him as she's leaving and he mentions the name of a town that he says is twenty-five or -six miles off. When it occurs to him that she's bewildered by what he's saying he writes the name down on the edge of a brochure. 'Not the full shilling', is an expression her father uses, and 'Nineteen and six in the pound': she wonders if the man is thinking that.

No one else can help her. She walks through the estate, investigating every road, inquiring in a do-it-yourself emporium and in Britannia Scaffolding. In OK Blast & Spray Ltd a woman draws a map for her, but when she follows the arrows on it she finds herself at a plumbers' supply warehouse that is closed. She returns to Pritchard's Garden Requisites and Patio Centre in the hope that the salesman isn't busy now. Crosser than before, he ignores her.

She tramps wearily back to the town, on the grass verge beside a wide dual carriageway. An endless chain of lorries and cars passes close, the noise of their engines a roar that every few moments rises as a crescendo, their headlights on because it has become foggy. The scrubby grass she walks on is grey, in places black, decorated by the litter that is scattered all around her – crushed cigarette packets, plastic bags, cans and bottles, crumpled sheets from newspapers, cartons. In the middle of the morning she had a cup of tea and a piece of fruitcake; she hasn't had anything since and she doesn't feel hungry, but she knows that as soon as she arrives back in the town she will have to find somewhere to spend the night. Her arms ache from the weight of the two carrier bags; her feet are sore, blisters in two different places, one of her heels skinned. She knew it wouldn't be easy; even before she set out she knew it wouldn't be; she hadn't been expecting anything else. What has happened is her own fault, due to her own foolishness in not making certain she had an address. She can't blame anyone else.

Yet in spite of everything she wouldn't not be here, closer to him. On the day of Aidan's wedding, when she was Connie Jo's bridesmaid, when she held her bouquet of autumn flowers, she hardly knew he existed, yet the day has been special ever since because it was then, suddenly, that he was there, the beginning of everything. In the Church of Our Saviour she had been thinking that her shoulders were ungainly, that her face hadn't responded to the softening attentions of Carmel's make-up, that no doubt her hair had gone limp. Tulle and lace stretched flatly over the upper half of her body and she wished she had taken Carmel's advice and puffed her brassiere up with wads of cottonwool. 'God, you're gawky,' Carmel used to say when they were twelve, and she felt she still was, at seventeen on the day of her brother's wedding. 'I will,' Aidan responded to Father Kilgallen at the altar, and Connie Jo said it too. Afterwards on the steps they smiled for the bald photographer – she and Connie Jo, and Moss McGuire with his best man's buttonhole, carnation and asparagus fern, similar to Aidan's. Confetti clung to their shoulders on the walk from the church to Hickey's Hotel in the Square, and was carried into the Kincora Lounge, where Connie Jo's kid sister was already asking for Pepsi Cola. Sister Benedict, who loved the weddings of her convent girls, was perched on the scarlet upholstery of a gold-painted chair, one of a set arrayed against the walls. The scarlet was soiled where it bulged, the gold of the legs worn away in patches, or chipped. Barry Manilow whispered softly through the speakers.

As Felicia progresses on the dual carriageway, the faces of that

October afternoon jostle in her thoughts; scraps of conversation echo. The Reverend Mother, and other nuns, joined Sister Benedict, specially invited because the father of the bridegroom was the gardener at the convent. Artie Slattery, who supplied the cake, stood near it with his buxom wife. Old Begley, who attended all funerals and weddings as a matter of course, waited for the first of the food to appear. Sergeant Breen, off duty, and Fogarty the tractor-repair man, crossed the hall of the hotel from the front bar to the Kincora Lounge at the invitation of the bride's father. Mr Logan, proprietor of the Two-Screen Ritz and the Dancetime Disco, was natty in a chalk-striped suit and blue bow-tie, as befitted the locality's most prominent businessman and bachelor. Welcoming guests at the door, Connie Jo's mother was unable to dispel from her expression the opinion that her daughter, by marrying a plasterer, had married beneath her. Connie Jo was Felicia's friend, had been since their time at the convent, which Felicia was privileged to attend because of her father's connection with it. Occasionally, when a nun was cross, Felicia had been reminded that she was there on sufferance. The nuns weren't always severe, but those who still favoured the tradition of honouring sacred figures in their names had seemed so to Felicia before she knew some of them better: Sister Antony Ixida, Sister Ignatius Loyola, Sister Francis Xavier, Sister Benedict, Sister Justina.

'How're things at the quarries?' Tim Bo Gargan inquired of Felicia's big twin brothers. Things were all right, they replied and left it at that, no more communicative at a wedding party than at any other time. 'How're you doing, Felicia?' Small Crowley asked, speaking out of the corner of his mouth the way he believed American gangsters did, eyeing Carmel while he spoke because it was Carmel he was interested in. 'How're you doing, Carmel?' he plucked up the courage to ask eventually, causing Carmel's cousin Rose to giggle. 'Any time you want it, Aidan,' Connie Jo's father offered, 'there's a place for you in McGrattan Street Cycles and Prams.'

Tim Bo Gargan tried for Scott Joplin on the piano, but desisted when there were protests. Trifle was handed round. 'Ah no, no, you look great, Felicia,' Connie Jo reassured her, and Carmel and

Rose agreed that of course she did. Small Crowley struck a match on his thumbnail and said he'd heard Fogarty had been out all morning trying to start a tractor in some farmer's field, which was the reason why a smell of petrol was coming off him. 'We'll have the cake soon,' Connie Jo's mother announced, interrupting the conversations in the Kincora Lounge, and then the cake was cut and there was applause, with glasses and tea-cups raised. In the hall the children opened and closed the lift doors. 'You're wanted! You're wanted!' they called up the stairs, and a girl Felicia didn't know told her that Dessie Flynn had put the remains of a chicken salad in a bed. 'Hold on to that confetti till they're outside,' Hickey of the hotel begged when the bride and groom were ready to go. 'Keep the confetti for the street, lads.' Everyone was moving out of the hotel behind Aidan and Connie Jo, and a cheer went up when they stepped into the car Connie Jo's father had hired for them. 'Bray,' Tim Bo Gargan knowledgeably declared. 'I'd say they're headed for Bray.'

The car drove round the Square. The guests re-entered the hotel, and it was then that Johnny Lysaght passed by on the pavement. It was then that he paused and looked, and saw her in her bridesmaid's dress. As long as she lives, Felicia has told herself many times since, that moment will never lose its potency: her father's back, his grey head as he passed through the swing doors, and how she turned to catch a final glimpse of her brother and her friend in their be-ribboned wedding car, and instead caught the eye of a man who was passing by; how she smiled because he smiled; how she said to herself afterwards that this was when she knew the beginning of love.

The moment is still vivid when she reaches the outskirts of the town that that love has brought her to. Dark-skinned shopkeepers are closing their small premises. Racks of newspapers are unhooked from doorways, displays of vegetables lifted inside. The houses that separate these solitary stores from one another are drab; discoloured concrete is dominant, the metal of skimpy window-frames rusting through its covering of paint. The prevalence of litter continues, blown in from the road or spilt out of dustbins, accumulating on a small expanse in front of each of the shops.

'You didn't have any luck?' a voice says, and Felicia turns to find the fat man she asked directions of smiling at her from a car that is keeping pace with her, close to the edge of the pavement. The car comes to a halt when she stops herself, a small green vehicle with an old-fashioned humped back, so modest you'd hardly think the man would fit in it. He's wearing a hat now; his features are shadowy in the gloom of the car's interior.

She shakes her head. She understands what he says more easily than she understood the others: having to try so hard on the estate added to her tiredness.

'No, it's not there.' A man wrote down the name of another town for her, she says, and takes the car salesman's brochure from a pocket of her coat. He nods over it, commenting that the man may be right about that town. It's the town where Thompson Castings is: he'd thought of Thompson's himself five minutes after she'd gone. But she won't get a bus in that direction tonight.

'I'll stay here so.'

'You have somewhere?'

'I'm just going to look for a place.'

Just before he spoke to her she'd decided to make inquiries about inexpensive lodgings. During the day she passed a bus station: they would know there, she'd thought, and was about to ask someone on the street to direct her to it when the car drew in beside her.

'Marshring,' the fat man says. 'That's where a lot of the accommodation is.'

She asks him where Marshring is and he says:

'Straight ahead, second on the right. Left at the bottom, that's Marshring. There's the Crescent and the Avenue. Ten minutes' walk.'

When she thanks him he nods and smiles. His glasses glint from the shadows as he turns his head away while still winding up the window.

'Thanks again.'

Felicia moves on and eventually turns into the road that has been mentioned. She follows it down a hill to Marshring Crescent, where there are notices in most of the windows, offering overnight lodgings. *Bed & breakfast with evening meal, £11*, one says. She pushes open a small ornamental gate and passes between two narrow areas of uncultivated garden. Then, wondering if she has closed the gate, she glances behind her to make sure. At the end of Marshring Crescent she notices what seems to be the humpbacked green car, but presumes she is mistaken.

That night, at five minutes to twelve, Mr Hilditch slowly mounts the stairs to his bedroom.

His Uncle Wilf went to Ireland after the First World War. He went to settle the unrest, and came back with a story or two, nothing spectacular, just army tales. He died a dozen or so years ago at eighty-eight, still telling his army tales about skirmishes in France and Belgium, and reading the riot act in Ireland.

It was listening to his Uncle Wilf as a child that made Mr Hilditch want to join a regiment himself, an urge that increased as he grew older. But they wouldn't take him when the moment came because of his eyesight and his feet. He pressed his application, having been eager for so long, thinking that maybe the quartermaster's department or the cookhouse wouldn't be particular, not knowing how these things were regulated. 'Not a chance, old son,' a recruiting sergeant said, a cold-faced little upstart with a black blade of a moustache. Ever since, the disappointment has remained, stuck there beyond its time.

Funny the way your thoughts go round, Mr Hilditch reflects. Funny the way they begin with a girl's face lingering and then get back to Uncle Wilf and that recruiting sergeant. Number 19 she went into.

4

Felicia wakes in the middle of the night, and fragments remain from dreams as they evaporate. 'I've brought you a shell,' Sister Benedict is saying, and a boy runs out in front of the Corpus Christi procession and someone waves from a window. *Flanagan's Quarries* is on one of the lorries her brothers drive, parked by Myles Brady's bar as the procession goes by. Passing Aldritt's garage, you can see petrol vapour in the bright sunlight, a man filling his car at the pumps. 'Angels flying low,' Sister Francis Xavier says, but that isn't something that began in a dream, although perhaps it came into one. Sister Francis Xavier said it whenever she referred to the Little Sisters who worked among the heathen of Africa. Just as the Reverend Mother used to tell how St Ursula set forth with her girl-companions, sailing the world because she wished to keep herself holy. 'You never considered the celibate life, Felicia?' the Reverend Mother inquired once, out of the blue. Afterwards, when she told them, Carmel and Rose said she had the face for a nun.

When people went to the sea they brought her back shells because her mother had died. She arranged them on the chest of drawers in the bedroom she shared, but her great-grandmother kept knocking them off by accident so she kept them in one of her drawers instead. The first time she saw the sea herself was when she came on this journey. '*The sea, the sea, the open sea . . .*' Reciting that in class one day, she couldn't remember what came next. She stood there, going red, ashamed because she'd known it off pat the evening before.

Felicia closes her eyes in the darkness, but does not sleep. The details of her journey impinge – the sickness, the woman who used her toothbrush in the washroom, the security man's questions, one train and then another, asking where the factory was, the hatchet-faced landlady who brought her shepherd's pie and tinned fruit in the empty dining-room, the cup of tea afterwards. Then Johnny is there, lightening the tiredness and frustrations of the day before: his grey-green eyes, his dark hair, the neat point of his chin, his high cheekbones. She sees him in a factory crowd, the first in a throng that comes out of Thompson Castings, hurrying as if he has a premonition that she'll be waiting for him, his deft, angular movement. 'The other day I thought it was you was the bride': the Monday after the wedding it was when he spoke to her on the street, coming up to her outside Chawke's.

She loves making it happen again, better than any dream or any imagining because it's real. 'Ah no, no,' she said, shaking her head, not adding that she didn't think she'd ever be a bride. A woman in Chawke's window was changing the clothes on the models, replacing the summer styles. 'Johnny Lysaght,' he said, smiling friendlily as he had when she was in her bridesmaid's dress. 'D'you remember me at all?'

She remembered him vaguely from way back, when he was still at the Christian Brothers'. He was seven, maybe eight, years older than she was; he didn't live in the neighbourhood any more; occasionally he returned to see his mother. 'How are you getting on?' she said.

Lying there with her eyes still closed, she hears her own voice boldly asking that because she couldn't think of anything else to say. He had never belonged with the Lomasney lot or Small Crowley's crowd; he'd been more on his own, going off to Dublin when he left the Brothers' and soon after that going to England. He had an English accent.

'OK,' he said. 'Yourself, Felicia?'

'Out of work.'

'Weren't you in the meat place?'

'It closed down.'

He smiled again. He asked why Slieve Bloom Meats had closed down and she explained; again it was something to say. A woman failed to report a cut on her hand that went septic, and an outbreak of food-poisoning was afterwards traced back to a batch of tinned kidney and beef. No more than a scratch the little cut had seemed to Mrs Grennan, even though it wouldn't heal. Dr Mortell had seen it and given Mrs Grennan a note, but she had gone on working because when you went sick you sometimes found yourself laid off when you returned: since 1986, when there had been another food scare – one that was general in the processed-meat business then – the factory hadn't been doing well. There was an opinion in the neighbourhood that sooner or later it would have closed down anyway, and with some justification Mrs Grennan believed she was a scapegoat. 'Sure, the work's gone and that's all there's to it,' Felicia heard another woman comforting her at the time. 'Does it matter whose fault it was?'

On the street outside Chawke's Johnny Lysaght asked her if she had ever worked anywhere else and she said no, only at Slieve Bloom, where she'd been since she left the convent. She didn't go into details. She didn't say that, being out of work for the past three months, she saw no opportunity for further employment, at least in the locality. What experience she had was with canning, and although very little skill was required she could rapidly make the movements she had become familiar with, and had developed an eye for a faultily sealed can. You had to be trained to work a till in a supermarket, and the smaller shops preferred casual labour – schoolgirls or elderly women. There was never anything these days at Erin Floor Coverings or the hospital. If you waited you might get something in the kitchen of a public house that did dinners or in Hickey's Hotel, but you'd easily wait a year. 'I have a word put in for you with Sister Ignatius,' her father reassured her from time to time, Sister Ignatius being the nun he had most to do with through his work in the garden of the convent. On the other hand, it eased matters, having her at home: she was company for her great-grandmother, who left neither her room nor her bed these days; she was able to attend to all of the cooking and the cleaning that previously had been shared.

'It's no joke being unemployed,' Johnny Lysaght said, leaning against Chawke's window. He undid the cellophane on a packet of cigarettes and offered her one. She shook her head.

'It's not, all right,' she said. 'No joke.'

Her freedom had been taken from her with the loss of her

employment – the freedom to sit with Carmel and Rose and Connie Jo in the Diamond Coffee Dock, an evening at the Two-Screen Ritz without first having to calculate the cost. Within a few weeks of the canning factory's closure she had spent what savings she'd accumulated, and it was only fair – as her father had made clear – that any dole money coming into the house should go towards board and upkeep. A family had to pull together, especially the family of a widower.

'Come down to Sheehy's,' Johnny Lysaght invited. 'A drink?'

'Ah no, I have to get back now.'

It was half past three in the afternoon. She had chops and greens to buy yet. The main meal was at a quarter to six because her brothers couldn't get back from the quarries in the middle of the day, and her father was given something at half-twelve in the convent kitchen. At four she would put the chops on to stew, with half a turnip cut up, and a sliced onion. It was necessary to have the stew beginning to bubble by a quarter past.

'Later on?' Johnny Lysaght suggested. 'Seven? Half-seven?'

In her lodging-house bed Felicia remembers wanting to say yes, but hesitating. She remembers feeling awkward, saying nothing.

'Half-seven?' Johnny Lysaght suggested again.

'In Sheehy's, d'you mean?'

'What's wrong with Sheehy's, Felicia?'

He laughed and she laughed, experiencing a surge of relief in her stomach. The cigarette packet was still in his hand; through his smile he blew out smoke. Why was he bothering with her? Carmel or Rose or any other girl she could think of would drop everything to go out with Johnny Lysaght. She hadn't their looks; she wasn't much.

'I'll see you,' he said softly.

The cadences in his voice, his smiling glances, flow through her night thoughts. As she walked away from him – to Scaddan's for mutton chops and suet, to McCarthy's for greens – a euphoria such as she had never experienced before made her almost want to cry. And it did not diminish while she peeled potatoes at the sink and blended ground rice with milk, while she beat up an egg and chopped the greens. From across the hall came her great-grand-

24

mother's occasional grunt of impatience or a call for assistance when her jigsaw pieces clattered to the floor, the bedroom door open, as it always was during the day in case of an emergency. 'How's she been?' Her father's first utterance was the same as ever it was when he entered the kitchen at a quarter past five, but that evening the repetition had an airy freshness about it. Nor was it an irritation when his lowered voice – still loud enough to cross the hall – regaled his grandmother with the details of his day: how he had raked up the last of the grass cuttings and layered them into his compost stack, how Sister Antony Ixida had been on about tayberries again. 'Who are you anyway?' came the old woman's familiar cry. 'What do you want with me?'

Not wishing to think about the old woman, Felicia is not entirely successful when she tries to divert her thoughts. She remembers how – that lovely, different Monday evening – she in error set a place at the table for Aidan, forgetting that his home was in McGrattan Street now, in the flat about his in-laws' bicycle and pram shop. At six her two other brothers came in from the quarries, as similar in their reticence as in their appearance, sitting down immediately at the kitchen table to await their food. 'Yes, she's struggling on,' her father reported, returning from his visit to the bedroom and bringing with him an aura of the old woman. Her presence rekindled a spirit in him, her history had long been rooted in his sensibilities: that seventy-five years ago her husband of a month, with two companions, had died for Ireland's freedom was a fact that was revered, through his insistence, in the household. The tragedy had left her destitute, with a child expected; had obliged her for the remainder of her active life to earn what she could by scrubbing the floors of offices and private houses. But the hardship was ennobled during all its years by the faith still kept with an ancient cause. Honouring the bloodshed there had been, the old woman outlived the daughter that was born to her, as well as the husband that daughter had married, and the wife of their only son. And when she outlived her own rational thought, Felicia's father honoured the bloodshed on his own: regularly in the evenings he sat with his scrapbooks of those revolutionary times, three heavy volumes of wallpaper pattern books that Multilly of the hardware had let him have when their contents went out of date. All her life, for as long as Felicia could remember, she had been shown, among dahlias and roses, dots and stripes, smooth and embossed surfaces, the newspaper clippings, photographs and copies of documents that had been tidily glued into place. At the heart of the statement they made – the anchor of the whole collection, her father had many times repeated to her – was the combined obituary of the three local patriots, which had been kept by his grandmother among her few possessions until she decided it would be more safely preserved in the pages of the scrapbooks. Next in importance came a handwritten copy of Patrick Pearse's proclamation of a provisional government, dated 24 April 1916, its seven signatories recorded in the same clerkly calligraphy. Columns of newsprint told of the firing of the General Post Office and the events at Boland's Mills, of Roger Casement's landing from a German U-boat on Banna Strand, of the shelling of Liberty Hall. The attacks on the Beggars' Bush Barracks and the Mendicity Institute were recorded, as were the British occupancy of the Shelbourne Hotel and the executions of Pearse and Tom Clarke. There were the Mass cards of the local patriots, and letters that had come from sympathizers, and a photograph of the coffins. An article about the old penal laws had been pasted in, and another about the Irish Battalion. Patrick Pearse's cottage in Connemara was on a postcard; on another the tricolour fluttered from a flagstaff. The Soldier's Song in its entirety was there.

The wallpaper scrapbooks, Felicia's father believed, were a monument to the nation and a brave woman's due, a record of her sacrifice's worth. In red ink he had made small, neat notes, and stuck them in here and there to establish continuity. Among peeping flowers were the hallowed sentiments of Eamon de Valera:

The Ireland which we have dreamed of would be the home of a people who valued material wealth only as the basis of right living, of a people who were satisfied with frugal comfort and devoted their leisure to the things of the spirit; a land whose countryside would be bright with cosy homesteads, whose fields would be joyous with the sounds of industry, with the romping of sturdy children, the contests of athletic youths, the laughter of comely maidens;

whose firesides would be forums for the wisdom of old age. It would, in a word, be the home of a people living the life that God desires men should live.

'No sign of anything?' Felicia's father inquired that Monday evening, referring to her unemployment.

'No.'

'I still have Sister Ignatius on red alert.'

The day Slieve Bloom Meats made it clear that the closure was permanent he'd spoken to the Reverend Mother when she had finished her office. Later he'd mentioned the matter to Sister Ignatius.

'Was there talk of something with Maguire Pigs?' He made a mush of gravy and potato for the old woman and spooned out ground rice for her.

'Bookkeeping. Lottie Flynn got it.'

'The dentist, what's his name, has a card in Heverin's for a cleaner part-time.'

She filled the pepper container at the draining board while her father placed a chop and potatoes and a spoonful of greens on each plate, and passed the plates on to the table. He took in the old woman's tray.

'In a shocking condition,' he said when he returned, 'the brass outside the dentist's. The same with the doctors' and solicitors'. Time was those plates would be gleaming to the heavens.'

When she was twelve Felicia had been in love with Declan Fetrick. He was older, already employed on the ready-meats counter of the Centra foodstore. She used to wander about the Centra on her own, pretending to read the labels on the soup tins, picking up jars of shrimp paste and chicken-and-ham, pretending to change her mind as she put them back again. One of the women who came to work there in the afternoons took to eyeing her suspiciously, but she didn't mind. She never spoke to Declan Fetrick, a scrawny boy who was trying to grow a moustache, and she never told anyone else about how she felt, not even Carmel or Rose or Connie Jo, but every day and every night for nearly a year she thought about him, imagining his arms tightening around her, and the soft bristles of his boy's moustache.

'Delaney that dentist's called,' her father said. 'No wonder we couldn't remember the name, the way you can't see it, the state the brass is. Wouldn't the part-time suit you though? Seventy an hour he's offering. Nine hours a week. When you think of it, wouldn't it suit you better than the full-time?'

It was what he wanted for her; he was relieved she hadn't been qualified for the opening at Maguire Pigs. Some little part-time arrangement would get her off the dole and allow her to continue to do the housework, and the cooking for himself and her remaining brothers. A full-time job would mean having to pay Mrs Quigly for looking after the old woman in the middle of the day, as the job at the Slieve Bloom had. He'd worked it out; he had probably discussed it with the nuns.

'I'd say it would suit you all right. If not the dentist's then something like it.'

'I'd rather have the full-time.'

'It's what's going, though, at the heel of the hunt. It's what's on offer, girl.'

'Yes,' Felicia said, and then the subject was changed, her father repeating what he'd told the old woman: that Sister Antony Ixida was bothering him about tayberries. When the meal was over and the washing-up completed Felicia changed out of her jersey and skirt and put on make-up in the bedroom, beadily observed by the old woman, who was always alert after she'd eaten.

'You're going out, girl?' her father asked, seeing her with her coat on. When she said she was he expressed no further interest. Her mother would have been curious, Felicia thought, from what she could remember of her. Her mother would have guessed that she wouldn't doll herself up, with earrings and eye-shadow and her coral lipstick, just to meet Carmel and Rose on a Monday evening. Her brothers, on their way out themselves to Myles Brady's, didn't even notice that she had her coat on.

'Hi,' Johnny Lysaght greeted her in Sheehy's ten minutes later. 'You're looking great.'

She loved his saying that. She wanted him to say it again. She didn't know a thing about eye make-up, yet he could say straight away when he saw her that she was looking great. 'Aren't you the pretty one!' Dirty Keery used to call out, lying in wait in Devlin's Lane. But that was different because he said it to all the girls going by, trying to get them to come close to him. And he was blind in any case.

'Take off your coat,' Johnny Lysaght invited, and she was glad he did because the shade of red her coat was didn't match her coral lipstick. Also, it was worn in places. She had put a dress on specially, her blue one with the squares and triangles. 'What'll you drink?' he offered.

'7-Up.'

'Drop of gin in it?'

'Ah no, no.'

'Keep me company. Cheer you up. Try a vodka and orange instead of that old stuff.'

He had been drinking beer himself. The label on the bottle was festive beside his empty glass. He'd go over to a short, he said, ring the changes. 'Cheer you up,' he said again.

'OK.'

He ordered their drinks from young Sheehy behind the bar. His expression changed a lot when he conversed, vivacious one moment, meditative the next. He referred to her perfume when he returned to their table, saying he liked it. *Love in a Mist* it was called; she'd put it on when she'd left the kitchen, on the street outside. 'Cheers,' he said.

She asked him whereabouts he was in England. She asked if it was London and he said no, north of Birmingham. He mentioned a town but the name was not familiar to her. He was a storeman in a factory, spare parts for lawn-mowers. He lit a cigarette. It kept the wolf from the door, he said; you could do worse.

'You're good the way you come back to see your mother.'

'You only have the one mother.'

'Yes.'

'Oh, sorry.'

She said it was all right. Most people wouldn't apologize; most people would forget, or remember too late and not know what to say.

'Is the old lady OK, these days?'

29

She said she was. In her hundredth year, she said, and he wagged his head in wonderment. He smiled again and she watched him smoking. *Marlboro*, it said on the packet on the table. In the Coffee Dock and the Two-Screen Ritz Carmel smoked the odd Afton Major. So did Rose.

'What's England like?' she asked.

'All right. You get used to it. You can get used to anywhere when you're there a while.'

'There's some gets lonely. Patty Maloney came back.'

'The likes of Patty Maloney would.'

'I don't know will things improve here.'

He didn't know either. She said there had been talk of Bord na Móna opening a factory, to do with compressing peat dust.

'Stuff people buy for their gardens,' she explained. 'My father was on about it.'

'But they drew their horns in, did they?'

'They shelved it in the end.'

'Have another drink?'

'Ah, no, no.'

He laughed. 'That orange has vitamins in it.'

'Just the orange then.'

He laughed again, picking up her glass and his own. She watched him at the bar, easy in his manner with young Sheehy. Carmel and Rose might come in; she wished they would. She wished they'd come over to where she was sitting and she'd say no, the seat was taken.

'Is the Dancetime still in business on a Friday?' he asked when he returned with their drinks.

'They have the Friday disco all right.'

She knew he was going to ask her, but he didn't at first. He was looking at her lips and she wondered what kissing would be like. The time of Declan Fetrick she had imagined it. Carmel hadn't liked it at first, when the fellow with the blackheads from the post office got going in the Two-Screen, when Carmel was thirteen.

'Would you be on for the disco, d'you think? Friday, Felicia?'

'I can't afford a disco these days.'

'You wouldn't pay if you were with me.'

She felt confused, in spite of having guessed he was going to invite her. She felt her face reddening and sat back a bit, trying to get out of the light. It was two months since she'd been to the Dancetime Disco, the night the Heart Stoppers came, the night Small Crowley first showed an interest in Carmel, the same night Rose got involved with the failed curate from out in the country somewhere, a man who hadn't appeared in the Dancetime before and whom Rose hadn't seen since.

'It was great running into you, Felicia.' Under the table one of his knees brushed hers when he moved. 'I'm glad you weren't the bride, Felicia.'

Carmel said you never knew why a fellow fancied you, why a fellow picked you out. You could be driven to distraction by fat arms or a flat chest, and then you'd discover that it was that very thing that drew a fellow on. Connie Jo used to say the same. Rose said you could never understand the male mind.

'It would be great if you came,' Johnny Lysaght said. 'Really great.'

He says it in a dream, when Felicia sleeps again. For four hours they danced at the Friday disco, neither of them dancing with anyone else, twice getting a pass and going to Sheehy's. When he took her hand, walking together through the silent streets at two o'clock in the morning, she wanted to tell him she loved him. She wanted to tell him a boy never kissed her before. In her dream he helps her through the barbed wire and his arms are around her in the field next to the old gasworks, hugging her to him, loving her, he says. There's the fragrance of his aftershave and he opens a button of his shirt, guiding her hand on to his warm flesh; everything about him is gentle. 'You're beautiful,' he whispers. 'You're great, Felicia.' His lips are moist when he kisses her again, and he closes his eyes when she does, in just the same moment, as if they are one person.

Then her dream is different. Her father says it's the way the country's going, brass plates unpolished, a holy show to the world. Her brothers eat without speaking. 'What's Lysaght *like*, though?' Rose asks, and Carmel giggles.

It is almost seven when Felicia wakes; a faint blur of light filters through flimsy curtains, marking the room's single window. She watches it intensify, shadows defining themselves as a chair, a table, a clothes cupboard, a wash-basin on a stand in a corner. The curtains are orange and green swirls; dun-coloured walls are scarred where Scotch tape has once adhered, pink paint is chipped. Her father would be on the way back from Heverin's with the *Irish Press*, her brothers' heavy morning footsteps just beginning. In the bedroom she left behind, the jigsaw pieces would be scattered on the bedclothes and on the floor, the few the old woman managed to interlock fallen apart, the jigsaw tray slipped down between the bed and the wall. In a moment there would be the bedpan, her father having to heave the old woman up on his own. The way she always does at this time, she'd feel under the rubber sheet for the clothes-peg bag she keeps her pension money in, and then she'd remember that some of it has been taken, that yesterday there was that unbelievable discovery. In the kitchen the panful of streaky bacon would be spitting on the stove, scattering little specks of fat on to the white enamel, on to the eggs still in their carton, waiting to be fried.

Felicia rises and washes in the corner of the room. She slips out of her nightdress and for a moment is naked, feeling shy to be so, as if she is in the room she shares at home. She dresses quickly, from habit also, then brushes her hair and smears on lipstick. She opens the door softly and finds the lavatory. As she crosses the landing, returning to her room, the sound of a radio comes faintly from downstairs. A few minutes later she descends to the dining-room, where a single place is laid, a plate of cornflakes already waiting.

When the woman with the hatchet face comes in she says something about sleep, and Felicia replies that she slept like a log. 'Boiled all right for you?' the woman offers, not waiting for a response. An overall, mainly blue, is wrapped tightly around her. She places a boiled egg in an eggcup beside the cornflakes and a plate of toast, and places a metal teapot on a coiled wire mat. She tells Felicia to help herself to milk and sugar. 'Call out if you need anything,' she adds before she leaves the room.

Felicia pours tea, finishes her cornflakes, and slowly spreads

32

butter on a piece of toast. She cracks open the top of her egg. In the kitchen her father would be easing the bacon slices from the pan, slipping a knife under them where they have become stuck. 'Like this, Felicia,' he said years ago, showing her. He would cut bread for frying and slice black and white puddings. He likes his eggs turned, her brothers done on one side only.

The landlady appears again, to ask if everything is all right. She mentions the balance of the sum that was agreed, and Felicia pays what is owing.

5

He stops from time to time, drawing in to the curb, allowing her to move almost out of sight before he drives on slowly in pursuit. He knows where she is going since she stated what she intended in their conversation. But of course there could have been a change of heart overnight; he has had experience of that.

In fact, she turns into the bus station, exactly as she said she would, the same red coat, the same two carrier bags. Mr Hilditch watches for a few minutes longer, then drives away.

There are no hills. Against a grey sky, tall bleak chimneys belch out their own hot clouds. Factories seem like fortresses, their towers protecting an ancient realm of iron and wealth. Terracotta everywhere has blackened to the insistent local sheen. The lie of the land is lost beneath a weight of purpose, its natural idiosyncrasy stifled, contours pressed away.

The bus that carries Felicia through all this is almost empty. Women with shopping-bags occupy seats on their own, staring ahead at the driver's back. A child perpetually cries, ineffectively hushed by its mother. A man mutters as he turns the pages of a newspaper.

As the bus approaches the periphery of the town where Thompson Castings is, the flat roadside fields dwindle, and the factories intensify in number, one rubbing against another. In one of them, Felicia imagines Johnny Lysaght, with spare parts arranged behind him floor to ceiling, in wooden drawers and on shelves. She imagines him in his work clothes, a brown overall, the same brown as the assistants in Multilly's hardware. He looks for something he has been asked for, and whistles the way he sometimes does. When she visualizes it, Thompson Castings is a place

34

like Queally's the agricultural-machinery depot on the Roscrea road.

'Happen it's out a bit.' A man in a uniform hazards an opinion at the bus station, lips pursed in irritation because he doesn't know. 'Never heard of it, to tell the truth.'

She walks into the town, which has an older look than the town she has travelled from but with the same insignia on banks and stores. Streets amble and twist and turn, petering away to become lanes and alleys, the picturesque preserved as if in protest at the towers and chimneys that mar the town's approaches. 'Excuse me,' Felicia interrupts a man in a wheelchair outside a teashop with small-paned windows that bulge out in a bow. 'Push me in, dear,' the man directs. 'We'll inquire inside.'

The cashier by the till asks a passing waitress if she knows where Thompson Castings is. The waitress shakes her head, but repeats the query to the people she's serving. 'Thompson's,' an elderly woman recalls. 'Used to be in Half Street.' But someone else says that was Thompson's the leather people.

In a shop that sells electrical goods a briskly mannered man, grey-suited, knows at once: Thompson Castings was taken over by some larger concern two years ago. Another victim of the recession, this man asserts, no doubt about it. You can't walk a yard without the recession impinging, tales of it everywhere. But when Felicia asks him if he knows what Thompson Castings is called now he says he's stumped. On the streets again no one knows either.

So Felicia returns to the teashop with the bulging windows and sits over a cup of tea because they were helpful to her there. The tables all around her are full, with housewives and office employees who've slipped out for a moment; the waitresses hurry, chivvied by the cashier, who leaves her till from time to time in order to find people seats. The two women at Felicia's table are talking about a third woman's unsatisfactory marriage. They are smartly dressed and made up, seeming younger than perhaps they are, fortyish.

'No one could put up with Garth,' one of them declares, eyeing the fingers of shortbread that have been placed on the table. 'Dire, that man is.'

'You have knowledge of Garth, of course.'

35

'You could say.'

She's becoming used to the accent, Felicia realizes, listening to further exchanges about this husband. Her carrier bags are close to her chair, where she can see them when she glances down. She has removed from her handbag the banknotes the security man who interrogated her didn't comment on, keeping only a few back: the bulk of them are stuffed into the arms of a jumper at the bottom of one of the carrier bags, safer there than in a handbag that might attract a thief. Connie Jo put her handbag down in a café in Dublin and when she turned to pick it up there wasn't a sign of it.

'You couldn't live with stuff like that,' the first woman maintains. 'I always said it.'

'Into swapping, the company Garth keeps. They offered her Bob Mather one time.'

'They never did!'

'Garth fancies Beryl Mather was at the root of that.'

'Excuse me,' Felicia asks the women. 'Would you know what Thompson Castings is called now?'

They look at her, surprised.

'What?' one says.

Felicia repeats the question, and the other woman says there's Thompson's in Half Street.

'The Thompson's I'm after was taken over two years ago,' Felicia explains. 'They make lawn-mowers. The place in Half Street is different.'

The women shake their heads. One of them says she has a Flymo herself.

'Only a friend of mine works there,' Felicia explains. 'I'm trying to find him.'

'Could be anywhere,' the woman who has a Flymo points out, reaching for a finger of shortbread.

'I know.'

When the two women rise to go Felicia asks the waitress who scribbles out their bill, a different waitress from the one who was helpful before. 'Half Street,' this waitress says, abrupt and in a hurry, and doesn't notice when Felicia shakes her head. She asks

36

the couple who occupy the table next to hers, but neither has heard of Thompson Castings, not even in the days before the takeover. She waits for the bustle of the tearoom to calm in the hope that the cashier will be less busy. She's certain now that Thompson Castings, under its new name, is the place she's looking for. She has a feeling about it: he lives in one town and works in the other, no reason why he shouldn't. She even wonders if he didn't say something like that, but then they talked about so much. 'Eleven days left,' he said and on every one of them they met. They walked out to Creagh crossroads in the October sunshine, and held hands in the little crossroads bar attached to Byrne's grocery. They hurried back through the Mandeville woods because it was a short cut, because he didn't like to leave his mother for too long since she saw so little of him.

'Thompson Castings got taken over,' Felicia tells the cashier when she pays for her tea. 'Apparently it's called something else now.'

But this time the cashier looks blankly at her, as if not recalling their previous conversation. 'Yes,' she says, and Felicia leaves the chatter of the tearoom and walks about the streets, asking other people.

She sits for a while on a seat, each hand gripping the string of a carrier bag, the strap of her handbag tight on her chest. They had always had to be careful not to cause difficulties with his mother. When they went to the Diamond Coffee Dock he chose a table at the back in case she passed by on the street outside and saw them. That would upset her, he explained: years ago she had been betrayed in love and had been distrustful of love since. Felicia didn't know his mother to speak to but she sometimes came across her in the shops: a small, tired-looking woman, a widow, Felicia had assumed until he told her that she'd been deserted. A fine white line — a bleached-out scar — ran from beneath her left eye to her jawbone, and this was what you noticed about her most. 'I understand,' Felicia said when he explained that there was nothing he'd have enjoyed more than strolling for longer through the Mandeville woods now that the leaves were on the turn, or idling for hour after hour in the little bar at Byrne's. But of necessity their meetings were often snatched, their coffee hastily drunk. There were glances at his watch even when they were in one another's arms down at the old gasworks. 'Will you be back soon again?' she asked him in the Diamond Coffee Dock on the day of his departure and he said maybe for Christmas. 'Could I write to you?' she asked, and he said he'd give her the address, not that he was much of a one for letters himself. He put his hand over hers on the diamond-patterned surface of the table. 'Every minute I'll think of you,' he said, his fingers still pressing hers. 'Every minute I'll have you by me.' He kissed her on the lips, not minding that the woman serving could see, and she asked him what the address was. He began to tell her, but unfortunately Shay Mulroone came in just then. 'How're you doing?' Shay Mulroone said, leaning against the wall in his working clothes. She prayed he would go away, that it would dawn on him they wanted to be alone, but he just went on telling jokes and laughing. 'Give me a Coke,' he ordered eventually, and plonked the money down on the counter. 'No, by the neck,' he said when the woman began to pour the drink out, and then he took the bottle and moved towards the door, drinking as he went. 'Cheers,' he said, and related a tale about a woodpecker that had got into a honeymoon couple's luggage. 'God, I creased myself laughing the first time I heard that one!'

A flow of bitterness returns when Felicia remembers Shay Mulroone that day, with his broken nose and funny eye, his voice going on and on, his noisy sniggers. If Shay Mulroone hadn't entered the Coffee Dock when he did none of this would be occurring now. They would have kept in touch; letters or postcards – anything at all – would have been exchanged; there might even have been a telephone number. 'Will you write down the address for me?' she said as soon as they were alone again, but everything was a muddle then because the bus was going in less than twenty minutes. 'Oh God, look at the time!' He was on his feet as he spoke and she thought he would write it out there and then, that he'd root in his pockets for a piece of paper and maybe borrow a ballpoint from the woman behind the counter, but instead he became agitated about catching the bus. He'd send her the address, he said, the first thing he did when he arrived. A moment later he was gone and she was left with nothing of him except an empty, sick feeling, as if part of her stomach had been scooped out. She carried her glass coffee mug to a table in the window, thinking that any minute she would disgrace herself by giving way to tears. The address she didn't have – which she had so tentatively asked for in the first place, not wanting to be pushy – had been snatched from her as a lifeline might be. She hadn't realized that even his handwriting on some scrap of paper would have been something to treasure, apart from anything else. From the window she could see Doheny's grocery, where the buses drew in on the other side of the Square. Ten minutes passed and then he was there, with a suitcase, his mother at his side, her arm in his. They passed beneath the statue of the gaitered soldier that stood on the Main Street side of the Square, pausing then for a moment to allow a car to go by before they completed their journey. On the pavement outside Doheny's they were the only two waiting, and within a minute the bus arrived, slowing to a halt while a fresh nagging began: how could he send her his address since he didn't know her own? She had never told him, not even the name of the street: on his journey he would realize that but then it would be too late. 'Bye,' the woman called from behind the counter when she hurried from the Coffee Dock but she was unable to answer, not even to respond by gesturing. Across the Square the bus began to move and then an elongated red setter – the ensign on its side – passed close to where she stood. For a single instant his face was there also, the dark hair, a hand raised in a farewell salute to the small, greyly dressed woman on the pavement. The back of the bus was so dusty that its red-and-white paintwork was obscured, misted into shades of brown.

'No,' a postman says in the town she has come to, pausing in the emptying of a post-box, shaking his head. 'Not known to me at all.'

She asks in shops. She asks two security guards and a woman at a bus stop. 'No, you got that wrong, dear,' a man who is waiting there confidently assures her. 'No way Thompson's was took over. Thompson's went bust two years ago.'

'Is there anywhere here that makes lawn-mowers?'

The man says definitely not and an hour later, in a police station, her question is repeated. 'Anywhere on lawn-mowers these days?' a desk sergeant calls through a hatch. Someone she can't see makes a suggestion, but someone else says that's history, packed it in in '89 they did. 'I doubt we can help you,' the desk sergeant informs her, closing the hatch again.

Already he has confirmed that Thompson Castings went bankrupt two years ago, but in spite of this and the response of his colleagues he consults a directory.

'Nothing here,' he reports.

A second directory is leafed through, two telephone calls made, before she is assured, with even greater confidence than before, that what she seeks does not locally exist: lawn-mowers are not manufactured in this neighbourhood. Lawn-mowers are sold; there are showrooms, which might also possibly supply spare parts; it's perhaps something like that she's after. She is given a list of telephone numbers and spends the next hour in a call-box, not surprised when she is not successful. Storeman in a factory was what he said, definitely a factory.

'No way we can help you further, love,' the desk sergeant makes clear when she returns to him. Best to go back to where she came from this morning, he suggests, since that is the town that has been mentioned by her friend.

Overhearing the conversation, a second policeman looks up from his paperwork to agree. Needle in a haystack, Felicia hears one of them saying to the other as she leaves.

6

At five past four, leaving the catering department early, Mr
Hilditch drives to the bus station and finds a place in a car park
from which he can observe the arrival bays. He is confident she'll
come back; as soon as she draws a blank she'll return in order to
pursue her search in another direction. That stands to reason, but
of course it doesn't preclude the chance that he might have missed
her. She might easily have decided that it was all no good after an
hour or two of making inquiries. All day he has been jittery on
that count; at lunchtime he was in two minds about driving over
to Marshring Crescent and hanging about there in the car for a
while in case she returned. He drove by Number 19 just now, but
naturally you can tell nothing from the outside of a house.

Alert to the buses that come and go, Mr Hilditch presses coins
into the pay meter in the car park and waits for a ticket to emerge.
Shoppers, laden with their purchases, pass slowly by, young women
shouting in frustration at their children, men dour and cross-
looking. There is so much of that, Mr Hilditch considers as he
makes his way back to his car, so much violence in the world, so
much prickliness. *Keep your Distance!* a sticker rudely orders on the
back window of a car. *Surfers Do it Standing Up!* another informs.
I Want Madonna! a T-shirt message asserts. Mr Hilditch finds it all
unattractive.

A bus draws in and Mr Hilditch watches the passengers stepping
off it: schoolchildren, an elderly couple, road repairers with their
snap boxes and empty flasks in grimy canvas satchels. A long-
haired man whom Mr Hilditch often sees on the streets is travelling
about in search of work, he guesses. Factory workers, men and
women, come in a bunch. The Irish girl is not among them.

Hunched in a doorway, he thinks about her. Where looks are

concerned, she's not in the same league as Beth, but then very few girls are. And she certainly doesn't have Elsie Covington's spunkiness, Elsie with her shiny little knees cocked out, sitting sideways the way she used to, her lipstick glistening like a cherry. The memory of Elsie Covington inspires an ornately framed image in Mr Hilditch's recollection, as if a photographer had once been present when she put on her film-star air – Barbara Stanwyck she used to remind him of, not of course that she had ever even heard of Barbara Stanwyck. Beth sits silent within another pretty frame, her long black hair reaching down to the slope of her breasts, her laced black boots ending where her thighs begin. Beth loved black. She used to blacken patches beneath her eyes, and whitely powder her face and neck to make a contrast. In Owen Owen in Coventry they bought a black dress with a lace bodice, the first of the many garments they bought together. All her underclothes were black: she told him that when he asked, the third time they were together it would have been, November 5th 1984, the Happy Eater on the A51, fireworks night, a Monday.

The Irish girl brings it all back, the way a new friend invariably does, stands to reason she should. Memory Lane is always there, always shadowy, even darkened away to nothing until something occurs to turn its lights on. Mr Hilditch likes to think of it like that; he likes to call it Memory Lane, not of course that he'd say it aloud. Certain things you don't say aloud; and certain things you don't even say to yourself, best left, best forgotten. Many a time he has lain awake at night and willed the glitter to come – the little floating snapshots of Elsie and Beth and the others: Elsie with her hand raised for attention, Beth in her yellow jersey, Sharon coming out of the Ladies at the Frimley Little Chef, Gaye waiting for him outside the electricity showrooms in Market Drayton, Jakki lighting a cigarette in the car.

The particular buses he's watching for come once every forty minutes, but he doesn't mind the wait because the potency of remembering is already running softly through his senses. The manager of an Odeon, in evening dress, flashed a smile at Beth in the foyer once: Leicester that had been, *The Return of the Pink Panther*. A boy attempted to pick up Elsie in the Southam Restful

Tray, grinning from a distance at her, and she gestured across the tables, indicating that she was engaged.

Jakki wanted to go to a church once, the time she had religion, and they went to a Baptist place in Coalville. In a Services on the M6 a boy was familiar with Gaye; no more than five foot that boy was, an ornamental razor blade on one of his ears and a shaved head, chunky, a trouble-maker, smelling of drink. In the Services near Loughborough Beth didn't speak for the entire meal, not that she was cross, just thoughtful, as any girl has a right to be. 'Five Foot Two, Eyes of Blue': Beth always reminds him of it, the lilting little rhythm somehow suits the memory of her.

Another bus comes in. The Irish girl is on it.

Stepping into the crowd, Felicia searches with her eyes. The buses in the bays, in differently coloured groups, are lined up at an angle, their destinations indicated, their waiting drivers standing about. Latecomers are goaded into a run by the occasional starting of an engine; those already seated are impatient. *The Friendly Midland Red*, *Midland Fox*, *Chambers' Coaches*, *Townabout*, are repeated designations.

Felicia wills her friend to step from a recently arrived bus, but he fails to do so; nor does she glimpse him anywhere in the crowd. For the first time she wonders if she should just go home again, and wonders what it would be like, walking into the kitchen to face her father and her brothers. Seeking some indication of her movements, they would by now have discovered the letters she had intended to take away with her but left behind by mistake: long, sprawling letters she had written even though they couldn't be posted. Every evening, in what seclusion the bedroom offered, while the old woman dozed or pored over another jigsaw, she wrote down what she thought would interest him: how Miss Horish from the tech backed her car into a petrol pump at Aldritt's garage; how Aidan – under pressure from Connie Jo and Connie Jo's mother and father – had already given up his trade and was now assisting in McGrattan Street Cycles and Prams; how the Pond's rep had been footless in the chemist's; how Cuneen the assistant with the short leg had been sacked from Chawke's for

43

falsifying. She made a calendar of the days until Christmas because he had mentioned Christmas as a time when, with a bit of luck, he might be back. She crossed each day off as it passed and then, when there were only nineteen left, she found herself writing a letter that was different from any she had written before . . . *It is a trouble but there it is. I was late the first month and then again this one. There is no doubt about it Johnny. I thought maybe being with you like we were might cause it to be late but it is different now. I will be two months gone at Christmas and then we will have to decide what to do Johnny . . .*

That letter -- the last she wrote — is with the others, secreted beneath her shell collection in the white chest of drawers beside her bed. On the night she wrote it, still lying awake hours afterwards, she wished that of all her letters she was able to post this one. The composing of the others — making up the sentences while she went about the shops or performed her household tasks -- had been a consolation; once written down, the trouble she recorded now — not shared with anyone — acquired an extra dread. As she lay there sleepless after she'd completed the letter, she tried to think of better words than the words she'd used, some softer way of putting it. But all there was was the church bell striking one o'clock, then two and three and four, and the old woman's watery gurgling, the bedsprings creaking as movement was attempted, the sudden gasp and then the breathing becoming regular again. When she was younger Felicia used to fear that her great-grandmother would die while she slept, that she'd be white and motionless in the morning, dead eyes staring.

Among the waiting buses, the melancholy of that long night returns and Felicia's spirits are as low as they were then — lower than on the ferry or in the desolate room where the security man interrogated her, or when she woke up on the train and didn't know where she was, lower than when the policeman said a needle in a haystack. Still searching among the faces around her, she again experiences the sense of punishment she was first aware of the night she wrote the last of her letters: a call to order, a call to account for the happiness she had so recklessly indulged in. 'Don't worry about that side of things,' he had reassured her once, as they hurried through the Mandeville woods. 'All that's taken care of by

44

myself.' Her face went red when he said it, but she was glad he had. 'There's nothing wrong in it,' he murmured, saying more, nothing wrong in it when two people love one another. Yet the night she wrote the letter she felt that maybe, after all, there had been: the old-fashioned sin you had to confess if you went to Confession; the sin of being greedy, the sin of not being patient. And why should she have supposed that the happiness his love had given her was her due, and free?

If she goes back now she'll wake up again in that bedroom. There'll be another dawn breaking on the same despair, the weariness of getting up when the bell chimes six, another day beginning. The cramped stairs will again be cleaned on Tuesdays, the old woman's sheets changed at the weekend. If she goes back now her father's eyes will still accuse, her brothers will threaten revenge. There will be Connie Jo's regret that she married into a family anticipating a shameful birth. There will be interested glances, or hard looks, on the street. God, you fool, Carmel will say, and Rose will say were you born yesterday?

Only being together, only their love, can bring redemption: she knows that perfectly. She knew it when Christmas passed and he did not return. She knew it during the snow that came in January; she knew it when the first week of February came gustily in, when she went to see his mother. 'I'm a friend of Johnny's, Mrs Lysaght': standing now with her carrier bags, hopelessly looking about her, she hears the echo of her nervousness, a stutter in her voice.

Is it being so separated from its reality that lends the recollection such potency, distance sharpening the ordinary trudge of time? His mother's stare, cold with suspicion and distrust, his mother at first saying nothing, seeming ready to close her front door on a whim. His mother asking her what she wanted, a dull inquisitiveness developing. The door held open then; the narrow passage, the way led to the kitchen. 'Yes?' his mother said, the white thread of the scar beneath her eye more noticeable in the better light. Bitter as a sloe, people called this woman.

The crowd is dwindling in the bus station, but Felicia still stands where she has taken up her position, by a refreshment kiosk that has closed. No buses are arriving now and only a few remain, waiting to set off. As clearly as she sees them, there are also the two figures in his mother's kitchen; as clearly as she hears the voices and the laughter of the people passing near by, there are the voices of his mother and herself.

'I was only wondering if you had Johnny's address.'

'What d'you want with Johnny?'

'Just to write him a letter, Mrs Lysaght.'

'My son wouldn't want his address given out to all and sundry.'

'It'd be all right giving it to me, Mrs Lysaght.'

'I'll be writing to him myself. I'll tell him you called in.'

His mother knew who she was: she didn't say so, but Felicia could tell. She knew her name and that her father worked in the convent garden, that his grandmother was still alive, almost a hundred years old. You could tell just by being in Mrs Lysaght's presence that she was a woman who knew everything.

'He wouldn't mind you giving me the address.'

'Why's that?'

'I know he wouldn't.'

'He didn't give it to you himself then?'

Felicia began to stammer. Mrs Lysaght sat down. A hand touched the lower part of her stomach, as if some pain had begun there.

'I have things to do,' she said, not rising at once but doing so a moment later before Felicia could collect herself. She moved towards the passage that led to her front door.

'I know he wouldn't mind,' Felicia said again. She felt a burst of heat in her face that tingled to the roots of her hair. 'I need the address badly.'

'Johnny has his own friends here, Cathal Kelly, Shay Mulroone, boys like that. I don't recall anyone like yourself mentioned.'

'I need the address, Mrs Lysaght.'

Felicia's predicament dawned in Mrs Lysaght's features then. Her mouth sagged; distaste crept into the coldness in her eyes.

'Leave my son alone.' She spoke without emotion. 'Leave him.'

'All I want to do is to contact him.'

'You've had contact enough with him.'

But Mrs Lysaght didn't move out of the kitchen, as she had

46

begun to do. She remained in the doorway and after a moment raised the fingers of her right hand to the scar on her face.

'I'm not well,' she said.

'I'm sorry, Mrs Lysaght.'

'It's why he comes back. Because I'm not well.'

'I didn't know —'

'When the rent man comes on a Friday I can see him looking at me. I haven't been myself since Johnny couldn't find work here. The worst day of my life.'

Felicia shook her head, trying to find something to say but unable to do so. On the mantelpiece, pushed between an ornamental china box and the wall, she could see a bundle of letters and postcards, and guessed whom they were from. The address would be there.

'I knew it,' Mrs Lysaght said, 'the first time he went out with you. "I think I'll get a few lungfuls of air," he said, and when he came in again he said he'd met Cathal Kelly. One time in Dublin, on his way back after being over to see me, he was seen with a girl coming out of an ice-cream parlour. That came back to me and I mentioned it. He laughed. "Mistaken identity," he said. They'd do anything,' Mrs Lysaght added, as though she had forgotten whom she was talking to, 'once they have their clutches round a boy. Sweet as sugar, and then they're working like adders.'

Her fingers ran slowly down the mark on her cheek. 'Wouldn't hurt a fly,' she said, 'until the moment comes. "What about Johnny?" I said to his father. He stood there, just come in from the rain, the drips falling on to the floor, a foot from where you're standing yourself. "Doesn't Johnny mean anything?" I said, and all he did was look away from me, with the pool of water at his feet. "Listen to me," he said, but what was there to listen to? He was off, and what's there to listen to in that? "You'll get money regular," he said. That's all he could think to say. Four years married, two miscarriages before Johnny, and then your husband's off. "Take it," I said to him, and I picked up the bread-knife off that table. "Do what you like with me. No better than dirt, that woman you're going to." I held the knife out to him, but he didn't

47

move. So I lifted it myself and I watched him watching me. And then the point broke the flesh and I pulled it down hard.'

Mrs Lysaght turned and left the kitchen when she'd said that, and Felicia followed her.

'If I gave you a letter would you send it on for me, Mrs Lysaght?'

The front door was opened, and since no reply had come Felicia repeated her request. She would stamp the envelope, she promised. All that was necessary was that it should be addressed.

'Very well,' Mrs Lysaght agreed at last.

But when ten days, and then a fortnight, passed without a reply Felicia knew that the letter had not been sent. It had not been sent because his mother hated her. Johnny was being stolen from his mother, in the same way as a woman had stolen her husband: that was how his mother saw it. She'd have read the letter and probably burnt it.

As she moves from where she has been standing by the refreshment kiosk, Felicia wonders if his mother guesses where she is now; and, knowing, if she hates her more. She wonders if his mother mentioned the visit when she wrote to him herself, and thinks she wouldn't have. Why should she, since it's not in her interest, since there's nothing to be gained? He never said his mother wasn't well; it explained his solicitude for her.

'I was worried about you,' a voice says, and the bespectacled face of the fat man who helped her yesterday is there in a doorway. He speaks softly, his expression full of the concern he refers to, his sudden presence, and what he says, bewildering Felicia. During the course of the day, he goes on, he has made inquiries about Thompson Castings and learned that she has been misled. He was so upset that he asked around and in the end tracked down the only factory within a reasonable distance that filled the bill. They did a mower with a Briggs and Stratton engine there, the bodywork cast in the works, Sheffield blades, rotary or cylinder.

'I think it's what you're looking for,' he says. 'I phoned up Ada from the office and she said to drop by the bus station in case I caught a sight of you coming back. When I told Ada last night what your problem was she was worried to think of you wandering about.'

He is pressed back in one corner of the doorway, shop windows displaying shoes on either side of him. His voice is no more than a whisper, not like it was when she accosted him yesterday to ask if she'd come to the right place, or when he called out from his car at her. Ada is his wife, he says, a caring woman.

'The only thing is it's a good fifty miles away.'

She begins to shake her head, but he says there are lots living locally who make a journey like that every day. No reason why her friend wouldn't. A girl in the office checked the whole thing out: up to sixty-odd miles people travel every day.

'They'd go to business in a locality like the one you drew a blank in today, or this one I'm mentioning. Coming back here for nights.'

'Yes, I understand. I worked that out.'

He is whistling beneath his breath, a soft breeze on his lips, soundless almost. It ceases when he speaks again.

'What I wanted to tell you,' he explains, 'is that the wife and myself have to drive up that way in the morning. What I'm saying is you'd be welcome to a seat in our little jalopy.' He laughs, the excess flesh on his face and neck quivering and then settling again.

'Oh, I don't think I —'

'No, of course you wouldn't. Naturally you wouldn't. It's just that Ada said I should mention it. But I reminded her it's an early start. You probably wouldn't want an early start.'

'Your wife —'

'Ada's poorly. We have to drop her into a hospital up there. Specialist stuff.'

'If you could just give me the name of the factory,' Felicia begins to say, but is interrupted at once by the doubt that spreads through the plump features in the shadows of the doorway.

'It's difficult, that. The girl wrote down the name and address on a notelet for me, but unfortunately I left it behind in the office. When the cleaners came on I was going to give them a ring and they'd read it out to me. But there's no call for that if you're not game for the early start.'

49

'If you could just give me the name of the town –'

'You'd be there for the duration, searching high and low. There's upwards of a hundred and fifty works you'd have to investigate, more like two hundred. Still, maybe I'll run into you again one of these days and I'll pass the info on. I have to be going now, to see how Ada passed the day.' He eases himself out of the doorway and begins to walk away.

Quickly Felicia says:

'Could I have the lift?'

'It's six-thirty sharp on account of Ada having to be in the hospital first thing. Sorry about that.'

'Six-thirty's all right.'

'We'll pick you up down Marshring. Junction of Crescent and the Avenue.'

He smiles and nods. He won't forget to ring the cleaners, he promises, then ambles off. Felicia watches his cumbersome form disappear into the car park before taking his place in the doorway, her glance again searching the crowd for Johnny Lysaght.

7

The house is silent and in darkness. No pet is there to witness the homecoming of its single occupant, not a goldfish or a bird. A key turns in the deadlock, a second one clicks in the Yale. The spacious hall is illuminated, the breathy sound of an aborted whistle begins.

Mr Hilditch hangs his mackintosh on the hall-stand, catching a single glimpse of himself in its octagonal mirror. Mechanically, he raises a hand to pat an area of his short hair. Other families' ancestors regard him from the portraits he has purchased over the years, a strangers' gallery that is no longer strange. In his kitchen he gathers together the ingredients of a meal.

The *frisson* of excitement that has been with him all day is charged with a greater surge now that he has spoken to the Irish girl again: never before has there been a girl as close to home as this one, a girl who actually approached him on the works premises. Elsie Covington cropped up in Uttoxeter, Beth in Wolverhampton, Gaye in Market Drayton. Sharon was Wigston; Jakki, Walsall. All of them, like the Irish girl, came from further afield and were heading elsewhere, anywhere in most cases. You make the rule about not soiling your own doorstep, not shopping locally, as the saying goes; you go to lengths to keep the rule in place, but this time the thing just happened. Fruit falling from a tree you haven't even shaken; something meant, it feels like. And perhaps to do with being approached rather than the other way round, Mr Hilditch senses a promise: this time the relationship is destined to be special.

The snapshot memories begin again: weekend appearances in towns and places where no one knows he is Hilditch, a catering manager; hours spent in the car, watching from a vantage point

51

near a disco that is due to end, or just parked anywhere on the off chance; up and down the motorways, alert on the approach roads in case there is another vehicle to keep close to; fatherly conversations with waitresses in bed-and-breakfast places, an invitation offered but not often accepted.

Mr Hilditch wonders if the breaking of his meticulously kept rule is in some way related to the fact that the Irish girl comes from so far away, a foreigner you might say, the first time there has been that. She is the ultimate in passing trade, more than just a new face for the A522 Burger King or the Forest East Services, or the Long Eaton Little Chef. Whatever the reason for his own behaviour, he finds himself exhilarated by the circumstances that have been presented to him, and only regrets that the ordained brevity of this relationship is an element in those circumstances also. Perhaps that, he reflects as he washes a pound of brussels sprouts, is how perfection in a friendship has to be, unenduring lest it lose its quality.

Grilling the steak he bought in Tesco's on the way back to his house, draining potatoes and the Brussels sprouts, he effortlessly keeps the girl's features in his consciousness. He lays the table in the dining-room, carrying in salt and pepper and a few slices of Mother's Pride on a side plate. He always eats in the dining-room in the evenings.

While waiting for the steak to grill, he scoops two individual trifles on to a plate, pours cream over them and sprinkles a spoonful of caster sugar. He carries the trifles to his long mahogany table, carrying, as well, his biscuit tin – raspberry creams and coffee creams, chocolate digestives, fig rolls, a couple of KitKats. Music plays softly: 'Bugle Call Rag'.

She walks about, still scanning the faces on the pavements. If the man hadn't told her what he had, if he hadn't sounded so certain, she might by now have convinced herself that she should go home in spite of what awaits her there. Again she wonders what they're thinking now, what conclusions have been reached. Do they dread her return as much as she dreads it herself? That thought strikes her suddenly, not having occurred to her before. Are they hoping she has gone for ever? Is there a plea in Mrs Lysaght's prayers that she should be lost, or even dead?

'Did you go out with young Lysaght?' her father asked, only a few hours after she handed to Mrs Lysaght the letter in a stamped envelope. 'A while back?' her father went on, his tone suggesting that some further turn of the screw was in store for her. 'October?'

A man on the street asks her something, smiling at her. She doesn't understand; she doesn't answer. She didn't answer, either, when her father asked those questions. She was polishing brass at the draining-board, ornaments and ashtrays which her father liked to see gleaming, as he did the brass on people's hall doors. 'Around about the time of the wedding?' he pressed.

'I know Johnny Lysaght,' she said. She bent her head over a piece that represented three monkeys, their paws obscuring mouth, ears or eyes. The television, which was on earlier, had been turned off.

'Did you go out with him, though?'

'I did.'

'I would avoid that fellow,' her father said. 'I would go out with some other young fellow.'

'What d'you mean?'

'You hear certain remarks made about Lysaght.' Her father's grey head was poked out in Felicia's direction, a habit he had when he was serious or intent upon being understood. 'I'm not saying it's gospel. All I'm saying is there are certain statements made.'

'What statements?'

'That he joined the British army.'

'Johnny works in a factory stores. Lawn-mower parts.'

He nodded thoughtfully and slowly, as if agreeing. He was frowning a little, which he tended to when endeavouring to establish an accuracy. He liked to get things right.

'It'd be a natural enough thing for him to keep it quiet about the army.'

'He has work in a stores.'

Her father continued to nod in the same slow fashion, and when he spoke the pace of his speech was unhurried also. He wondered, he remarked, where something without foundation would have come from, and added:

'There's better boys round here than that, girl. Irish boys belong in Ireland.'

'Johnny went to England because he couldn't get work here.'

'A member of the British forces could be sent into the North. He could be set to killing our own.'

'Johnny's not in any army. It's someone else you heard about.'

'There's plenty of decent Irish boys you could go to Sheehy's public house with, girl. That's all I'm saying to you.'

There was a silence in the kitchen then. Her father sat straight and upright in his chair, not doing anything with his hands, gazing in front of him at nothing. Felicia picked up another piece of brass.

'Johnny and myself love one another.' The words came tonelessly, when several minutes had passed. She didn't cease to polish the brass while she spoke. 'There's no one can do anything about that.'

There was no reply. Had she still been employed she might have brought up with one of the women at Slieve Bloom Meats the plight she found herself in, a plight that could not be mentioned in the kitchen. She remembered the women's lowered tones when they spoke of such a predicament, or joked about it. She could have said she had a friend who was in trouble; anything like that would have done. Instead she had still told no one that punctually every day, at eleven o'clock in the morning, nausea afflicted her. Not Carmel nor Rose nor Connie Jo, nor Sister Benedict, who always listened to your troubles; naturally not her brothers. The very thought of confiding in someone she knew well made her feel nervous all over, prickles on her skin.

But while waiting that evening for her father to launch into further condemnation of Johnny Lysaght, and perhaps because the women at the canning factory had come into her thoughts, she remembered Miss Furey. 'You're no more than a child, Felicia,' her father commented eventually, on his feet and already going from the kitchen. He hesitated by the door, as if about to say something else, and just then her brothers returned from Myles

54

Brady's and sat down at the table to eat slices of a pan loaf and spreadable cheese, which every night at this time they did. Her father closed the door behind him.

Would she have been able to confide in her mother? Would she have confessed and said that an error had occurred, that there was no doubt? Would her mother have gone silent, and been unable to disguise her disappointment, have even cried for a while, but then have known what to do? Would she have cried herself, and been comforted in the end?

She pushes her way into a public house, the Pride of Lions, still pondering that. It's crowded and noisy: drinkers are flushed with laughter and good humour; the barmaids hurry with glasses. The surface of the bar is marble, brown flecked with green and grey. There are shaded lamps on the walls between dark-framed mirrors, and green velvet on the banquettes that stretch beneath them. Glass-topped tables have ornamental metal clasps at the corners. On one of them, beside her, a lipstick-stained cigarette is smouldering in an ashtray. At the bar a man is demonstrating a mechanical chimpanzee in a tartan dress.

No one notices her, standing there with her bags. Music is playing, the air is smoky. There are football colours, red and white; a gang of youths. 'Here we go! Here we go!' their song begins, and a voice calls out that singing's not permitted, not tonight or any other night. A black girl leans against the bar, her head thrown back in amusement. Felicia stays a moment longer, making certain: he isn't there.

Cold on the street again, she picks up the thread of thought this conviviality has interrupted. There is no way she can know if she would have confessed to her mother. Her mother is too far away now, too shadowy and lost, little remaining of her besides that last glimpse of her features, and the memory of running to keep up with Father Kilgallen in the Square, and her father being there when the moment came, and the old woman saying she has outlived another one. 'Excuse me, miss,' a bearded face begs. 'Bit of loose change at all?'

Strange to think it was Miss Furey she confessed to, or as good as confessed to: a stranger who once a fortnight sold duck eggs and turkey eggs in the shops. Middle-aged, unmarried, a woman to whom no man had been known to pay attentions, yet about whom there had once been a rumour that she was pregnant. When abruptly her condition changed and she returned to normal it was said with certainty that no child existed in the farmhouse where she lived.

Felicia drops a coin on to the proffered palm. The man looks at it, not thanking her, not saying anything. Guiltily, she adds a second coin, still thinking about Miss Furey. She hadn't hesitated when she remembered the story that had got about: the night after her father brought up the subject of her love affair she rode out to Miss Furey's farmhouse, a frosty night, the moon almost full. Dogs barked as she approached the yard. Miss Furey herself opened the back door.

'I'm sorry to come like this,' Felicia said, and gave her name. 'Could I ask you something, Miss Furey?'

Miss Furey was a big-shouldered woman, with large and protrudent teeth. Her nose was large also, heavy about the nostrils. These were her dominant features. Her hair, cut short, was sandy.

'Are you lost?' she asked in reply to Felicia's query.

'No, no, it's not that. I think maybe you could help me.'

'Come in.'

She held the door back and Felicia walked straight into a big, cluttered kitchen. Miss Furey's brother, heavily made also, was seated in an armchair by a Rayburn cooker, watching television. Cats slept at his feet. The dogs that had barked were sheepdogs, one of them diseased, something the matter with the skin of its head, around its eyes. Four dogs in all there were, and as many cats.

'I don't know do I know you?' Miss Furey's bewilderment, mingled with the curiosity of a woman who did not have many visitors, had not abated.

'No, you don't. I hope you don't mind me coming out.'

'Why'd I mind?'

There were unwashed dishes on a table in the centre of the kitchen, and saucepans and a frying pan piled up in the sink. All the surfaces – windowsills, shelves, table-tops – were untidy. Two pairs of wellington boots stood by a door that was half open at the far end of the kitchen. Coats hung on hooks; there were sacred pictures, and a calendar. Dishes of food for the cats littered the soiled linoleum on the floor.

'We paid that tax thing,' Miss Furey's brother said. He didn't take his eyes from the television screen. His clothes were ragged, as Miss Furey's were, cardigans and jumpers with holes in them. Both of them wore trousers.

'Sit down at the table,' Miss Furey invited, and Felicia could feel her curiosity getting the better of her suspicion. She wanted to hear; already there was an eagerness about her. It was the News on the television.

'I have a cheek coming here,' Felicia said.

'Well, you're here now. Don't mind him,' Miss Furey added, for Felicia had glanced in the direction of the man in the armchair. 'He's deaf on the left side.'

Felicia let it all tumble out. She wanted to close her eyes while she did so in order not to have to see the woman's reactions, in order not to have to pay attention to them when Miss Furey took offence. At the time it had been said that Miss Furey had travelled to Dublin to consult a chemist who performed operations. The women at Slieve Bloom Meats said her brother was the father. One of them contradicted the theory that a Dublin chemist had been involved, claiming that the infant had been got rid of more crudely and been buried on the Fureys' land.

'God above us!' Miss Furey exclaimed. 'What are you telling me this for?'

'I remember years ago –'

'That's a slander you're about to say. Don't say it.'

Miss Furey kept her voice down, even though it was thick with emotion. Deaf on the left side or not, the man hunched in the armchair had sharply turned his head when she exclaimed.

'Could you help me, Miss Furey?'

'People will say anything. Any lies that will come to their lips. Go home now.'

Miss Furey rose. In her tattered garments she hastened to the

57

door that led to the yard, the four sheepdogs roused by her movement.

'Take care I wouldn't go to the Guards,' she threatened. 'Get off our property now.'

Riding back, Felicia wept and the oozing of her tears became a flow that blinded her. When finally they ceased she dismounted in order to wipe away the traces from her cheeks and to blow her nose. 'Please, God,' she prayed. 'Please, God, help me.'

But no help came. Instead, on her return, her father pursued his harangue. 'Now, listen to me, girl,' he began the moment he saw her, a hardness distinguishing his features and his tone as he advanced on to the territory that mattered to him most, territory on which he was unable to believe he could ever be wrong, on which his own expertise was unassailable. Her face tingling with cold, the rims of her eyes raw from her tears and the chill night air, Felicia listened.

'You will not live in this house and keep company with a member of the occupying forces. This family knows where it stands, and always has done. Your great-grandfather and his patriot companions journeyed from this small community to the cockpit of war, and perished in their valiant efforts. For eight centuries, not an hour less, the Irish people have known only the suppression of language, religion and human freedom. A vision was born on the streets of Dublin seventy-five years ago during those Easter days. It was not fulfilled, the potential has not been realized: you have only to look around you. On top of that the jackboot of the British bully is still in six of our counties; there is still the spectre of death and torture on the streets of towns as humble as our own. No child of mine will ever be on that side of things, girl.'

Felicia said nothing, and for a moment closed her eyes. What was being said about soldiers was pathetically irrelevant.

'This fellow'll be back, girl, but associate with him and you'll leave this house. That's said and it needn't be said again.' Her father paused, then went on less harshly. 'You're at the beginning of things, girl. One of these days there'll be work for you to go out to again. I heard yesterday a farmers' co-op might be set up, with every item stocked that a farmer would want – gum boots, pig-wire, roofing felt, all that type of article and more. Within a six month there could be as many employed as there used be in the canning, maybe twice the number. When you're a child you take advice, girl. That's what I'm saying to you now. I've said it and we can leave it.'

Felicia did not acknowledge this either. She remembered, years ago, when she was too young to understand, her father playfully drawing her attention to a little Union Jack that was the trade mark on the bonnet of Miss Gwynn's old Wolseley car. She had been holding his hand, out for a walk with him on a Sunday morning. 'A good thing the Wolseley went out of business,' her father had remarked with humorous satisfaction, and at the time it had seemed a natural thing to say. Yet now, just because someone worked in England, just because he had an English accent, he had to be condemned, and lies made up about him.

'I'll say one last thing to you, girl: look no further than that brave old woman who sleeps across the room from you. Not much older than yourself she was when the lads went off, knowing the colour of their duty. Three days later and she's a widow. She wasn't married a month and he was gone. Don't talk to me of some back-street romance, girl.'

He nodded in his emphatic manner, still lost in the fervour that inspired his statements. Then he rose and left the kitchen, as he had the evening before. But when she was cooking the breakfast the next morning he suddenly said:

'Has Lysaght got you pregnant?'

She didn't pretend otherwise. There was no point in pretending anything. No point in telling a downright lie now that the word was there between them.

'We're both responsible,' she said.

'How long are you gone?'

'I've missed a few times.'

'How many?'

'There's no doubt about it.'

He crossed himself. He called her a hooer, looking at her over the smoke from the frying pan, not raising his voice. He said he was glad her mother wasn't alive. No better than a dirty hooer, he furiously repeated.

'I feel sick in the mornings,' she said.

By ten o'clock Mr Hilditch has read everything in the *Daily Telegraph*: the foreign news, the financial news, the sports news, the home news. He has no interest in sport, but usually finds himself acquiring information about sporting matters because he finds the knowledge useful in conversation. A high court judge, he has learned, is in some trouble after revelations made by a youth; a woman has been found, still living, in the locked boot of a Ford Escort; the dogs of New Age travellers have ravaged a herd of sheep; a woman has decapitated her husband. Such detail engenders a mild gloom in Mr Hilditch and he rouses himself to place a record on the turntable of the old, wind-up gramophone he bought at an auction the week Number Three became his own. 'I Got it Bad and That Ain't Good' cheers him considerably, and pleasurably he speculates on what tomorrow holds for him.

8

The little hump-backed car is waiting at the end of Marshring Crescent even though Felicia is early. Its windows are misted up, but one of them is wound down as she approaches. The fat man smiles at her. He whispers, as if anxious not to disturb the sleep of the people in the nearby houses. He tells her to get in at the other door, remaining in the car himself.

It isn't yet fully light. As she settles her bags at her feet, she feels it is wrong that she should be sitting in the front and the man's wife in the back. But she doesn't say so because the engine has already been started. The car is actually moving before she realizes that the back seats are empty.

'Your wife,' she begins, suddenly alarmed.

'I had to take Ada in last night. No warning whatsoever, they rang up to say the little op was put forward to ten this morning. I had to drive Ada over so's they could prepare her.'

Bewildered and still uneasy, Felicia says she hopes he isn't making this second journey on her account.

'Ada'll need me when she comes through. I have to be at the bedside. Digs all right, are they?' His voice is squeaky. She hasn't noticed before. He isn't a man you can be alarmed about for long.

'What?'

'The house you're in? OK, is it?'

'It's fine.'

'I'm glad to hear it. I wouldn't like to think I'd misled you about Marshring.'

The huge shoulders beside her are motionless as he drives. Hands, ungloved and pale, seem disproportionately slight on the steering wheel. There's hardly any traffic about. A joy to drive in the early morning, he remarks, and adds:

'First time I met up with you I could see you were in an upset.'

'It's just that I've come a long way.'

'And then again you're in a country that's strange to you.'

'Yes, I am.' She explains how at first she found it hard to understand what people were saying to her, but that this is getting better the more she listens.

'I hope I didn't offend in that respect.' An unexpected gurgle of laughter startles her. Two small eyes gleam humorously behind the thick spectacles. Pouches of flesh blur the features that are turned in her direction, teeth smile evenly. He smells of soap, a pleasant early-morning freshness that reassures her. The cuffs of his shirt are crisp and clean.

'Soon as you spot your friend you'll be tickety-boo. Soon as you know the state of play.'

'Yes.'

'Do you mind if I ask you your name?'

She tells him; he doesn't tell her his. 'I never heard that one,' he says instead. 'Felicity we have over here.'

'My father found Felicia. Some woman he'd heard of.'

A woman who'd manned the barricades in 1916, who'd met her death there. There is a newspaper cutting about this person in her father's albums, a photograph of a hard-faced woman in military uniform.

'It's nice,' he says, ignoring the information about the revolutionary woman. 'Felicia has a ring to it.'

'Yes, I suppose so.'

'I was never in your country, Felicia. Though I had a relative who used to talk about it. Beautiful country, I understand.'

'It's all right.'

'You work at something, Felicia?'

'I had work in a canning factory. It closed a while back.'

'The unemployment's terrible. Strictly speaking, you're unemployed then?'

'Yes, I am.'

'And have you other family, Felicia? Father and mother still with us?'

'My father is. So's my great-grandmother. I have three brothers, two of them twins.'

'*Great*-grandmother? She'd be an age, eh?'

'She's nearly a hundred.'

'Well, I never!'

The landscape they are driving through has become familiar to Felicia: the well-used fields, grass drenched in a greyish fuzz, furnace chimneys breaking the flat monotony, the brick of factories.

'That old lady would remember the Boer War.'

Felicia doesn't know when the Boer War was, but she nods none the less. Once she would have known, at least for the length of one of Sister Francis Xavier's history classes, but then she'd have forgotten because she had no interest. Her great-grandmother wouldn't have been interested in a foreign war either.

'Two relatives went down to the Boers,' her companion divulges. 'I'm from a military family.'

'I see.'

'I've had a regimental career myself. The army's in my blood, as you might say.'

'You're not in the army now?'

'I came out when Ada was first ailing. She needed care, more care than I could give, having regimental duties. No, I still help the regiment out, but it's office stuff now.'

'At the factory where I met you —'

'Oh, no, no. No, not at all. I happened to call in there to see a friend. Well, as a matter of fact, to tell him Ada was going into hospital. People like to know a thing like that. No, I keep things straight for the regiment on the bookkeeping side now. Gets me out of the house, Ada says.'

Again Felicia nods.

'You'd stagnate if you didn't, Felicia. You'd stagnate in a big house, caring for an invalid wife, nursing really.'

'Your wife's an invalid?'

'Best to think of Ada as that. Best for Ada, she says herself, best for me. It's what it amounts to, as a matter of honest fact, no good denying it, no good pulling the wool. You follow me, Felicia?'

'Yes, I do.'

'If you face the facts you can take them in your stride. I had a sergeant-major under me said that, top-class man. You meet all sorts in a regimental career.'

'Yes, I'm sure.'

'Not long now, Felicia. You're jumpy, aren't you?'

Again there is the smile, the small eyes glinting at her, clear behind the thick glass discs. This is a kind man, Felicia reflects through her apprehension, kinder than the desk sergeant of yesterday, who became impatient in the end. 'God, here she is again,' she heard him muttering when she returned to the police station in the hope that he might have come by some further information.

'Anyone'd be nervy in the circumstances, Felicia. This chap's a boyfriend, is he?'

'Yes.'

'Well, there you are. Naturally you'd want to locate a boyfriend.'

'Yes.'

'Family at arm's length, eh? Boyfriend not approved?'

'My father's against him.'

'It can be awkward when there's that. In conversation with you, Felicia, you can sense a spot of bother. I thought it might be family.'

She explains about her father, how he has got it into his head that Johnny is in the British army, how her great-grandmother was left widowed by the Troubles when she was married only a month, how there is always that in the family, a feeling for that particular past.

'He'd have told me if he was in the army.'

'Of course he would. And if he has steady work and isn't some fly-by-night why should the family worry? If he's your choice and if you're his, why should they interfere?'

'My father's unreasonable.'

'I know what you mean, Felicia. Some of the young squaddies I had under me in the regiment had a problem or two of a similar nature. Trouble over the girlfriend, family at arm's length. I used to father the poor lads, if you get my meaning. I'd bring them back to the house and Ada'd give them tea and pies and cake, a whole spread she'd have. We never had kids of our own, a great disappointment to Ada and myself. Fond of the boyfriend, are you?'

'Yes.'

'Not hard to believe he's fond of you.'

For a further hour the conversation continues. Felicia hears more about the regiment, and about the factories they pass near, how the motorways have changed the face of England, how new towns have come to these parts, how people from Pakistan and the West Indies have begun to settle, changing the look of things also, how prosperity has given way to poverty in certain areas. At ten to eight the little green car creeps cautiously into a factory car park.

'Thanks very much indeed,' Felicia says.

'I'm not due at the hospital just yet.' In the same cautious manner the car is driven to the edge of the car park; and Felicia is informed that you have to be careful in case you plank yourself down in a space that is reserved for management or where parking is forbidden. Before you know where you are you could find your head being chewed off by some officious attendant. 'We'll see everyone who arrives from here,' the fat man adds. Most would come by car, he says, and there'll probably be a couple of buses just before half past eight. If somehow they miss her friend she can always make inquiries at the security barrier.

'I don't want to keep you from the hospital.'

'Ada'd want me to give you what help I could. A young girl wandering isn't recommended in this part of the world, you know. You hear shocking things sometimes.'

'It's very nice of you.'

'She's always worried about a young girl wandering. Well, I told you. It was Ada who said to find out about any works where mowers would be manufactured. It was her initiative. Well, being a woman, I suppose.'

'I hope she's all right.'

'I'd go in and have a word only they don't like you to bother the patients before the ops. Better not to cause an excitement, I think it is. You know how it is, Felicia, a patient might want to go to the toilet if she got worked up due to a visitor.'

'Yes.'

'They don't like that before an op. I know it from sad experience.'

She nods, only half hearing what's being said now that they have reached the factory. In the night she dreamed that her father called her a hooer again, and a soiled young bitch. Her mother was alive, saying she wouldn't have believed it of her, striking her with her fists, saying it was she who should be dead. In her dream she could see the sprawl of the convent at the top of steep St Joseph's Hill, and the Square with its statue of the gaitered soldier, and vegetables lank outside the shops in the summer heat. There was the chiming of the Angelus; turf smoke was pungent on the air. Her father said they wouldn't be able to hold their heads up when the sniggering began in the back streets. Carmel and Rose talked about it in the Coffee Dock.

'Here's something now,' her companion remarks when cars begin to arrive. She is advised to wind down her window to give herself a clearer view.

It is not impossible that the boyfriend may actually appear. It is not impossible, but it is hardly likely. When he telephoned this works yesterday he spoke to the only person employed in the stores department, and that was a woman. The kind of store-keeping the boyfriend is doing is clearly in a retail outlet, after-sales service. Either she'd got it wrong about a factory or the boyfriend had been pulling the wool. Most likely the father was right when he said the army; pound to a penny, it was a young thug she'd got mixed up with, his eye on the main chance, which he'd been offered and had taken.

Cramped behind the steering wheel, a slight ache beginning in the lower part of his back, Mr Hilditch watches the cars arriving and employees of both sexes moving into the factory. There are greetings, names called out, groups formed. At twenty past eight the buses arrive.

'He's not here,' the girl declares in a woeful tone of voice when these buses have emptied. 'The siren's gone and he's not.'

66

'You just slip across, dear, and ask at the barrier. It could be he's nights. Or late turn. You never know. Better sure than sorry, eh?'

In her absence he goes through the two carrier bags she has left in the car. At the bottom of the second one, stuffed into the sleeves of a navy-blue jersey, are two bundles of banknotes. He hesitates for a moment, before transferring the money to an inside pocket of his jacket.

'No,' the girl reports when she returns. 'He doesn't work here. They don't have a stores like the kind he described.'

'I'm sorry, Felicia. I'm really sorry.'

When, without warning, she begins to cry, the flesh of Mr Hilditch's face creases in sympathy, puffing up around his tiny eyes. Between sobs he hears about a breakdown of communication, how the boyfriend failed to leave an address or telephone number behind, how she'd been frightened of seeming pushy. She was shy, the girl says, and he is put in mind of Elsie Covington, who couldn't walk into a crowded room without suffering palpitations apparently.

'I know, I know,' he sympathizes. 'It's a horrible affliction, shyness.'

The boyfriend's mother hadn't been agreeable to handing over the address, and seemingly there was no one else who might have known it. All of it is worse, the Irish girl insists, because she knows that if she'd pressed for it he'd have given it to her immediately, no doubt about that.

Pull the other one, is Mr Hilditch's silent response before he turns the ignition on and drives slowly from the car park. He knows where the local hospital is: he went there once on the off chance that one of the night nurses might be tired enough to accept a lift. Walked off their feet, some of them, and the next thing is they could be giving the whole thing up, in need of help and advice from an older man. When the car is parked he says:

'I'll just pop in, dear, find out the state of play.'

The girl blows her nose in a tissue that looks to Mr Hilditch as if it has been used before. Young Sharon had a dreadful habit of keeping used tissues on her person, and cotton wool she dabbed her make-up with, and half-smoked cigarettes.

'I'll make off now,' the girl says. The rims of her eyes are almost scarlet. Tears come again. 'I'm OK,' she says.

'You be a good girl and hold on, Felicia. I'll be gone five minutes, just get a report on her. Then we'll maybe have a cup of tea and see what's what.'

When her teeth show they glisten, due to a coating of saliva. Gaye had a gap between her two front teeth where saliva used to gather, but of course you can't have everything.

'I don't want to be a nuisance to you.'

'You're never a nuisance, Felicia. You'd never be that.'

In the hospital reception area he asks where the lavatory for visitors is, and follows the direction he's given. He finds a telephone and rings the catering department to say he has been delayed that morning as a result of having to assist a neighbour who suffered a stroke in the night. Slowly he returns to the car park.

She will have to walk back to that factory to make certain. She should have made further inquiries, not just asked the security man. She shouldn't have got into the car again; she should have said she'd like to be on her own, so that she could think about what to do next. But the disappointments that have accumulated, and the addition of this latest one, form a necklace of despair that shackles her will. Wearily she reflects that the man has been good to her: the least she can do is to accept his concern, and what use is there, anyway, in her searching? What point is there in endlessly asking and endlessly being told that people can't help her, in tramping about, looking at the faces on the streets?

She hears, again, the outraged protest of her great-grandmother when she burrowed beneath the old woman's rubber sheet, extracting the clothes-peg bag and then returning it. 'Get off out of that!' came the cry from the depths of sleep, muzzy and confused. By now, they'd have been told at Doheny's that she took the Dublin bus; by now Mrs Lysaght would have passed it around that while she was out at early Mass a week ago someone climbed in through her kitchen window, leaving mud on the sill and the spotless surface of her sink. *Went to an airshow Sunday*, a postcard with barges on it had said, his handwriting tidily sloping, loops and dots and crossed t's. On the lined exercise paper of his brief letters there was never an address at the top. Father Kilgallen will summon her if she goes back now, the Reverend Mother too, both of them intent on preserving the life of the child that is her shame. 'God damn you to hell!' her father's greeting awaits her.

The car lurches on its springs as the fat man re-enters it. His breath is noisy in the small space.

'I'm sorry,' he whispers, hoarse from his exertions.

When Felicia turns to look at him his pinprick eyes are staring vacantly. He makes no attempt to start the car. She watches him trying to steady the quivering in the hand that is closer to her, pressing it against the steering wheel.

'Is something wrong?' she asks, her attention wrenched away from her distress. 'What's happened?'

'A cup of something,' he mutters, reaching into a pocket for his car keys. 'We're both in need of a hot beverage.'

9

Buddy's the café is called.

An electrician is on a step-ladder, working at a fuse-box just below the ceiling. The ceiling is brown, stained with pools of a deeper brown. Behind the bar where the tea and coffee and food come from there is a row of Pirelli calendars, half-dressed models in provocative poses. An old man is smoking and reading the sports news in the *Sun* at a table in a corner.

'I think a coffee,' Mr Hilditch requests. 'Would you mind fetching me over a coffee, dear?'

He closes his eyes and keeps them closed until she returns.

'Is something wrong?' he hears her ask again.

'Ada's not so hot,' he whispers, with his eyes still closed. 'They did an emergency on her, five this morning. She's not so good.'

'Oh, I'm sorry.'

'I'll be all right in a minute.' The first time he took Beth to the A361 Happy Eater he observed the woman at the till deciding that Beth was his daughter, and he laid his hand for a moment on Beth's knee the way a father never would. He glanced in the direction of the till and the excitement began because the woman was still staring, deciding now that the relationship was different.

'I'm sorry,' this present girl is repeating, and Mr Hilditch opens his eyes.

'You get a shock like this you don't want to be alone. Both of us with a shock, Felicia.'

Her red coat, unbuttoned in the café, has fallen back, and for the first time he sees the other clothes she is wearing: a navy-blue skirt and a red knitted jumper. Her hair has gone lank, the rims of her eyes have recovered a bit. She still wears the little cross on a chain around her neck: a Catholic girl, Mr Hilditch speculates, which stands to reason, coming from where she does.

'You're pregnant,' he says softly.

'Yes.'

They sit in silence. In many ways, he considers, there is nothing as tasty as a toasted bacon sandwich. Sometimes you find a café like this won't do you one, but this morning they've struck lucky. *Bacon sandwich's*, a handwritten sign advertises.

'I think you should have something to eat, Felicia.'

'I'm not hungry.'

A mouthful or two is a comfort in distress, he quietly explains, better for you than a coffee on its own. They sit in silence again. He finishes the coffee she bought and rises to get them some more.

'Mine was tea,' she says.

'Not a coffee, dear?'

'Coffee doesn't agree with me at the moment.'

'Ah yes, of course.' He pushes himself to his feet and goes to the counter. 'Two bacon sandwiches,' he orders from a small Indian woman, no taller than a dwarf, he considers. 'A tea for my girlfriend and a coffee for myself.' He smiles at the woman, knowing that the smile cannot be seen by the Irish girl. 'Look lovely, those bacon sandwiches you do.'

The woman doesn't acknowledge that. Often they don't. He counts out one pound fifty-four, recalling an occasion when he was seated beside an Indian woman in a cinema and tried to strike up a conversation but she rudely moved away. Younger than the one serving him, she'd been on her own or else he'd never have presumed. 'Sugar for the tea?' he inquires. 'My girlfriend likes a spoon of sugar.'

A sachet of sugar is thrown on to the counter and then, at last, there is a flicker of interest. Still not responding to his smile, the Indian woman notices the girl in the red jumper and for a passing instant – he's certain of it – considers their relationship. He nods, confirming what he believes the woman's speculation to be. They're having a day out, he confides, his fiancée and himself.

'You'll find your friend,' he says when he returns to the table. 'If we failed at the factory, Ada said to me last night, we'll find him where his abode is.'

'I thought I might run into him on the street. I didn't realize the town would be so big.'

'Of course you didn't. It's understandable, that.'

'The town I come from myself –'

'It would be smaller, of course it would.' Mr Hilditch inclines his head understandingly. Naturally it wouldn't be the size of an English town, he agrees, you wouldn't expect that. He wonders if the girl is religious since she's a Catholic. It would account for a lot if she turned out to be religious, like Jakki was. She says again she's sorry about his wife.

'You don't mind keeping me company for just a few more minutes? Only she's dozy at the moment and they said best I should go. I told them I had a friend in the car and they said I'd be better off in the company of a friend.' Mr Hilditch risks the shadow of a smile. 'To tell the truth, it lifts my mind, just sitting here with a friend.'

He lets another silence gather. He likes to look at something tasty before he takes the initial bite: he was no more than five or six when that was first noticed in him. He likes to think about it. 'Eat up, dearie,' his mother used to press. 'Mustn't be a Mr Dawdle.'

'I have to tell you, Felicia, it isn't a bolt out of the blue. A shock certainly, but not a bolt from the blue.'

She nods. She begins to say something. He watches her changing her mind.

'"I'll maybe not come out," she said on the way over last night. She faced it months ago. We all face it one day, Felicia.'

She nods again, at a loss for words, as any girl would be. There is a tiny dimple, almost unnoticeable, that comes and goes in one of her cheeks, affected by her change of expression.

'I'm glad you're going to have a baby, Felicia. It's a help to me, that.'

'A help?'

'Another life coming. Ada going in at this particular time and

72

you being here, and Ada concerned about you when I told her. A young Irish girl, I said, and she asked me what you looked like.'

She doesn't comment on that. He bites into the crisp toast of his sandwich, savouring the chewy bacon and the saltiness.

'Don't you want the baby, Felicia?'

'I don't know what to do until I find him.'

Again she struggles with tears, and then pulls herself together.

'The father's the young man we're looking for, Felicia?'

'Yes.'

'To tell you the truth, I thought there might be something like that.'

'I don't want to bother you with it.'

'Another person's trouble can lift the mind, Felicia.'

'Yes.'

'You understand me?'

'Yes.'

'I'll drive you back when I've been to the hospital again.'

She says there is no need. She says she'll maybe go out to the factory and make sure there hasn't been a mistake. He shakes his head.

'I don't think there was a mistake, dear.'

The Indian woman is engaged in a shrill conversation on the telephone. Neither the electrician nor the old man in the corner has displayed any interest in them, but then they wouldn't, people like that. Another thing is, the condition she is in hardly shows; you can tell all right, but it has to catch your eye. If she were bigger it might be a different kettle of fish, with the Indian woman noticing and speculating further.

'Ada'd like to know I was still keeping an eye on you.'

'Will you be all right yourself?'

He shakes his head. You couldn't be all right in circumstances like these, no one could. Finishing the second bacon sandwich, he wipes his fingertips with a paper napkin.

'What I'm thinking of is your condition, Felicia. I'm just thinking that walking about with those carriers mightn't be a help.'

To his surprise, she appears to lose track of the conversation.

She starts on about the missing address, saying it's all her fault. She says again she didn't want to be pushy.

'I know what you mean, dear. I know how you feel, I've had experience. Some of the young squaddies I had under me were in a shocking state due to emotional harassment. Terrible to see them – decent, innocent young fellows, bowels all to pieces.'

'I'd have stayed at home waiting for him if it wasn't for the baby.'

Mr Hilditch nods sympathetically. He allows a silence to gather before he says:

'Are you thinking of having the thing terminated, Felicia? Do they have that over there?'

'There's difficulties.'

'You could have it done here, of course. Any day of the week you could have the matter attended to.' He pauses. 'Old friend, is he? Your sweetheart?'

Bit by bit, it all comes bucketing out, as he knew that sooner or later it would. In a misty, uninterested way Mr Hilditch envisages the wedding there has been, the youngest of his companion's three brothers marrying above himself, a priest conducting the ceremony, the gathering in a hotel lounge. Then, when the bride and groom are driving off, the young thug happens to pass by on the street and the trouble begins. Smiles in a dancehall, walks in the countryside, autumn leaves in the woods, hands held under a café table. And in no time at all he's off with a suitcase, leaving her to fend for herself.

'He'd have come back at Christmastime only I'd say his mother said not to when she heard about us. God knows what she told Johnny.'

'God knows indeed, dear. I know the kind the mother is. I've had experience there too.'

'He was always protecting her because of what happened to her.'

Mr Hilditch listens while he is told about that, encouraging the flow of revelation, keen now to form a picture of the circumstances.

'I take to the sound of your friend,' he says when the picture is complete.

'He didn't have my address any more than I had his. We both forgot about that. I thought at one time he might have phoned up someone he knows – Cathal Kelly or Shay Mulroone, someone like that. I thought he might get them to pass a message on to me.'

'You can't blame him for not thinking of it.'

'I'm not blaming him for anything.'

'What I mean is it's surprising the things you don't think of at the time.'

There is more about the mother, who by the sound of her knows the price of carrots. It's not an unfamiliar story, Mr Hilditch reflects as he listens; give or take a few details, a similar tale buckets out of most of them. Twice, seemingly, Elsie Covington had a go at her wrists before their paths crossed. Teenage depression she called it, although she was more than halfway through her twenties.

'You've had a time of it,' he says, remembering saying the same thing to Jakki in the Dewdrop near Brinklow. Weals on her back, Jakki reported she had, after some fellow took a buckle to her.

'I didn't mean to tell you all that. At a time like this –'

'It does you good to get it out, Felicia.'

He adds that he's glad she felt she could. They're being eyed now by the old man, who has tired of his newspaper. Two people with a trouble, he says again: it's strange the way things turn out. No one ever looked after another person as beautifully as Ada did, he says. '"You get yourself ready for it, dear" she warned me – oh, must be six months ago.'

But the girl isn't listening; her mind isn't on it, which again is understandable in the circumstances. He knows what she is preoccupied with, and alludes to it.

'There are inquiries I could make, Felicia. As to his whereabouts.'

She shakes her head: the usual thing, not wanting to be a nuisance. He says:

'The girl I have in the office is very good. If we put our heads together we'd track him down, no problem at all.'

'How would you?'

'The girl would phone up every lawn-mower outfit in the

Midlands. Coventry. Nuneaton. Derby. King's Brompton. You name it. Added to which, there are citizens' registers and rates registers and housing registers. Would it be an intrusion to inquire as to your friend's name?'

'Johnny his name is. Lysaght.'

'And how are you spelling that, Felicia?'

She tells him; he writes it down.

'But I couldn't put you to the trouble. Not with your wife —'

'Ada'd want it, dear. A heart as big as a house. I don't know what I'm going to do.'

'Maybe it'll be all right. Maybe when you go back to the hospital they'll tell you —'

'I know what they'll tell me, Felicia.'

He doesn't mind crying in public. His sobs come softly, tears caught for a moment against the rims of his glasses. Ada has her ways, he whispers, but she'd never hurt a fly. A face blinks in his consciousness, its shape lost in excess flesh, stupid eyes. A woman who came to Number Three to make chair-covers, called Ada by his mother.

'Don't blame me for putting off going back to that ward, Felicia. Just for the minute I can't face them there.'

He blows his nose. He slips his spectacles off and wipes them. It will take only a few minutes in the hospital, he suggests. When he has been there they can go back to that factory if it's what she wants.

He returns to the counter for another cup of coffee and a packet of biscuits. She protests again that she can't go on being a nuisance to him, and again he contradicts her, saying she is a help. They leave Buddy's Café soon after that and return to the hospital.

He spends the time in the staff canteen, where the biscuits are of better quality than the biscuits in the café. 'They still want to keep her undisturbed,' he announces in the car, and when they've driven to the factory he waits while further fruitless inquiries are made.

Later, on the journey back to his home ground, he pulls up suddenly in a lay-by. He can't go on, he whispers. He can't face the empty house alone. He wipes his spectacles clear and sits staring through the windscreen, willing the girl to speak, willing her to say that they'll keep together for a while, that together they'll look for her friend. He has words ready, to explain that in the neighbourhood where he's known it wouldn't do for him to be seen in the company of a young girl, that if she wouldn't mind crouching down in the back of the car when they reach the outskirts of the town it would help a lot. Especially with Ada in a hospital it would help. But the girl still doesn't respond to what he has said about not being able to face the empty house alone. The girl doesn't say anything at all.

'It's hard for me,' he whispers, and drives on, not asking her to crouch down in case it upsets matters further, telling himself it's not unusual that she should be silent. But when he turns into the driveway of Number 3 Duke of Wellington Road – taking a chance he has never taken before by arriving in daylight at his house with a girl in his car – she reaches for the door handle as soon as the car is stationary. Two people in a trouble, he begins to say, but she shakes her head, again insisting that she can't be a nuisance to him at a time like this. Then, like a rabbit scuttling off, she is gone.

IO

Waking at ten past seven, her black nakedness clad in a frilled red nightdress, Miss Calligary is aware all over again that Miss Tamsel Flewett has walked away. Miss Tamsel Flewett has gone and will not return: Miss Calligary has lain in her bed with that glum reflection, before rising and washing the walls of her room and of the communal bathroom and lavatory. It is her practice to wash something when discontent assails her, discontent being a snare. The dull flow of time while she scrubs and cleanses is soothing; peace will return.

While she works she hears the people of the Gathering House going out, one by one or in groups, setting forth on their day's business. Then, without Miss Tamsel Flewett, who has accompanied her on her own business for the past seven and a half months, she goes out herself, her territory this morning the new Brunel estate.

'I don't want nothing,' an old white woman protests when Miss Calligary rings the first doorbell.

'Of course you don't.' Miss Calligary is soothing, shaking her head as she speaks. 'Course not, honey.'

'What's all this then?'

'Usually I come by with a young friend, Miss Tamsel Flewett, because sometimes a Jamaican lady on her own don't go down too good. But today Miss Tamsel Flewett cannot be with us. May I inquire if you read the Bible?'

'The what?'

'The Bible, honey. Today I have brought the Bible to you. For instance, do you ever consider the future there is for the one who dies?'

'Are you from the Security?'

Miss Calligary says she isn't. But nevertheless she brings security with her – security of mind and heart, security of purpose.

'What's this about dying then? We all have to die, stands to reason.'

'I've come this morning to talk with you about that.'

'There's *Gloria Live* coming to an end. I was watching Gloria when you rang on the bell.'

The old woman is slightly humped, small and wrinkled, with sparse grey hair. She hasn't a use for a Bible, she states; if she had a use for a Bible she would buy one in a shop. Miss Calligary ignores that. She says:

'In busy times there isn't always the opportunity to think about the future there is for the one who dies.'

The old woman shakes her head. *Dish of the Day* is starting, she points out.

'Could I perhaps step in?' Miss Calligary smiles a wide, brilliant smile. 'Ten minutes out of your day, that's all I'll take, honey.'

She had the waterbed man the day before, the old woman replies. She doesn't want a waterbed; she doesn't even know what a waterbed is. She says she has enjoyed their chat, and makes to close the door, but Miss Calligary's elbow obstructs the motion.

'For the one who dies the future is wonderful. That is the Message I bring you this morning. Our Father Lord's purpose is for a paradise earth. Our Father Lord's promise is for life without end. In return only for obedience. I'm not endeavouring to interest you in a waterbed.'

'Happen you've come to the wrong house. Number 5 this is. Mrs Crimms I am.'

'Mrs Crimms, it's not by chance that a Message is brought to you. I am here to gather, to gather you and other good folks in. Take a minute to consider, Mrs Crimms, that we awake in the morning and survey the day. We all do that, Mrs Crimms, you and I and the whole wide world of mankind. At night we look back into the day that has passed. Each night of our life there is a day that is passed into the darkness of this night. But if there has been no brightness we do not bow our heads.'

'I don't want no Bible.'

'I'm not selling Bibles, honey. The Task that is given to me is to gather folks in. "Shall we gather at the river?" is the words that I am saying to you.'

'I'm missing *Dish of the Day*.'

'We'll watch *Dish of the Day* first, Mrs Crimms. We'll watch *Dish of the Day* without a single word spoken. *The heavens are my throne*, is what is written for today. *The earth is my footstool. I shall glorify the very place of my feet*. You stand to gain, Mrs Crimms.'

This final statement has the desired effect, and so Mrs Crimms' small sitting-room is glorified, while cooking takes place on her television. And when the programme ends Miss Calligary explains how Mrs Crimms may be released from the inevitability of death, and Mrs Crimms speaks of her son, Rod, who is in gaol. She has twenty-two grandchildren, Mrs Crimms reveals; all of them born to the same son's three wives. Rod hasn't had luck with his wives, she divulges, weeping as she recalls that. Eighteen months he got the last time, for a thing he never did.

'I would speak with Rod,' Miss Calligary offers. 'I would take the Message to him.'

'Twenty-two kids and not one of them lifts a finger to bother with him. Rod never had luck.'

'I would bring your son reading matter,' Miss Calligary promises. 'I would convey letters and parcels, I would gather Rod in. My Church thinks in terms of families.'

Mrs Crimms repeats that she has twenty-two grandchildren. All kinds of work they are in. 'A garage, then again computers, then again a Payless and on the buses. Another's in refuse.'

'Pass on to your grandchildren the Message I bring to you today, honey. When you read the words I am leaving with you you'll discover that the Father Lord makes all things new. You'll discover your life without end, and your son and your grandchildren will discover theirs. *Out of the abundance of His love, the Father Lord lent His Son, that the world of mankind might be brightened, as lightning brightens His sky*.

'Poor Rod's in the Scrubs.'

'I'd go to the Scrubs. I wouldn't hesitate.'

But Mrs Crimms does not appear to be much interested in this offer. Vaguely she shakes her head. It is time for Henry Kelly's game show. She likes a game show best.

'You have rooms going spare in your house.' Miss Calligary speaks softly, smiling and seeking to make eye contact. 'In the springtime the folk come for our Prayer Jubilee. From the far corners of the earth folk come and we need more beds and bedding, and the use of bathroom and kitchen and all that.'

Mrs Crimms turns up the volume of the television and Miss Calligary's promise that she will return in a day or two is lost in the tumult. On the street outside the roar of the game show continues, and then abruptly ceases as the volume is reduced. Plenty of room in that house, Miss Calligary says to herself as she continues on her way, obedient to her Task.

All that morning blank faces stare back at her animated presence, at her smile and the vigour in her eyes. She taught Miss Tamsel Flewett to be cheerful no matter what their reception was. Two smiles are better than one, she used to say, and this morning it is lonely. At door after door she explains that she conveys the Message of the Church of the Gatherers, but she receives in return only rebukes for her folly.

It is then, when her spirits are low, that she notices a girl in a red coat on an isolated seat in a walkway, with litter blowing all around her. Miss Calligary observes this figure from a distance, noting the two green-and-black carrier bags and the tired hunch of the girl's shoulders. There is unhappiness here, Miss Calligary silently remarks to herself, and strides forth to gather the girl in.

For three days Mr Hilditch dwells upon the fact that anyone can make a mistake. Anyone can attempt to advance a friendship too quickly: enthusiasm, he supposes, a surfeit of keenness. He recalls the one he ran into once in a Debenham's Coffee Bean, who said she'd rather not when he suggested meeting up again, and the one who told him she came from Daventry: Samantha, whom he'd assisted when her car wouldn't start. It could happen to a bishop, he reflects, recalling this expression of his Uncle Wilf's: advancing too swiftly is an understandable human error.

Since he has never felt the need of a telephone at Number

Three, and does not wish to be overheard in his office, Mr Hilditch telephones the barracks on Old Hinley Road from a call-box during the lunch hour. The voice at the other end is matter-of-fact and cold.

'Who's making inquiries about this soldier?'

Mr Hilditch states that he is a family friend. There has been an emergency of a personal nature: the young man's father in an accident at a level-crossing, signal failure.

'What are you asking me?' the clipped, uninterested tones inquire.

'The family's uncertain which barracks the lad's stationed at owing to the father being unconscious in a hospital. We're ringing round all barracks in the area.'

'Name and rank?'

'Lysaght, J. A squaddy I'd say he is.'

'A what?'

Mr Hilditch says a private and is told to hold on. Nearly ten minutes go by, during which time he repeatedly feeds money into the coin-box.

'We have a Lysaght here,' he is told then. 'We'll pass the message on after fatigues.'

'Excuse me, but maybe it'd be better if the family broke the news to the lad. Now that we know where he is we'll contact him pronto.'

Mr Hilditch smiles agreeably, projecting this bonhomie into the mouthpiece, but the receiver is replaced at the other end without further effort at communication. He extracts his unused coins and steps out of the telephone-box. No way there isn't a chance that the girl could run into the tough who got her up the pole, no reason why she shouldn't if she continues to wander about the place. Even so, knowing his location is somehow a comfort: being a jump ahead, as the expression goes.

Since he has half an hour to spare, and in order to avoid having to shop later on, Mr Hilditch drives slowly to Tesco's car park. Finding a trolley, he pushes it through the chromium swinging barrier and makes his way to the refrigerated area, where he chooses cod in batter, faggots, garden peas, broccoli spears, four bags of chips and two tubs of strawberry and vanilla ice-cream. In the fresh meat section he picks out pork chops, chicken portions and prime steak, adds celery and carrots and more potatoes from the fresh vegetable shelves, and bourbon creams, custard creams, lemon flakies, chocolate wafers and chocolate wholemeals from the biscuit shelves. Since Mr Kipling's Bakewell Slices are reduced, as are Mr Kipling's French Fancies and McVitie's treacle cake, he helps himself to a selection, and to packets of jumbo-size crisps and Phileas Fogg croutons near the pay-out, as well as a six-pack of Bounty bars. He smiles at a woman who ungraciously pushes in front of him, saying it doesn't matter in the least.

In the car park he stacks his purchases in the boot of his car, and returns to his catering department, consuming a Bounty bar on the way. Most of the lunch hour has gone, but something hot will have been kept back for him in the kitchens, as he requested earlier. 'Sorry to give you the bother,' he apologizes when a plate of gammon and parsley sauce, creamed potatoes and sauced cauliflower is placed in front of him. 'Had a bit of business to attend to. I'll have to stay late to catch up on the figures.'

He does not intend to do that. He intends to drive down to the Marshring area in the hope of a sighting. As he eats, and afterwards in his cubicle of an office, an anger he has suppressed gradually begins to seep through his defences. Anyone could have seen her hurrying away from Number Three. He broke his rule for her, and then that: hardly evidence of gratitude, after she'd been driven upwards of a hundred and ten miles, with cups of tea paid for, and all that guff about some woman left a widow seventy-five years ago patiently listened to. And although it should be, it's no satisfaction to know that the boyfriend has been guilty of porkies.

Unable to help himself, Mr Hilditch imagines this soldier, tidy in his uniform and engaged in cheerful afternoon fatigues. He envisages him off duty later on, relaxing with his mates, feet up on a table in the day room of the barracks, the kind of camaraderie he had once looked forward to himself, before the recruiting sergeant with the bladelike moustache rejected him because of his feet and his eyesight. With his legs still cocked up in front of him, ankles crossed, the young thug guffaws that keen bints like the one he had are two a penny, pick them off the bushes, no problem at all. And one of his companions looks up from *Big Ones* and recalls the first time he'd had it, with a fat nurse behind a public house, the Flight of Birds up Scunthorpe way, a summer's evening. Another of them throws in that the first time he had it he was thirteen, a plumber's wife.

At a quarter to six Mr Hilditch drives down to the Marshring area and waits for a while in his parked car. 'Thanks very much,' was what she said as she scuttled off. 'I hope it'll be all right about your wife.'

At ten past six he drives away again, disappointed.

No iron bars are needed, for all the animals are at peace with the happy people. The lion and the lamb are friends. See those brightly coloured birds as they flit here and there! Hear their beautiful song and the children's laughter filling the air! Smell the fragrance of those flowers, hear the rippling of the stream, feel the tingling warmth of the sun! Oh, for a taste of the fruit in that basket, for it is the best that the earth can produce, the very best, like everything that is seen and enjoyed in this glorious garden . . .

The happy people, the flowers and animals and fruit, are brightly illustrated on the cover of the brochure. Flamingos stalk about, rabbits nibble grass but not the flowers. A child hugs a swan, yachts sail on a distant lake.

'That, now, is the paradise earth,' a black woman asserts, a long forefinger drawing Felicia's attention to a trickling waterfall, to giraffes and then to cockatoos. The black woman is tall and slender, with rings on several of her fingers, and earrings. 'That is the promise and the place,' she states, 'of the Father Lord.'

'Yes,' Felicia agrees.

'Come with us, child. You hear of the Flood, honey? Noah in his Ark? You hear of that?'

'Yes, I have.'

'The Flood is a proved event,' the black woman reminds her.

'Yes, I understand.'

Only a few other people are about. Gusts of wind blow the litter into the doorways of shops. It is colder than it has been.

'Where you live?' the black woman peremptorily demands. 'You have rooms going spare there?'

Felicia replies that she is a stranger: she has been lodging in bed-and-breakfast places. She reaches for her carrier bags and says she must be getting on.

'Where you go off to, child? Where you run in a hurry from the Father Lord?'

'I'm looking for someone.'

It is late in the day. She has to find another bed-and-breakfast place, in an area that isn't familiar to her. The more she moves about the more chance she has of running into the person she is looking for: she explains that, but the black woman doesn't understand. She doesn't listen. She says there is happiness for the one who dies.

'Child, we live in a miracle. Look here at this garden, honey. See the fruits of the trees and the peoples of all nations. See the juice to drink and the smiles of the children. Look, child, the Father Lord is gathering all things in.'

'I have to get a room for the night.'

'I can offer you a room, child. No charge made. Miss Tamsel Flewett is gone and I have the knowledge in my heart she is gone from us for ever. A lady from Jamaica don't go down too well on her own when she rings folks' doorbells.'

Again the leaflets are pressed on Felicia, the heavenly picture of fruit and flamingos and well-behaved rabbits.

'No, really. I'm sorry.'

'What things you have to do, child? What things more important than the work of the Father Lord?'

'I'm looking for someone.'

'There's all kinds stay at the Gathering House. You need a pillow for your head? Well, here we have it for you, honey. I do not like to see you sitting out here in the wind, a prey to the coming night.'

Felicia feels tired. She fell asleep, just sitting there on the wooden seat, and even dreamed: that they were in Sheehy's again, the first time he took her there, that they were at the Creagh crossroads, in the warm little back bar. She should have insisted when she went to see Mrs Lysaght. She should have told her everything, and refused to leave without the full address. She should have screamed at her and made a scene. After all, it is Mrs Lysaght's grandchild.

'Come with me, honey,' the black woman commands in her firm manner, and Felicia goes with her because it's easier than looking for somewhere else. 'Miss Calligary,' the black woman introduces herself. 'It isn't far.'

She hurries them through deserted streets to a brick-built house in a row with others. She leads the way upstairs, to an attic with pictures on the walls that are similar to the brochure illustration. Miss Calligary's clothes hang from two rows of hooks on either side of a casement window, dresses and skirts and coats. Her shoes are neatly in line along one of the walls. A suitcase, on the floor also, bulges with underclothes and other possessions. The only pieces of furniture in the attic are two upright chairs, a trestle-table and a narrow bed. 'I'm forever on the move,' Miss Calligary explains. 'I gather in where the Message leads me.'

She prepares a meal of tuna fish and salad, and when they have eaten this food she makes tea. They drink it, then wash the dishes up in an enamel basin. Miss Calligary disposes of the dregs from the teapot, and the tea-leaves, in a small lavatory on a half landing, pouring away the washing-up water here also. No sound comes from the rooms below.

'It's quiet in the Gathering House tonight,' Miss Calligary comments. 'Each and every one is out and about.'

'Do a lot of people live here?'

'Black and white, child, old and young. All that are called to gather in.'

Later these people return. The hall door bangs frequently. Voices exchange greetings. A piano plays a hymn tune. An odour of food cooking rises to Miss Calligary's attic.

'Love! Joy! Peace!' So exclaiming, a man in a maroon anorak smiles a welcome at Felicia when, an hour later, Miss Calligary leads her into a large, unfurnished downstairs room. Others come up and shake her hand: black and white, as Miss Calligary has said, old and young. A bed-roll, Felicia is told, will be spread out for her in the room where the people are now congregated, the Gathering Room it is known as. A girl called Agnes, with softly tinted fingernails and trim black hair, reveals that she's in dental care, but would prefer to devote all her time to distributing the Message.

'Mourning will be no more,' Agnes avers. 'Nor outcry nor pain. When we have gathered together, when it is known again by all that a future awaits the one who dies.'

Every evening, she further reveals, the people meet in the Gathering Room in order to exchange their day's experiences. An elderly Ethiopian relates his to Felicia, most of them to do with the ringing of doorbells. 'You are not amongst us by chance,' he adds, 'for there is nothing that can happen but by the Commandment that began in the garden of pleasure. Adam was taken from out of the ground of the paradise earth, and the Commandment was drawn in the dust. Look close and see the serpent's spit.' The old man's face is as wrinkled as a walnut, his darting eyes bloodshot. He nods at Felicia and passes on.

'Bob's the name.' Small and balding, the man who addresses her next is the man in the maroon anorak. 'Ours is the bed-roll,' he now declares. 'Ruthie's and mine. We keep it for newcomers, since not long ago we were newcomers ourselves. We met in this room, Ruthie and myself. We were married from this house. Our children were born in our upstairs room. Two beautiful children. It is they who will bring down the bed-roll.'

'Everyone is pleased that you have come to us,' a tall woman assures Felicia. The woman's breath is sweet, as if scented. She pushes her face close to Felicia's, articulating her confidences clearly. 'I was lost as in a forest until the Way was revealed to me through the Message.'

A Japanese man says his name is Mr Hikuku. Felicia can't understand anything else he says, but the woman with the sweet breath explains that he works among the people of the East, bringing them the Message. He lives modestly in the Gathering House, the woman adds, in one small room, sharing lavatory and bath like everyone else. But in commercial terms Mr Hikuku is twice over a millionaire.

A middle-aged couple, Mr and Mrs Priscatt, wear rimless spectacles and are similar in appearance, pale-faced and brownly dressed. Mr Priscatt's brown suit is carefully pressed, his shirt is fresh and clean, his tie has a business emblem on it. Mrs Priscatt's cardigan is a lighter shade of brown than the jumper beneath it, perfectly matching her pleated skirt. Unlike Miss Calligary and the other women who have congregated, she wears no jewellery.

Her husband, Mrs Priscatt informs Felicia, is in the claims department of the Eagle Star insurance company and is looking forward to retirement. She herself devotes all her time to the promulgation of their discovered faith. Mr Priscatt adds that it is heartening to welcome a new face.

'You are pregnant with a child.' The statement is neither a question nor an accusation. It is made by Mrs Priscatt, and both she and her husband nod their confirmation of the assumption before Felicia replies.

'Yes,' she agrees, feeling that in spite of their confidence in this matter some comment from her is required.

'Mrs Priscatt can always tell.' Accompanied by a sideways inclination of the head in his wife's direction, Mr Priscatt's tone is complimentary.

'A girl child,' Mrs Priscatt predicts, and Mr Priscatt suggests that Joanna is a lovely name.

Felicia is questioned then, and she passes on details of the circumstances that have overwhelmed her. Everything she says is sympathetically received, and later, when she has talked to other people in the room, she senses that already all of them know how her troubles have come about, although only the Priscatts have questioned her on the subject. Without condemnation, the knowledge is there in their expressions. A child will be born in the Gathering House, Felicia hears Bob whispering to Ruthie, another child born, as their own two beautiful children have been. Listening, not saying much herself, Felicia feels that all of it is more like a dream than reality: she has never in her life met people like this before, nor even known that such people exist.

One by one they bid her good-night and repeat that she is

welcome. Pamphlets are left with her as reading matter, should she be wakeful. Her bed-roll arrives and thankfully she rests, her worries lost in oblivion.

Mr Hilditch has seen them about: nutters, is his view. He has noticed them on the streets, imposing their literature on people, bothering people with religious talk.

Somehow or other the girl has become entangled with them; certainly she's lodging in their house because he has seen her entering it. An innocent girl from the bogs of Ireland, susceptible to any suggestion they'd make: what chance would she have under pressure like that? The only consolation is that the house she's in is well away from the Old Hinley Road barracks, two miles at least, maybe two and a half. The lads from the barracks use the Goose and Gander, and Hinley Fish 'n' Chips at the Stoat roundabout, or else the Queen's Head down Budder way. Mr Hilditch remembers that from the Elsie Covington days, when a young thug from the barracks had her out a couple of times. The area isn't part of the town, never was. Apart from the barracks, there's nothing much doing there: weekends or a heavy night out, the squaddies are on the motorway down to Brum.

Mr Hilditch plays 'Falling in Love Again' on his gramophone, then 'Stella by Starlight' and 'Makin' Whoopee'. The records are old seventy-eights: being an antique, the gramophone doesn't play anything else. Mr Hilditch relaxes in an armchair, the *Daily Telegraph* – all of it read – on the carpet beside him, the melodies a solace in his worry about the well-being of the girl he has befriended. '*Ev'ry rolling stone gets to feel alone,*' sings Doris Day, '*When home sweet home is far away.*'

Mr Hilditch calls this room his big front room, the expression used privately to himself because there never has been a call to use it to anyone else. The oil paintings of other people's ancestors gaze benignly down at him. His billiard table, rarely used, is in a corner; a cabinet contains someone else's collection of paperweights. Two grandfather clocks, wound every Thursday evening and adjusted daily, tick agreeably, one between the heavily curtained windows, the other by the door. On the black marble mantelpiece, above a mammoth electric fire with glowing coals, there are china mugs, and ornaments: a seal balancing a ball, ballet dancers, a comic orchestra of Dalmatians, highland cattle. The room's wallpaper is mainly crimson, roses on a trellis. Books of military history, back numbers of the *National Geographic* magazine, bound volumes of *Punch* and the *Railway and Travel Monthly* fill a bookcase.

'*Never thought my heart could be so yearny,*' sings Doris Day. '*Why did I decide to roam?*'

The song concludes and the needle whines softly as the record continues to revolve. It's a pleasant sound, Mr Hilditch considers and listens to it lazily, much calmer now than when he entered the room an hour ago. Tomorrow he'll try again for an encounter.

For several days Felicia lodges in the Gathering House, leaving it every morning to make inquiries, to scan the faces on the streets and to travel to factories she has heard about, in other towns. Often she is sent in error to a factory that has changed its function, and in this way she becomes familiar with plant-hire yards, and sheds where diggers and tracked excavators are repaired, and engineering works where compressors and rammers are manufactured. In her continuing search for anywhere that has to do with lawn-mowers she passes by scrapyards in which old motor-cars are disembowelled before being heaped on top of one another, and timber yards and builders' yards and brewers' yards. When she asks, she is sometimes told – if she happens to ask an elderly person – about the great mowers of the past: the days of the Dennis, and the Ransome and the Atco in their prime. Nothing is as it was then, such informants agree, shaking their heads over her hopeless task as if it, too, is an aspect of nothing being as it was.

Every evening in the Gathering Room the other inmates ask her if she has found her friend yet and she says no. No one comments and still no one condemns. She eats with Miss Calligary, as she did the first evening, and every morning Miss Calligary makes tea for both of them, and offers cornflakes and toast. Felicia guesses that Miss Calligary has been in touch with the Father Lord on her behalf, that Mr Hikuku has, and the woman with sweet breath, and the Priscatts, and Agnes and Bob and Ruthie, and the old Ethiopian whose face resembles a walnut. Joyful expectation greets her every evening when the people congregate, their concern for her apparent all over again, their forgiveness offered afresh: hers is the soul that has been saved on the premises; she is the sinner whose redemption is present for each and every one to witness. In the shining brightness of the Gatherers' love an infant will be made aware of the Message and the Way, its infant's inheritance the future of the one who dies, a girl child who shall be called Joanna.

The heady, unreal atmosphere becomes cloying in the end. Aware that her mute presence has misled the people of the Gathering House, Felicia does her best to dispel the illusion her arrival has engendered, but no one listens. And the more they do not do so the more it is borne in upon her that she is accepting their hospitality under false pretences. She is a pregnant girl who is desperately hunting for the father of her child: there's no more to it than that.

So early one morning she goes, leaving a note on her bed-roll, thanking everyone. As she did before she was taken in at the Gathering House, she moves about then from one bed-and-breakfast place to another, changing districts in the hope of finding herself by chance in the neighbourhood of the missing address, still travelling by day to factories she has been advised about. *You have all been good to me,* the note she left behind in the Gathering House says, but when she catches a glimpse of Mr Hikuku on the street she feels guilty about leaving in the way she did. Once she catches a glimpse of the little green humpbacked car, and she feels guilty then too.

At the very last moment, when she is suddenly there one afternoon, asking directions of a couple with a guide-dog, prudence restrains Mr Hilditch from the encounter he has been anticipating with some fervour. All he has to do is to cross the street and say hullo when the couple have moved on. If he's noticed by a local person to whom he is known, by sight or otherwise, the chances are that not much significance will be read into it, the assumption made that further directions are being given. But the fact remains that this is still home ground and you never know. No way could they walk an inch together on the street. And what if she turned her taps on, or acted familiar? And how much of value could be exchanged in the minute or two it would be safe for him to stand there in the broad light of day, gesturing as he supplies the directions the guide-dog couple have been unable to assist her with? It is contact enough, Mr Hilditch decides during his hesitation, to know she has left the religious set-up, which he can tell she has from the fact that she's on the streets with her carriers again. Patience will bring her back to him. Sooner or later she'll turn to him for help, since he has offered it.

In a public lavatory, with the door locked, Felicia feels her way through the belongings in the heavier of her carrier bags, to the jersey in which she has secreted the greater part of her money. She has two pounds and seventy-three pence left in the purse in her handbag.

But the sleeves of the jersey are empty and, thinking she has made a mistake, she searches the other bag. Since it yields nothing either, she returns to the first one. In a panic she takes everything out of both, littering the floor of the cubicle, unfolding the navy-blue jersey and shaking out all the other clothes. The money is not there.

She tries to calm herself. Could the notes have somehow worked their way out of the woollen sleeves and become displaced when she took something from the bag in the room she first occupied overnight, or in the Gathering House, or in one of her other lodging places?

'Nothing was found,' the hatchet-faced landlady in Marshring Crescent states when she returns there. 'What is it you're missing?'

Felicia says it is money. She might have taken it out from where it was and put it down somewhere, although she doesn't recall doing so.

'No money was found.'

'Would it be possible to look, just to make sure?'

'The room was done out the day you left and every day since. I do the cleaning myself.'

Felicia explains that as a result of what has happened she has very little money left. All she wants to do is to make certain she didn't leave anything behind.

'You left nothing.' The woman is emphatic. Felicia goes away.

She makes the rounds of the other bed-and-breakfast houses, but without success. She is not surprised because by now it has become apparent to her that the money could not have made its way unaided out of her hiding place, and in none of these rooms did she leave her bags behind by day since in each she stayed no more than a single night. Only in the Gathering House did she do that, considering the bundle of banknotes safe among religious people.

'So you return to us, child?' Miss Calligary greets her a little stiffly when she rings the bell, not smiling in her usual manner. 'So you are here again.'

'I had to go to look for my friend.'

'And now the friend has said to you, "I cannot assist". Is it a friend who will say that to a girl heavy with child?'

'He doesn't know.'

'Child, they always know.'

Not invited into the Gathering House, and sensing no sympathy whatsoever from Miss Calligary, Felicia suddenly feels tired. The loss of her money is a disaster almost as great as her failure to locate the right factory. The money isn't even her own; if she wanted to turn round now and go home she wouldn't be able to; she hasn't enough left for a single night's lodging.

'I lost some money while I was here.'

'Money?'

'I had money in one of my bags.'

'What you saying to me, child?'

'I had money that was with my clothes. I had it hidden away and it's been taken.'

'Not in this house. Never that, child.'

'It's missing.'

'Stolen? You saying stolen?'

'Ah no, I'm not at all. Only I left it here during the daytime, I don't know what I was thinking about. If we could just look –'

'You go away without a word, child. You come back here with this talk.'

'I have hardly any money now.'

'You are asking me for money, child?'

'Maybe I took it out here by mistake. Maybe it slipped out. If we could look in the room.'

Not deigning to reply, Miss Calligary opens the door a little wider and then leads the way to the empty Gathering Room. But there is nowhere there where the money could be, no drawers to pull out, no carpet on the parquet floor, and only the radiators behind which Felicia hopelessly looks.

'You leave us, child. You turn your back on our people and our true belief and now there is accusations.'

Tears run over Felicia's cheeks as she shakes her head, denying that she has turned her back. Everyone was kind to her, she says; everyone was sympathetic; she was ashamed that she moved on so hurriedly. It was all her fault; she should have looked every day to see that the money was still there. She should have divided it more evenly, half in the jersey, half in her handbag. In an effort to control her sobs, she clenches her fingers into her palms until it hurts.

'I don't know what to do.'

Miss Calligary waits for Felicia's distress to subside, then reminds her that soon the inmates of the house will arrive with news of the day's gathering. When the folk are fully congregated she will inform them of what has occurred, and make inquiries about the possibility of the money having been found lying around and put away for safety.

There is a wait, and there is silence between them. Then, when everyone has returned, when Felicia has been greeted – though without the warmth she previously experienced – Miss Calligary puts it to the assembled Gatherers. Their response is to stare at Felicia with disappointment that is not disguised. All trace of friendliness has drained from the bloodshot eyes of the old

Ethiopian and from Mr Hikuku's, peering out of their narrowness. The hurt in the other faces distorts them; loathing sours Agnes's prettiness. No one speaks. Miss Calligary has become so still her features might be cut in ebony.

With nothing left to say, Felicia goes away.

12

Mr Hilditch draws up the figures for the January expenditure and canteen takings, spreading the monthly subsidy lightly in the hope of holding on to a bit extra for February. At four o'clock a vending-machine representative begins his sales pitch: install a bank of food machines in the canteen and you dispense with all canteen staff. The machines would back directly on to the kitchens, the prepared portions loaded straight into them: at the drop of a coin the dishes would emerge when and how they're required, piping hot or chilled. Drinks likewise: load the machines with the necessary ingredients – tea, coffee, chocolate, softs, no more than ten minutes' labour a day. 'You can't lose, Mr Hilditch,' the vending man assures him, but Mr Hilditch has no intention of making a change. He likes the old ways. He likes to see his canteen staff, the women's hair tied up under their caps, the chatter and bustle of the queues, steam rising from the pans, mashed potato scooped up, an extra spoonful of sprouts jollied out of the server. Yet in spite of this preference he is always prepared to see a catering representative in the lull of the afternoon. He enjoys the interruption, a cup of tea and a plate of biscuits shared. He feels it gives a shape to the day. Tomorrow the Colman's mustard man is due.

These passing days are shaped in another way also: with speculation, with reassurance following doubt, with the steadying of his thoughts. The unknown factor is how much money she retained in her handbag, how long she can manage to keep going. The nag is that while she's hanging about on the streets there's the danger of her running into the boyfriend. Added to which it could dawn on her at any moment that there might be something, after all, in her father's astute suspicions: anyone she cares to ask would direct her to the barracks. Driving home on the evening of the vending salesman's visit, Mr Hilditch shakes his head with renewed finality: all that is a chance that has to be taken. What matters more is that she's still around, and is likely to be.

But that night, having deadlocked his front door and shot the bolts at the back, Mr Hilditch mounts his stairs feeling nervous in case he has let everything slip away from him. In the days that have passed since his sighting of the girl she could have stumbled on her quarry. At this very moment he could be making a clean breast of his deception, buttering her up with devious excuses. At this very moment she could be getting herself up the pole all over again.

Savagely Mr Hilditch brushes his teeth, painfully attacking his lower gum as he reflects on the way the world is these days: crazy God-botherers enticing young girls, lying thugs taking advantage, you name it and it's there. *GP Ruined my Sex Life! says Boob-Op Fourteen-Year-Old Mum. Dog-Collar Dougie Had Sofa Sex with my Pal for Revenge! Kids in Black Mass Sacrifices!* The headlines race through Mr Hilditch's memory, culled from the newspapers he sometimes carries away from the canteen because he likes to see it tidy. Every day of the week, seemingly, cigarettes are stubbed out on the flesh of infants. Every day of the week women in their nineties suffer rape and violence. Flaming petrol is poured through letter-boxes for the fun of it. Cars are stolen, televisions are stolen. Company directors spend their employees' pensions on motor yachts. Drug addicts get their fixes over the counter in Boot's. Teenage girls are set alight on city wastelands.

Mr Hilditch cools his face with water. Calm again, in bed, he recalls an evening with Bobbi in the Welcome Spoon at Legge's Corner near Junction 18. They sat for hours, maybe even three, while she poured out her troubles, in much the same way as the Irish one has. 'You wouldn't credit half of it,' Bobbi said: the abuse she received at the hands of the man her mother took in after her father went off; the home she spent six months at, where men in belted overcoats arrived at weekends intent on the same. With Bobbi's almost pretty face for company, Mr Hilditch drops off.

The following evening, distancing himself equally from his place of work and Number 3 Duke of Wellington Road, Mr Hilditch drives to a supermarket where he is not known. He purchases hairnets and tights and women's underclothes, talcum powder and skin cream. Already, at a Saturday jumble sale, he has selected outer garments and two hats. After he has eaten, he arranges these articles about the house, filling a wardrobe with coats and skirts and dresses, and drawers with underclothes which he takes the trouble to crumple up, even to tear a little. He half empties bottles of lotions and squeezes cream from tubes. He packs the talcum powder, with lipstick and eye make-up, into the bathroom cabinet. He drapes the tights over the rails of the ceiling-drier in the kitchen. He locks away his spike of receipts, and any envelopes and papers that bear his name, old cheque-books and bank statements.

When Mr Hilditch's mother died he sold her belongings to a clothes dealer who sent in a card, but he later discovered that the cardboard box he'd filled with her shoes had been overlooked. Planning to dispose of these on some future occasion, he stored them in an outside shed. On the kitchen table he wipes off the mildew and later arranges them in a row by the side of the wardrobe.

'I require your national insurance number.' The clerk speaks through glass, making it difficult to hear him. He repeats what he has said.

'I haven't one over here.'

The clerk directs her to where the forms are, pointing behind her. He mentions a permanent address, stating that that will be necessary.

'I haven't anywhere permanent. I've had my money stolen.'

'An address is required on a benefit application.'

Overhearing this conversation, a middle-aged man with waist-length hair and torn clothes says Felicia is wasting her time, an opinion confirmed by a girl trailing a dog on a string. The girl has a safety-pin hanging from a nostril. Her hair is pink and blue, tomahawk style.

Felicia says she has been staying at the Salvation Army hostel, but they tell her that won't do for an address. The man says the benefit's no loss: if he was beginning again himself he would keep well clear of the System and its computers. Once you fill in a form you're harassed for ever. Earn a wage for a day and half of it's taken off you to buy false teeth for old-age pensioners.

'Play music, do you? Pity,' the girl adds when Felicia shakes her head.

That evening the hostel is full when she arrives. In a Spud-U-Like she spends some of her money on a cup of tea and asks the people whose table she shares if the bus station remains open all night. It's not something they'd know, they say. On the street again, she is accosted by two men loitering outside a pool-hall. They want to know her name and when she tells them they want to know where she's from. They say they can fix her up, but she doesn't understand. She feels frightened and hurries on.

'Get off out of this street,' a woman whose face is green in the night-light orders when she sets her bags down for a moment in a shop doorway. 'Move yourself.'

The woman is big, with artificial fur on the coat, and earrings shaped like hearts. Felicia says she is only having a rest.

'Rest yourself somewhere else then.'

'D'you know is the bus station open all night?'

'What d'you want the bus place for?'

'I need somewhere for the night.'

A car draws up beside them. 'Business, love?' The woman simpers as the driver winds down the window. 'She ain't on the game,' she adds, jerking her head towards Felicia. The man opens the car door and the woman gets in beside him.

'How're you doing?' another voice asks when another car draws up.

'No,' Felicia says.

She walks on, reaching streets that are familiar to her, where the night-time traffic is busy. Clothes are displayed in the fashion windows, their bald-headed models prancing in affected motion, pouting at nothing. Building societies offer mortgage rates. A cardboard man and woman stride forward, holding a roof above their heads: 8.25% the enticement is. Sports equipment and ski clothing vie for attention with furniture and shoes. Washing machines and microwave ovens are in a sale. *Every Camera Slashed!*

another message is. *Olympus! Minolta! Praktica!* A Pizzaland is brightly lit, people occupying all the tables along the windows, a girl in a red beret talking urgently to her companion, a man with a ponytail who keeps nodding. A crowd of eight share a single table. A couple with a child gesture at the child, cross because she won't eat the food. A man wearing a cap is on his own. 'I'll go for a Kentucky,' someone passing by on the pavement says. 'I'd rather a Kentucky.'

Cartons are thrown down outside the Kentucky Fried Chicken, and Colonel Sanders is reassuring in the window, his honest gaze, his white goatee, Finger Lickin' Good. The voice of Sheena Easton on a ghetto-blaster is drowned by Michael Jackson's. Bright neon sparkles: *Coca-Cola is a Way of Life*, it says in the sky.

Two women rattle charity boxes. A West Indian is talking to himself, gesturing with his hands. A gang of hooligans push through the pedestrians, pretending to elbow them aside. In a gambling arcade men and youths, grim-faced, play the machines.

Felicia's eyes dart about as she continues on her way, still searching in the crowd. When she arrives at the bus station she settles herself on a seat, but an hour later she is told that no further buses are due either to arrive or depart, and is asked to go. She finds the railway station, and lies on a wooden seat in the waiting-room, but from there, too, she is eventually moved on.

She rests in the entrance to a shop that is more than just a doorway: a wide secluded area hidden from the street by a central pillar with windows in it, displaying watches. She sits there, crouched on the tiled ground. One of her shoes has come through in the sole. She roots in her bags and when she has changed her shoes she remains where she is because it is quiet.

She wanders on eventually, resting sometimes on a pavement seat, moving again when it becomes too cold. At a stall beneath a bridge where taxi drivers stand about she buys a sausage roll that is reduced to fourpence because it's stale. The air is dank with mist.

Already, hours ago, the homeless of this town have found their night-time resting places – in doorways, and underground passages left open in error, in abandoned vehicles, in the derelict gardens of demolished houses. As maggots make their way into cracks in masonry, so the people of the streets have crept into one-night homes in graveyards and on building sites, in alleyways and courtyards, making walls of dustbins pulled close together, and roofs of whatever lies near by. Some have crawled up scaffolding to find a corner beneath the tarpaulin that protects an untiled expanse. Others have settled down in cardboard cartons that once contained dishwashers or refrigerators.

Hidden away, the people of the streets drift into sleep induced by alcohol or agitated by despair, into dreams that carry them back to the lives that once were theirs. They lie with their begging notices still beside them, with enough left of a bottle to ease the waking moment, with pavement cigarette butts to hand. *Homeless and hungry* is their pasteboard plea, scrawled without thought, one copying another: only money matters. All ages lie out in the places that have been found, men and women, children. The family rejects have ceased to weep into their make-do pillows; those brought low by their foolishness or by untimely greed plead silently for sleep. A one-time clergyman no longer dwells on his disgrace, but dreams instead that it never happened. Rejected husbands, abandoned wives, victims of chance, have passed beyond bitterness, and devote their energies to keeping warm. The deranged are lulled by voices that often in the night persuade them to rise and walk on, which obediently they do, knowing they must. Men who have failed lie on their own and dream of a reality they dare not contemplate by day: great hotels and deferential waiters, the power they once possessed, the limbs of secretaries. Women who were beautiful in their day are beautiful again. There is no arrogance among the people of the streets, no insistent pride in their sleeping features, no lingering telltale of a past's corruption. They have passed the stage of desperation, and on their downward path some among the women have sold themselves: faces chapped, fingernails ingrained, they are beyond that now. Men, in threes and fours, have offered the three-card trick on these same streets. Beards unkempt, hair matted, skin darkened with filth, they would not now attract the wagers of their passing trade. In their dreams there is occasionally the fantasy that they may be cured, that they may be loved, that all voices and visions will cease, that tomorrow they will discover the strength to resist oblivion. Others remain homeless by choice and for their own particular reasons would not return to a more settled life. The streets, they feel, are where they now belong.

'Looking for a kip, dear?' Felicia is addressed by a limping woman who is pushing a pram full of rags, with plastic bags tied around the belt of her coat. The woman's face is crimson and gnarled, her eyes bloodshot. Wisps of white hair escape from beneath a woollen muffler that's tied under her chin. Scabs have formed around her mouth.

'Nowhere to settle, dear?'

'The hostel's full.'

'Happen it would be.'

'I had my money stolen.'

'Am I right you're an Irish girl?'

'I am.'

'I'm from the County Clare myself. A while back.'

'I'm looking for someone.'

The lame woman isn't interested in that. She has been going about the streets for forty-one years, she says; forty-one years, two months and a day. 'I keep the count. Sharpens you to keep the count.'

Feeling safer in company than alone, Felicia walks with the woman through a neighbourhood that becomes quieter and darker as they advance. Their progress is slow, each litter-bin investigated, the remains of food rescued and gnawed, bottles drained of their dregs. 'What age would you call me?' Felicia is asked during such a pause, and she says she doesn't know.

'Eighty-two years of age, still going strong. I've been all over. Liverpool, Plymouth, all the sailor towns. I was in Glasgow one time. I knew all sorts in Glasgow. I knew the cousin of the Queen. Lovely, considerate man. Lovely in his uniform.'

Skirting an area of waste ground, they have left the streets and are approaching the tow-path of a canal. The water lies below them, at the bottom of an incline, reached by a path through scrub and weeds. Good shelter down on the cut, the lame woman promises, and delves among the rags in her pram. She holds a few up to demonstrate their usefulness as blankets, and Felicia shudders, affected by the fetid odour this rummaging has brought with it.

'Lena's out!' a voice cries, near them somewhere, and then two figures emerge from the mist, one of them waving and exclaiming again that Lena is out. From time to time weak moonlight filters through the clouds, and as the figures come closer Felicia distinguishes a skinny young man with a boyish face and clipped fair hair, and a scrawny middle-aged woman with matchstick legs. The man is attired in flannel trousers and a knitted jersey under a tweed overcoat torn at one pocket, a tie knotted into the collar of a grubby shirt. Orange dye is growing out of the woman's grey hair; in a skeletal face her lips are sensual, pouted into a tulip shape, shiny now with lipstick. Stubble sprouts on her companion's chin and upper lip and in a soft growth on the sides of his face. In the misty twilight the woman's clothes seem shabby.

'How are you, George?' the lame woman inquires after she has welcomed Lena back. Lena was released that morning at eight, subsequent exchanges reveal, and got a lift on a narrow boat to the Flowers and Castle, where George was waiting. They've been drinking barley wine. 'I'm off if you're not coming,' the lame woman abruptly threatens and, not waiting for Felicia's reply, she disappears into the scrub of the slope, the wheels of her pram rattling and juddering over the uneven surface.

'Haven't you a place for the night?' the skinny young man asks Felicia. 'Are you stuck?'

'I've nowhere tonight.'

Still preferring to be in company than on her own, Felicia remains with the two, returning with them the way she has come with the limping woman. They are curious at first: she tells them that she has been looking for a lawn-mower factory because a friend works there. She gives a description: dark hair kept short, medium height, greenish eyes, grey you'd probably call them. Johnny Lysaght, she says, and tells about the money that has disappeared from the sleeves of her jersey.

'Typical, that,' is Lena's response, the description Felicia has given eliciting no interest. 'Turn your head and you're robbed while you'd blink.'

As they walk, Lena talks a lot. Stale as old cabbage, a prison social worker is; another one's called Miss Rubbish. She was lucky, this time, with her cell-mate. 'Wants me to go in with her when she gets out, Phyllsie does. Some type of dodge she has with the benefit. I wouldn't go in with no one, Felicia, I give it to her honest. Now I've found the boy I ain't looking for nothing else. Me and George stick together, Felicia, know what I mean? I wouldn't want nothing dodgy there, not with young George. Don't know the meaning of it, the boy don't.'

'You're hungry, Felicia?' George interrupts.

His voice is the most beautiful Felicia has ever heard. Each word he utters is perfectly enunciated, undistorted by accent or slurred delivery. Lena speaks roughly.

'Yes, I'm hungry.'

Felicia adds that she hasn't any money to spare for food, but George says that doesn't matter and Lena agrees. In the street-light Lena's threadbare coat has acquired colour: a faded yellow, with ersatz gold buttons.

They buy portions of chips in a fish-and-chip shop and eat them on the street. She's London herself, Lena says, bred and born. She and George met up there and decided on a change of scenery a while back on account of a problem they had, a woman who gave a description. They were sleeping under cardboard in London, and previous to that she was on the game, playing the motors. She never took to it. Before that, a man she met in Westbourne Grove persuaded her to have snow-capped mountains tattooed on her back. They're there for ever now; act on an impulse and you have a landscape all over you for the rest of your days.

George is silent while Lena talks, content to nod sympathetic-ally when the tattooing episode is recounted. His eyes screw up when he's sympathetic, spreading geniality into his soft, boy's features.

'Wet as draining-boards some of them magistrates is,' Lena comments, but adds that the judge who sent her down this time was a different kettle of fish, loving every minute of his sentencing.

She describes the hot, red face, excitedly stern. 'Example-to-others stuff. Know what I mean, Felicia?'

'Yes.'

'You pregnant then, Felicia? Bun in your tin, have you?'

'That's why I'm looking for Johnny.'

'Johnny-come-lately, eh? Johnny-I-hardly-knew-you?'

'It's not like that.'

'Course it ain't. Course not.' Lena pauses, then adds: 'I'm not the boy's mother, Felicia. Did you think I was his mother? He's sixteen, you know, mother of his own down London way.'

'Drives a Daimler,' George says.

'Don't stand for a word against her, Georgie don't. I hear that boy called a saint, Felicia, many's the time. Bring him into a Pricerite or a Victor Value or a Lo-Cost, he don't lift nothing, never has in his life, not so much as a tube of pastilles.' All the time she was inside, George was out begging, sleeping rough, making do on cups of tea, never touched a thing. 'Sends a card to the bishops on their birthdays, never forgets one of them. Education done that to him, Felicia, know what I mean?'

They arrive at a house with scaffolding around it and a temporary front door, made of unpainted blockboard. 'No charge here for a doss,' George reassures Felicia, pressing a bell that hangs on its wires, no longer attached to the door frame. From somewhere within the house comes the thump of music, and occasional hammering.

'You're welcome.' A man in a bomber jacket, with a mug in his hand, greets them when the door is opened. 'Come on in.'

He leads the way through an uncarpeted hall, towards uncarpeted stairs. Wallpaper has been partially removed from the walls, torn strips of it still hanging. Pieces of plaster, bricks, wood shavings and lengths of electrical wire are strewn about in the hall and on the stairs. Bags of cement, shovels, buckets and a stack of concrete blocks almost fill the first-floor landing. Coming from behind a closed door from which the paint has been burnt off, the music is louder at the top of the house. In another room the intermittent hammering is louder also.

'So they've turned you loose again, Lena.' Opening the third door on the landing, the man in the bomber jacket has to shout to make himself heard. 'Remit, eh?'

'That's it, Mr Caunce.'

An unshaded bulb dimly lights a small room, empty of furniture. Several rust-marked mattresses, two of them occupied, lie close together on the floor.

'There you go.' The man in the bomber jacket smiles another welcome at the three newcomers. 'OK then?'

Lena says the accommodation is fine. 'Good-night, Mr Caunce.'

The occupants of the mattresses are a young man and a girl, fully dressed, without further covering. Both are lying on their backs, staring at the ceiling. Neither addresses the newcomers, nor ceases to gaze upwards.

'The toilet's across the way.' Lena directs Felicia before she makes the journey herself.

When she returns, George and Felicia go in turn. Felicia doesn't like the lavatory. There is no bolt on the door and it isn't clean. The floorboards are sodden because the bowl is cracked and oozes water. A piece of rope has replaced the chain. A single tap protrudes from the wall, but the basin that was once beneath it has been removed. There is no lavatory paper.

She doesn't like the room when she returns to it. She doesn't like the house. Lena has taken her coat off, revealing a tight black imitation-leather skirt and a black jumper, which she now removes also. George has taken off his overcoat and his shoes.

'All right for you?' Lena asks, not pausing for a response. 'Looks like our friends is on the needle.' Lena and George share one of the mattresses, with George's overcoat spread over them. Felicia lies down on the remaining one. Lena asks her to turn the light off. Mr Caunce doesn't charge, George assures her again.

Felicia lies listening to the noisy breathing of the drugged couple, and the music and the hammering. These sounds and the rank smell in the room pass into Felicia's sleep, until another sound wakes her. A woman is shouting. From somewhere lower down in the house come desperate, hysterical cries of distress.

The breathing of the couple does not alter. Neither Lena nor George wakes up. Then the music ceases, and with it the hammer-

ing, leaving behind only the woman's shrill cries, words occasionally articulated. 'Bestial! Bestial animals!' Sobbing begins when the
woman becomes exhausted, then silence until the music starts
again, and the hammering.

Felicia does not sleep after that, even though both sounds cease
when the darkness lightens. She sobs herself, wishing she could
have stayed asleep, not knowing what to do when the day begins.

'Fancy a tea?' Lena's voice interrupts. 'Tea, Georgie?'

The two they have shared the room with are disturbed by their
going, their eyes dilated and unfocused. Not speaking, they inject
themselves, one passing the syringe to the other.

'Who was that screaming?' Felicia asks on the street. 'That
woman?'

'A Spanish lady.' George looks sorrowful, his high spirits of the
night before gone.

'Singer from way back,' Lena adds. 'Nightclub stuff. She objects
to the noise, see. Plus there's that toilet dripping down through her
ceiling, plus she has a tale about her telephone breaking down.
Caunce has the music and the hammering going, plus every kind
of derelict up and down the stairs, so's he can get her out.'

'Mr Caunce is not a very nice man.' George offers the opinion
with reluctance. 'I'm afraid we have to say that.'

'I often think of her crooning in the nightclub,' Lena says, 'back
in her heyday. Sixty or so she is now.'

'That screaming was terrible.'

'Shocking,' Lena agrees, and the subject is left.

They queue for tea outside a church hall, its doors not open yet.
You don't get much, Lena warns: tea, and bread with something
on it, more if you queue a second time and they don't notice.
'Good morning!' a woman greets them, propping open the doors
after twenty minutes have passed. *Beryl* it says on a badge she is
wearing.

Inside, trestle-tables and benches are set out in rows. In a corner
there's a sink, beside a refrigerator and a gas stove. Three other
women are spreading sliced bread with margarine; a fifth is pouring
tea from a large metal teapot into rows of mugs with milk already
in them. There's a smell of gas and washing-up.

The morning visitors shuffle in, mostly men, all of them unkempt. They are silent except for two who mutter quarrelsomely. Lena has begun again about her colleague in gaol and the scheme she has devised for extracting extra benefits from the social-security system. 'That'll do there,' the woman pouring tea sharply calls out, a reprimand to the men who are quarrelling. They're not running a beer garden, the woman adds jollily, doing her best to cheer the men out of their disagreement. But the men remain morose.

'Phyllsie'll never get away with it, know what I mean, Felicia? Poor Phyllsie hasn't the way with her for stuff like that.'

Two more women, clearly not intent on sustenance, and younger than the women supplying it, enter the hall. Swiftly they survey those gathered there, and choose Felicia and her companions to approach first. 'The Aids brigade,' Lena remarks.

'Ever prick yourselves with a needle you pick up,' one of the women begins in a hectoring manner, 'you squeeze the blood out of the prick hard as you can. Really hard, much as'll come out. D'you understand?'

'We're not on the needle,' Lena says.

'No one's saying you are.' The second young woman picks up her companion's petulant tone. 'All that's being said to you is you might handle something by chance.'

'Hold the finger under a hot tap for a good ten minutes. Then dip it into household bleach.'

When the Aids women have passed on, and in a tone that suggests he has been giving the matter thought during their harangue, George says:

'We wouldn't know about lawn-mowers.'

He nods repeatedly to emphasize this conclusion, and Lena says she agrees. Not in their line, she adds, but there you are. They finish the breakfast they've been provided with and Lena says:

'Coming over to the park, Felicia?'

It isn't far away; they sit there watching people going to work. On soil as black as coal, roses have not yet begun to sprout their new season's leaves. The grass, cropped close months ago, still shows no sign of growth; flowerbeds are free of weeds. The wooden seat they occupy is dedicated to Jacob and Mir Abrahams. *Died with others, 1938. Remembered here.*

'What I'd have is one of them big brown dogs that has their mouths open,' Lena remarks. 'First thing if I came into money I'd get one of them dogs. Nice friendly fellow you could take on to the streets. Know what I mean, Felicia?'

A sedate couple pass by, arm in arm. Retired, Lena speculates; taking it easy now. Funny to be out so early, funny they don't have a dog. 'Anyone today, George?' she inquires, and George says yes, today is the birthday of the Bishop of Bath and Wells.

'I'm sorry we don't know about the lawn-mower thing,' he says.

He stands up, and so does Lena. Felicia realizes her encounter with them is over. He didn't forget, George says: yesterday he sent the Bishop of Bath and Wells a card with a squirrel on it. He smiles, nodding again when he adds that the Bishop of Bath and Wells is probably opening it at this very moment. There was a sermon once, he says, when he was at school. In which it was stated that bishops were lonely.

'Good luck, Felicia,' Lena says. 'Good luck with your fella.'

'I put a little rhyme I know on it,' George says, and pauses to recite with his clear enunciation:

> '*Of all the trees that grow so fair,*
> *Old England to adorn,*
> *Greater are none beneath the Sun*
> *Than Oak, and Ash, and Thorn.*'

They go, and Felicia watches them sauntering through the flowerbeds, while George's voice continues, before it fades away to nothing.

13

Mr Hilditch is in his big front room. 'Blue Hawaii' is playing. The *Daily Telegraph* is limp on his knees.

When the doorbell sounds he doesn't move. He knows she won't go away, she'll ring again. When she does he rises slowly and crosses the hall at the same leisurely pace, all the nagging doubts he has experienced dissipating so swiftly that they have gone completely by the time he reaches the door. 'Blue Hawaii' has come to an end, but he continues the tune with his breath, passing it softly over his lower teeth. He raises a hand to the mourning tie he's wearing, straightening it before he opens the door.

'We meet again,' he says, his smile agreeable.

Mr Hilditch doesn't press his visitor to enter his house. He stands on the doorstep with her, having to peer at her because it is dark. He recalls as a child trying to entice a mouse into a trap that was made like a cage. You put the cheese down and then go away. Every day you put the cheese down a little closer to the metal wire and in the end the mouse goes in of its own accord, confident that it knows what's what.

'You've had no luck in your searchings?'

Mr Hilditch speaks coolly, not wishing to give the impression of any satisfaction on his part. He listens while he's told that the Irish girl has been all over the place. He leaves it to her to tell her story.

'I've had my money stolen.'

'Stolen?'

'Well, it disappeared. It was hidden away in one of my carriers and when I looked it wasn't there.'

'You've been in doubtful company, have you?'

He listens while he's told about the religious house, and then contributes the view that any kind of fanatic isn't to be trusted.

The Irish girl says she doesn't know what to do. She has been in other bed-and-breakfast places, she says.

'How long have you got?' Mr Hilditch pats his stomach. 'You know.'

'I'm four months gone.'

'It hardly shows. Just a little. Just beginning to.'

'You said could you – you said could you help me that day . . .' She begins to stutter, then steadies herself. 'I was wondering . . .' Again she breaks off, and he nods to encourage her. 'I was wondering if you could lend me the fare to go home.' The stutter sets in again when she tries to say it's a cheek asking a stranger. She says she doesn't know where to turn.

'You want to go back?'

'It was a mistake coming over here, I shouldn't ever have come over.'

'What about your friend though?'

'I'll never find him.'

When the girl says that Mr Hilditch realizes she has lost heart. In spite of his reservations, he should have approached her again when he saw her on the street. It may now be too late: from his experience he knows that once they get a notion into their heads it isn't easy to disabuse them of it. If she feels she has turned up every stone, that may simply be that. Mr Hilditch is aware of a coldness in his stomach, the feeling that something he considered to be his may be clawed away from him. Alert to the danger, he speaks deliberately and slowly, simulating a calmness that does not reflect this inner tumult.

'The irony is, if your friend knew all this he'd be doing his nut with worry. I've had experience of that. If he knew what you've been through, all the hoo-ha at home and then looking for him in a country that's strange to you, the poor fellow'd be beside himself.'

There are tears then, as he suspected there might be. It's all down to the boyfriend's mother, he hears again, and experiences a measure of relief, he's not sure why. He listens while it is repeated that the mother wrote lies in a letter; that she said don't come at Christmas, inventing some reason or other.

'Do you know that for a fact, Felicia? Have you heard from someone it was the mother?'

'It was her. I'd swear to it now.'

'So you've heard from no one back home since you got here?'

'No one knows where I am.'

'But they know you came after Johnny?'

'Only she knows the town he's in.'

'And of course she wouldn't tell him you'd taken off. Naturally.'

'No, she wouldn't.'

She mentions a loan again, embarrassed, as she was before. She mentions the sum that is necessary, which she has calculated. He doesn't respond directly, but says:

'It doesn't seem a pity to you to give up so easily? Since you've come so far with so much at stake? For starters, will they welcome you back?'

She has her carrier bags with her and hasn't put them down. 'I'd rather find Johnny,' she whispers, sobs catching on the words. 'Only I never will now.'

'What I'm thinking is, after all you've been through maybe we should make one last effort. D'you understand me, Felicia? I could ask the girl in the office to ring round like I suggested to you. D'you remember I suggested that, Felicia? If Johnny said a lawn-mower works, it must be there somewhere.'

She shakes her head, wiping her nose with a tissue. 'I must have got it wrong.'

Slowly he shakes his head also. 'Just an hour or two it would take, nothing great. That girl's smart, she knows a thing or two. Another thing is, there's places I've heard of where the Irish boys meet up of an evening. For instance, the Blue Light. Have you checked out the Blue Light at all?'

She says she hasn't and he puts it to her that it could be worth looking at, it and a couple of other places. Just to make sure before she throws in the sponge.

'It was understandable, you scuttling off like that the other week, dear. I passed that incident on to Ada when she had a bright moment and she said it was understandable. I only mention it because I wouldn't want you to think there was offence taken.'

'Is your wife getting better?'

'Ada died, dear.'

Her hand goes to her mouth, a swift, uneasy motion. 'Oh, I'm sorry.' The words come out in a rush, with a hint of the stutter again. 'Oh God, I'm sorry.'

'Three nights ago.' He lets a silence develop, since one is called for. 'As a matter of fact,' he continues eventually, 'we have to say a blessed release. We have to use that expression, Felicia.'

He can sense her trying to make a response, but she cannot find the words. He senses what she's thinking. She's thinking that you get caring and kindness from a person who has worries of his own and you turn your back on him in his moment of need. All he asked for that day was a couple of hours' company, the only request he made.

'Well, I'll say good-night.' He hesitates, experiencing an impulse to recall 'Blue Hawaii', to breathe it soundlessly over his lower teeth. 'Unless you'd care for a beverage of some sort?' he offers, resisting this urge to honour the melody. 'You'd be welcome of course. I'm making tea.'

After a moment's hesitation on her part also, she mounts the steps to the hall door.

The kitchen is enormous, the biggest Felicia has ever been in. Its wooden ceiling is stained with the vapours of generations, a single ham hook all that remains of the row there must once have been. Two dressers are crowded with china; a long deal table occupies the central area; pairs of tights hang from drying-rails on a pulley. There are four upright chairs, a step-ladder against one wall, an old sewing-machine in a corner, a mangle. The refrigerator and an electric stove seem out of place.

'They're near by,' the man who hasn't yet told her his name says, running water into an electric kettle. 'The places where the Irish boys meet up. I could run you over.'

'You mean now?'

'It's early yet. The Blue Light's a fish bar. I have high hopes of the Blue Light, a feeling in my bones. To tell you the truth, it would lift me to go out. If you wouldn't mind a drive.'

Half-heartedly, Felicia shakes her head. 'No. No, I wouldn't mind.' Her tone is bleak. It won't be any good. All that's left is the chance of borrowing money.

'We'll have a bite to eat first.'

She wonders if his wife's body has been brought back to the house, and as though something of this thought has crept into her expression he says the funeral was this morning. She sees him noticing the tights on the drying-rack. He turns away from her while in silence he lowers the rack and clears it. When he has folded them and placed them in a drawer, he deposits liver and vegetables on the table and sets about preparing them. He opens a tin containing different varieties of biscuits and invites her to help herself while she is waiting, inviting her also to sit down.

'That's very bad about your money,' he says.

'I know.'

'Have you nothing left at all?'

She tells him: how much she has now, how because the Salvation Army hostel was full she spent last night in a house that was being rebuilt.

'You'll try the Sally hostel again tonight?'

'I don't know.'

She doesn't want to say it will be too late if they go out to the places he has heard about, but from the way he nods ruminatively, while cutting the green off carrots, she can tell that this has dawned on him. And he says:

'Perhaps we should leave it for tonight. I've delayed you enough with my talk. I'm sorry about that.'

'I'd like to go tonight.'

He nods again, in that same way, as if he has guessed this would be her response.

'I'm sorry about your wife,' she says.

With his back to her, he washes the carrots under a running tap. Ada was devout, he says; she came of a devout family. All that was a help to her towards the end.

'She would be happy to see you back with us, dear. She'd be happy to see us going out to look for Johnny.' Slicing liver, he tells her about the funeral: the Reverend Arthur Chase, and a large turn-out, a great spread of wreaths.

'I apologized on account I couldn't invite them back to the house, not being up to anything social. But the Reverend Chase said come in for a bite and a few of us did. A few of my regimental cronies were there, always had a soft spot for her. And of course her friends from the voluntary service, out in force. I have to say it was touching, what they commented about her.'

They eat in the dining-room. Felicia's deadened gaze passes over the mahogany expanse of dining-table and sideboard, the tallboy in the bow window, the portraits in pride of place on three walls, the set of brown Rexine-covered chairs. On the mantelpiece there's a framed photograph of a plump-cheeked woman with a black ribbon trailed around it. 'A crematorium service,' he says, and she imagines a church, not knowing what a crematorium is. When he has poured tea and offered the tin of biscuits again, they collect up the dishes they have eaten from. Pausing by the photograph before they leave the dining-room, his massive shoulders heave, and the bulge of his neck heaves also. When he turns to address her, to remark that his wife was a wonderful woman, his pinprick eyes are lost behind his misted spectacles. She feels ashamed all over again that she took fright after he'd been so good to her, having time for her when there was the worry of his wife's operation. No one has been as concerned: she remembers the hostile faces in the Gathering House, and the suspicion in Mrs Lysaght's face, and her father calling her a hooer. Lena and George walked off, wanting to be on their own. She remembers Miss Furey warning her to be careful about what she said.

'It's good of you to say it,' her benefactor replies when she stumbles through an apology for going off. 'Like I say, dear, no offence was taken.'

There is a generosity in his voice, a warmth that cheers her up.

Mr Hilditch is careful. He brings up the subject of crouching in the back of the car by explaining that it's necessary because the wrong complexion might be placed on the presence of a young girl in his company so soon after the death. 'Sorry about that,' he apologizes when they are clear of the immediate neighbourhood, adding that he wouldn't want Ada's memory insulted by talk. He draws into a lay-by so that she can join him in the front.

'So you've been around?' he prompts, and hears more about the religious house while they drive, and then about two down-and-outs, one of whom seemingly sends birthday cards to bishops. There's a man who's endeavouring to rid himself of the nuisance of a sitting tenant, and a bag woman who wheels her belongings about in a pram. Soft in the head, the one with the birthday cards sounds.

'You meet a rough crowd when you're out and about,' is the only comment he allows himself. 'I'd take good care if I were you. Well, you know to your cost.'

They call in at a Happy Eater on the way to the fish bar, which is a good thirty miles further off; then at the Dog and Grape, where he took Beth a few times. He chooses the saloon bar because he remembers the public bar has a juke-box. A middle-aged couple glance their way once or twice, but a foursome with a poodle are too engrossed in the jokes one of the men is telling to pay any attention. '7-Up', she asks for and he has the same himself, with a packet of crisps. When a lull occurs in the conversation he says:

'A Malaway, Ada was. Ada Daphne Malaway, Daphne after her mother. A manufacturing family. Ball-bearings for the heavy-vehicle industry.'

She sits there, glancing about her for the face she's after, not drinking her 7-Up.

'We often looked back to our wedding day, Ada and myself, in later days. Walking beneath the drawn swords, and then of course we cut the cake with a sword. All sorts of comradely traditions there are at a regimental wedding – champagne drunk from a regimental helmet, fellow officers embracing the bride. Nothing untoward, of course.'

With a friendly nod, Mr Hilditch acknowledges the presence of the middle-aged couple when he goes to the bar for another packet of crisps. The woman looks away, the man just stares. Pointless remaining here, Mr Hilditch reflects, and stuffs the crisps into a pocket, to nibble in the car.

'The Blue Light's our best bet,' he confidently predicts as they drive off. He has taken them all to the Blue Light at one time or another, it being their kind of place, Gaye's particularly. He doesn't care for it himself, even though the chips are good. On the rough side in his opinion, which is borne out as soon as they enter, when a crowd of rowdies begin sniggering.

'No?' he murmurs when she looks about in a way that had been eager in the places they went to earlier, but now is jaded. 'No go, dear?'

She shakes her head. She listens to the voices around her, and says in a defeated voice that they aren't Irish.

'Happen the Irish lads'll come in later. Give it twenty minutes, would we?' He pushes his way to the counter to order plaice and chips. When he returns to her she has found a seat in a booth. She tells him she doesn't want anything to eat, and he says she should take in some nourishment because of her condition. It's a disappointment for her, of course: he understands that, he says.

'Bear with me a minute, Felicia, while I put in a quick call to check out the state of play. Only it's occurred to me there's a bloke I know who employs Irish labour – manager of a smelting works about a mile off. Won't take me a jiffy to get the info about where the lads go of an evening if they've changed from coming here.'

He stands about in the Gents for a minute or two, not long enough to allow his food to become cold. When he gets back to their booth two of the rowdies are trying to pick her up.

'Can I be of assistance to you?' He smiles at them agreeably, but immediately they become abusive, then go away. He guessed that if he left her on her own they would approach her, giving him the opportunity to make it clear what's what.

'No dice,' he reports. 'Out for the evening seemingly.'

The rowdies are leaving now, and only a few couples occupy the booths. A slatternly girl is sweeping the floor.

'Tell me more about yourself, Felicia.'

He prompts her, asking questions to cheer her up: about her home life, if pets are kept, the friends she has and if any of them knows where she is. She shakes her head: she told no one, she asserts again, and repeats that if her father has gone to the police and they question the boyfriend's mother she'll probably mislead them as to his whereabouts. A picture of this woman has begun to form vividly in Mr Hilditch's imagination, but he doesn't want to think about her now. When the moment is suitable he says:

'I hope it's not a presumption on my part, Felicia, but have you considered your condition at all?'

He has raised his voice a little. The slatternly girl is quite close to them now, obviously interested.

'It's lovely news, of course,' he says, and then lowers his voice again. 'I'm only thinking, Felicia, that no matter what the outcome of tracking Johnny down is you don't want to let yourself get caught. Don't let it go too far was always the advice Ada gave, and my own as well. Enough to say you lost it, a form of words that is, covers a multitude. You understand me, Felicia?'

'Yes.'

'It's beggars and choosers, Felicia. I know what you mean when you say you'd want to talk to Johnny first. You and myself would both rather that and of course we'll try for it, but it isn't looking like an option at the moment.'

She doesn't appear to be listening. There's a faraway look about her, as if his inquiries about her home life have drawn her back into it. He rouses her with a practicality.

'Would you care for something, dear?'

She asks for tea. He smears ketchup on the last of his chips before he rises to fetch it for her. They remember him behind the counter, of that he's certain. They know him by sight even though it's a long time since he last was in, even though they didn't greet him and never have. They remember him because of the girls, one girl and then another, and now a new one, who's in the family way. A little tick of pleasure begins in him somewhere as he carries the plastic cartons back to the booth.

Her head is turned away and he knows there are tears. Another thing, he puts it to her, is that if they don't locate Johnny and she goes back home the way she is now, it'll definitely be too late when Johnny turns up there himself. And it stands to reason he will, being in the habit of regularly visiting the disagreeable mother.

'What I'm saying is, you'd be in Johnny's better books if you weren't wheeling out an infant he didn't know a thing about. I could be wrong, dear, but there you are.'

'I don't want to do a thing like that.' A sound like a sob comes from her and he moves around the table so that he's sitting beside her. He puts an arm around her shoulder, and she begins a long palaver about visiting some woman in a farmhouse who apparently had intimacy with her brother.

'Wipe your eyes, dear.'

Before he knew Sharon she'd got rid of three little errors in that department. She mentioned the place she went to the third time, paid for by the manager of a dry cleaner's. Scared out of his wits, Sharon said. The Gishford Clinic, up Sheffield way. Posh, Sharon said.

'Sorry.' The present girl blows her nose on a tissue she has been twisting between her fingers. People are definitely noticing now, a man and a woman waiting for chips at the counter, a girl and a youth in a booth across the aisle.

'Don't say anything, Felicia. Don't try to speak until you're recovered.' Mr Hilditch's small hands grasp one of hers, and out of the corner of his eye he can see that the couple in the booth and the couple at the counter are still noticing. There's been a lover's tiff is the assumption in their expressions, a little misunderstanding that is now being put right.

'Drink up that tea while it's warm. The good's in the warmth, they say. No, I only mention it because the night I came in and told Ada I found you wandering she said, "I wonder if she's in the family way?" A woman can tell, you know, even at a remove. Whereas I had no idea myself, although I'd actually been in your company. The thing is, a doctor's obliged to fix you up over here if you request it in the early stages. On the other hand, if it's left too late you're shown the door.'

'A lot come over for it.'

'Of course they do.'

A new excitement possesses Mr Hilditch. He remembers Sharon saying she was beyond the limit, twenty-nine or thirty weeks gone, the time the dry cleaner took her to the Gishford. It always has to be private, he remembers she said, if there's anything dodgy. Sheffield's easily far enough away.

'The only thing is,' he says, 'I think I'm right in stating that if there's any irregularity you can be going back and forth to a local surgery till the cows come home. Anyone who hasn't paid the health contributions. Anyone who's an alien. You could be hanging about for weeks.'

'What?'

She hasn't been listening. He half closes his eyes, seeing himself with her in the Gishford, as Sharon has described it. He sees them in a waiting-room, a clear implication established by his presence beside her. Carried away for a moment, Mr Hilditch breathes heavily, then calms himself.

'You cut the red tape if you go private, is what I'm saying to you.'

'I don't know what to do without a chance to talk to Johnny.' It's Johnny's baby, too: she repeats that twice, her voice raised. She repeats that she doesn't know what to do.

The images in Mr Hilditch's imagination recede. The emotion his passing reference to her condition has engendered alarms him. People are noticing now all right, but the pleasure of that is tinged with the fear that he has been clumsy, that again she is slipping away. When she quietens he says:

'It's only that Ada mentioned it before she went, but you're right; it's best left for now. We won't refer to it again. I'm sorry about the Irish boys not being in tonight. The trouble is they're never more than passing trade. A spot of trouble one night and they find somewhere else. Sorry about that, dear.'

'It's not your fault.'

He hopes she'll continue, but she doesn't.

'You're downcast, dear?'

'A bit.'

'You're looking chipper, as a matter of fact. If it's any consolation.'

She doesn't reply.

'I'll get the girl in the office to make her inquiries first thing in the morning, and then we'll see where we are. How's that look?'

'She won't find him.'

'If anyone can find your friend that girl can. I promise you that, Felicia.'

When the fish bar closes they move on, and only call in once more, at a Little Chef that surprisingly is still open. Later they stop in the lay-by they stopped in before.

'I hope it's not uncomfy.' He doesn't know if his solicitude reaches her through the rug he has suggested she should drape over her face when she has crouched down in the back again. He has recommended the rug because of the street lights. 'It's great the way you understand about that,' he adds, again endeavouring to induce cheerfulness.

When the car comes to a halt on the gravel outside Number Three he repeats that the girl in the office will get cracking first thing. She'll ring round every possibility she can lay her hands on; she'll get through to the personnel departments at the different works the way a private inquirer wouldn't be able to; she'll give the name John Lysaght, with a detailed description. As he said when he first mentioned the matter, she'll check out the electoral register and any other listings she can find.

'By eveningtime we'll know the score. We'll have Master Johnny in our sights.'

'Will I come back to find out from you?' From the way she says it — the tiredness in her voice — she is clearly already convinced, in spite of everything he has just said, that he won't have news for her. What's on her mind is the money she came to borrow.

'Any time after dark. Maybe about six?' He raises a hand to his mouth to stifle a yawn that does not develop. Then, as casually as he can manage: 'You'll find somewhere for tonight, will you?'

'I'll try for that house again. Mr Caunce's.'

'Take care in a place like that, Felicia.'

'Yes, I will.'

Her carrier bags are in the hall, where she left them by the hall-stand. He watches her endeavouring to find the words to raise the matter of the money, but she's too shy to return to the subject. It's natural enough, since touching a total stranger for anything up to fifty pounds is a delicate undertaking. He wonders about mentioning the money himself, just to keep her interested, but decides against that.

'All right in the toilet department before you set off?' he inquires instead, casually also.

'Yes, all right, thanks.'

She still hesitates. She begins to say something, but only manages a word or two before she interrupts herself and says good-night. Less casually now, his intonation furred with concern, he wonders if she's wise to go wandering about at this hour of the night?

'You're welcome, of course,' he offers next, 'to lay your head down here.'

14

'Morning, Mr Hilditch!' a man with a bad leg calls out on the forecourt, one of the canteen cleaners.

'Morning, Jimmy. Better spot of weather, eh?'

'Does your heart good, Mr Hilditch.'

The drizzly weather of the last day or two has passed on; it's frosty now, with a clear sky. Rissoles in batter it is today, or pork roast or fish; prunes and custard or roly-poly: the Thursday menu. He'll probably go for the rissoles, with french fries and mushy peas, unless the roast tastes special, which once in a while it does.

'Morning, Mr Hilditch,' someone else calls out from a distance, and he smiles and waves.

It seems extraordinary that he is greeted as he usually is. It seems extraordinary that no one looks differently at him on the forecourt, or in the kitchens when he enters them ten minutes later, or through the glass of the offices adjacent to his own. Mr Hilditch finds it hard to believe that none of these people is aware that less than eight hours ago, at twenty past one in the morning, standing in his own hallway, he issued the invitation he did and as a consequence has an unknown Irish girl under his roof. All your adult life you live to a rule. Every waking minute you take full precautions on account of wagging tongues. Then, in a single instant, you let it all go. Not once did he experience an urge to take Beth or Elsie Covington, or any of the others, under his roof. Never before has he made reference to a wife, or spoken of a wedding with regimental traditions, and swords. There has never been a call for anything more than the meetings, the hours spent together, and people noticing where it was safe for people to notice.

Last night in that Little Chef a woman collecting used dishes definitely muttered something to another woman, and both of them looked across to where the Irish girl was shaking her head after he'd drawn her attention to a young man who'd just entered the place. Clearly the two women had established that she was pregnant. It still hardly shows, but women can tell the way a man isn't able to, as he knows from what is sometimes passed on to him in the canteen. He even put it to her; something about a woman's perception, making conversation.

Shivering through him, akin to the fever that accompanies a bout of flu, the excitement that began as a tick of pleasure in the Blue Light fish bar became intense when later he stood with the Irish girl in the hallway, her carrier bags waiting for her to pick up, the little metal cross just visible at her neck. He invited her under his roof because he was impelled to do so, just as he'd been impelled to take Gaye's arm as they were leaving Pam's Pantry at the Creech Wood Services – a premature action because it was the first time they'd gone out together. Yet he couldn't have stopped himself if he'd tried, even though Creech Wood wasn't far enough away, not by a good twenty miles. Two minutes later, in the car park, he noticed a man who looked like Bellis from the spraying sheds, and tightness knotted in his stomach, a warmth becoming icy. 'Your daughter, Mr Hilditch?' he imagined the man saying the next time they met in the canteen; and having to shake his head, saying he'd never been at Creech Wood Services in his life. But to his vast relief he was mistaken: the man was someone else.

To be seen by the wrong pair of eyes when you'd linked arms with a friend seems a little thing now; tiny compared with it being known that you've taken a girl under your roof. For the first time in his adult life the sensation of risk feels attractive, and instinctively he is aware that this is because the risk he has taken is so great. It seems to Mr Hilditch, also, that he has been journeying for a long time to the destination he has reached, that all his previous actions have lacked the panache of the one that has brought him here. The Irish girl spent the night in his big front room, saying she'd be all right there, although he offered her a room with a bed in it upstairs. She lay down on the sofa, where he saw her when he tiptoed downstairs before he retired himself. As he recollects her shadowy, sleeping form now, Mr Hilditch knows that that sofa will never be the same for him again. Already this girl has used the forks and spoons he uses himself, and used the toilet and maybe has had a strip wash. 'Make yourself an egg or two,' he said before he left, 'if you're peckish later on, Felicia.' She is welcome to all he has.

The morning passes slowly for Mr Hilditch, a difficult time to concentrate. He knows he can trust this girl. He knows she will stay in the house, not venturing to the shrubberies or the backyard because he has said it's best she shouldn't. She will be careful at the windows, keeping well back although they're only partially visible from the road; in particular she will keep clear of the downstairs windows in case some deliverer of junk mail chances to glance in.

Yet even so, naturally, he is nervous. It would be agreeable to draw things out, to drive off this evening in another direction, to sit down again with her in the kitchen for a late-night snack after they've visited a few more cafés. But he can tell she's not in the mood any more for drawing things out; she has given up and she's beginning to be edgy. Again Mr Hilditch sees himself in the waiting-room of the Gishford Clinic, murmuring to her that she mustn't worry. There has never been anything like that either, nothing even approaching it.

'Keeping fit, Mr Hilditch?' is a query at lunchtime in the canteen.

'Fine, thanks. Yourself?'

Some reply is made; Mr Hilditch hides his lack of interest beneath a smile. Surely the Asian woman dishing out mushy peas can tell he's not as he was yesterday? How can there fail to be something in his expression reflecting the *frisson* of unease that caused him to remain awake all night just because she was under his roof, only a flight of stairs separating them? 'Oh, what a timid one you are!' his mother used to say when he was six. He smiles again, pleased that the remark has come back to him. He thanks the Asian woman and picks up his tray, not feeling timid in the least.

She'll maybe be turning the pages of a *Geographic* now. She's different from the others, nothing tough about her. Simple as a bird, which you'd expect her to be of course, coming from where she does. And yet, of course, they're all the same. The truth stares out at them and they avert their eyes. Beth, with her extra glass or two, couldn't tolerate it for an instant; Elsie had made herself immune to it by the time she hit the streets. The more lies they are told the more they tell them to themselves – Jakki about her so-called company director, Sharon up the garden path with the dry cleaner, father of five. The first time he met up with Bobbi she had a black eye: from walking into a door edge, she said.

'What would I go for, Mr Hilditch?' an employee whose name he can't recollect wants to know, and he advises the pork because of the crackling. 'Happen I will, Mr Hilditch. Looks champion, that pork, eh?'

She's maybe having her boiled eggs now. She maybe put on 'Lazy River' in the big front room and the melody comes softly to the kitchen. Curiosity has drawn her upstairs, to the dresses hanging in the wardrobe, and the shoes on the linoleum beside it.

'Third extractor's clogged, Mr Hilditch,' someone reports later that afternoon, and he can hardly tell if it's a man or a woman, it doesn't matter anyway, some shadow in an overall such as they all wear, some covering on the head by European law.

'Dearie me,' he responds, as he always does in a calamity. He watches while a crowd gathers round the faulty extractor, Len from the finishing shed who's always called in for this kind of repair, and most of the kitchen staff.

'I think you'll find us competitive,' the Crosse and Blackwell's rep contends later still, in the office. 'Grossed up, I'd say those terms are out of competition's reach.'

It's not of interest; it doesn't matter. A clogged extractor or bargain prices, how can any of it compare with a runaway from the Irish boglands passing through the rooms of his house, a girl with a cross on a cheap metal chain? 'Excuse me a minute,' he apologizes to the Crosse and Blackwell's man, and telephones the Gishford Clinic from the staff call-box outside the canteen. 'Yes, we can arrange an immediate,' a soothing voice assures him. Very civil, the place sounds, as Sharon said.

'You give us a shout,' the Crosse and Blackwell's man invites when he returns to the office. 'Any time you've thought it over.'

'Yes, I will.'

He shakes hands with the Crosse and Blackwell's man, trying to remember his name.

'Always good to see you, Mr Hilditch.'

'And yourself.'

Pregnant in his house, examining his mother's likeness draped in mourning on the dining-room mantelpiece, going from room to room upstairs, eventually at her strip wash. Mr Hilditch drops the lids over his eyes in the hope that the images will intensify. He turns his head away, taking off his spectacles for a moment to disguise his concentration on a private matter, while the Crosse and Blackwell's man fastens his briefcase.

'I'll leave another card,' the man says, placing the card on the edge of Mr Hilditch's desk. 'Just a reminder.'

Her clothes draped over the chair and the towel-rail in the bathroom: not since his mother was alive has there been anything like that in Number Three.

In the vast kitchen the remains of the tea Felicia made an hour ago is cold. Her head softly aches, muddled with the worries that have occupied it all day. Somehow or other, she'll pay back the money she took from the old woman and no longer possesses. She'll settle for part-time cleaning, an hour a day, anything there is. And whatever she is lent for her journey home she'll pay back by borrowing from Carmel, or from Aidan and Connie Jo, even Sister Benedict; she'll get it somehow. When Johnny comes – maybe for St Patrick's Day or Easter – he'll help her when she explains. When Johnny comes they'll disentangle his mother's distortions and she'll tell him every single thing, what she had in mind when she rode out to see Miss Furey, how in a final bout of desperation she sought the advice of the two women who had distributed leaflets at the canning factory when the rumour began that it was going to close. There was help at hand for any woman in difficulties, the leaflets promised, and someone had pasted one on to the door of the outside lavatory, which was still stuck there when she went to look, the telephone number underlined. 'You come on over,' a voice invited when she dialled it, and gave an address in a town twenty miles away.

After she has washed up her cup and saucer and the teapot, Felicia sits in the big front room, remembering that cold afternoon. Her carrier bags are beside the sofa, where she left them when she lay down last night. Sans Souci, the bungalow the women lived in was called, pebble-dashed in a shade of pink, on a small estate. The women wore chunky knitwear and glasses, and called her 'love', telling her not to worry. They gave her coffee in a mug, and she didn't like to say it didn't agree with her at present. A child came into the room when she was talking about her troubles, and was told to go away. The women sat on the floor, drinking mugs of coffee themselves. 'He's liable,' the one whose glasses had darker rims than her friend's pointed out. 'He can't run away from it.'

But she said it wasn't like that, and began at the beginning: how she and Johnny had fallen in love, how he had done his best to protect both of them against what had occurred, but something had gone wrong. She felt shy, saying that. She felt ashamed of having to tell strangers, and became flustered in the middle of it. 'Are you saying the man doesn't know?' the other woman asked, so she explained about Johnny leaving in a hurry, how between them they had failed to make arrangements to keep in touch. 'Before you do anything,' the same woman laid down, 'you have to get hold of the father. You have clear rights in that respect. You have a father waltzing off like he's a prince or something. That man was liable from the moment he abused you.'

She protested again it wasn't like that, but the woman insisted that was the way you had to see it. It was abuse if a man couldn't give a toss, if he was gratifying himself with girls all over the shop. Wherever he was now, an order could be obtained from the courts; as soon as the child was born, maintenance could be withheld from the father's wages. Figures were quoted: the number of women, nationally, recorded as having being left in this manner. The callousness of it was touched upon, the monstrous selfishness of it.

'Give us the offender's name,' the woman with the darker rims urged, reaching across the floor for a piece of paper on which the child had been drawing with a crayon. 'Full name and address in Ireland if you can't supply the present whereabouts.'

In the big front room Felicia remembers shaking her head, and soon after that she left. At the hall door of the bungalow the women told her that they were single parents themselves, each with a child. One-parent families were accepted these days, they both assured her; there were some who chose it. They offered to help her in the matter of the court order; fifty per cent of the time they were successful in cases where there were orders.

Daylight begins to fade in the room; gloom turns to darkness, and then the tyres of the car crunch on the gravel. A door of the car bangs, and there's his key in the lock. No dice, he says, the first words he utters, shaking his head sorrowfully. All day long the girl has been ringing round. Not a sausage. No sign of a John or a Johnny Lysaght anywhere.

It's not a disappointment. She knew; she said it would be this, it isn't unexpected. At least they know the score, he says; at least all that's out of the way. 'You been OK?' he asks.

'Yes, fine.'

'We'll have a bite to eat and then map out a plan of campaign.' He smiles. 'We'll get you home somehow.'

He cooks food for them, which, again, they eat formally in the dining-room. He talks about his regimental days, action he has seen. He asks her if she has been interested in the geographical magazines on his shelves, or the bound volumes of *Railway and Travel Monthly*. He asks her to tell him more about herself and she says there's not much really, but when he presses she tells him about her mother's death, and going to the convent, up steep St Joseph's Hill every morning with Carmel and Rose and Connie Jo, the same journey her father made every day and still does. She describes the Square because he asks her to: Doheny's where the buses draw in, the statue of the soldier that commemorates those who lost their lives in the national struggle, the Two-Screen Ritz. She tells him how Mr Hickey didn't want confetti thrown in the hall of the hotel on the day of the wedding because of the mess it made; and how Aidan has given up his trade under pressure from the family he married into, how he's serving in McGrattan Street Cycles and Prams now. She tells him about Shay Mulroone coming into the Diamond Coffee Dock; and how her father would like her to have part-time work only, so that she could continue to look after the house and do the cooking, so that Mrs Quigly needn't be called upon to see to the old woman every midday. She tells him that when she was a child people brought her back shells when they went to the seaside, all shapes and sizes, that she used to display on the chest of drawers in her room but which she keeps in a drawer now, the one where the letters she wrote are.

All the time he listens, pouring cups of tea for them when they have finished their main course, only interrupting to offer her biscuits to go with the jelly he made that morning. Then, when they are still in the dining-room:

'I know you don't care for the subject, Felicia, but I'm afraid I'm duty-bound to raise it again. I've had experience, as I've explained to you, with some of the young chaps under me in the old days. There wasn't one of them, not a single one in my entire recollection, Felicia, who didn't want the matter taken care of when it arose. Every man jack, not one out of step.'

She nods, knowing what he's referring to.

'You came over here to ask Johnny that question, but you never got an answer, Felicia. That's the way we have to look at it. If the girl in the office had struck lucky today it'd be a different kettle of fish, I'm not saying it wouldn't. But she didn't, and I'm definitely of one mind with you now: we won't find Johnny.'

'Johnny'll be over, St Patrick's Day or Easter. I was thinking about that the entire day. It'll be all right when I'm back there and we're together again.'

'But, dear, didn't you ride out on your bike to see that woman you told me about? Didn't you want to get the thing done then?'

'I wasn't right to think about it without Johnny knew. It was only I couldn't think what to do for the best.'

'I'm cognizant of all that, dear. I appreciate every word; I appreciate you've had a change of heart. But what we're trying to work out now is what Johnny'd want without having access to him. D'you understand me, dear?'

'Yes, I do. It's only –'

'If Johnny comes back and finds you in a certain condition he'll say to himself he's been trapped. Any young fellow would.'

'I'm not trying to trap him.'

'That's what I'm saying to you. That's what you and myself know. What Johnny'll choose to know mightn't be on the same lines at all.'

'Johnny and me love one another. He wouldn't think anything like he's been trapped.'

'It's not in doubt that Johnny loves you, dear. There's nothing you've said to me that contradicts that. The point I'm making to you is that a situation like you and Johnny are in can all too easily be affected by misfortune.' He pauses, looking away from her for a moment, before he continues. 'Ada used to say that, Felicia. Ada had considerable insight into matters of the heart.'

'I wish we could have found him.'

'I wish we could have. I'll be honest with you, Felicia: there's nothing in this world would please me more than if Johnny rang the bell this instant minute.'

'Johnny doesn't know –'

'I know, dear, I know. I was only putting a hypothetical case to you. The thing is, Felicia, you're over here, where a certain facility's available. What I'm saying to you now is what I'd say to any daughter Ada and myself might have had. I'm giving you the benefit of long experience. There's no doubt in my mind, Felicia.'

She is silent at the big dining-table, her headache worse now. She tries to work it out, to think how it would be: Johnny arriving home, and meeting him, Johnny looking at her and knowing before she can tell him. She tries to see his face. She tries to make him speak.

'I've given it thought since half past two this afternoon, Felicia, when the girl turned to me and shook her head. I sat there and said to myself it isn't only Johnny. There's her father too, I said to myself, a man in distress due to what's happened. There's her brother who got married that day, and then again the two lads out in the quarries, and the old lady who's her great-granny. There's that girl's whole life, I said to myself.'

'There's people would call it murder.' She explains that the nuns would. She explains that there are people who would never forgive it. Her mother wouldn't have.

'But your mother's no longer —'

'I know.'

'I understand how you feel, Felicia. Nobody understands better. But I'm an older man, that chance has sent your way. I have a little put by that I'd gladly donate in order to do the decent thing by your father and your brothers and the old lady. We're not put into this world to cause pain. I used to say that to the young lads I had under me, I used to make the point. You have to think of yourself on occasion, I used to say. You have to sometimes, I'm not saying you don't. But there're other people too, which is something you're daily more aware of as you get older. No one's denying you've been through it, Felicia, but so has your unfortunate father and the old lady, and your brothers trying to hold their heads up. That's all I'm saying to you. We all have to do terrible things, Felicia. We have to find the courage sometimes.'

Her eye is caught by a face in a painting above the mantelpiece, pink-cheeked and solemn. Again the tin of biscuits is offered to her. It's because he knows so much about her by now that he's able to advise her, he says. All he's intent upon is helping her.

'I know.'

'We'll get you home afterwards. Don't worry about that.'

'Anything you lend me I'll send back. Every penny.'

'I have no doubt, Felicia.'

Afterwards they sit together and he plays her old songs on the gramophone. When one of them comes to an end he repeats that looking after her is what his wife would want, deprecating his own kindness and his patience. But she knows they're there; she knows he's doing his best to help her. Tonight she'll sleep upstairs, in the room he wanted her to sleep in last night.

'I'm sorry we never found Johnny,' he says. He puts another record on. '*Do nothin' till you hear from me*', a lugubrious singer begs.

Later, in the kitchen, he makes Ovaltine. He tells her not to worry, not to lie wakeless. The night can be an enemy, he says, and she understands what he means. When she asks if he has anything for a headache he makes a fuss of her, watching while she takes aspirins, getting her a glass of water.

'They can do an immediate at the Gishford.' His back is to her now. He pours the milk he has heated into two plain white mugs.

'A what?'

'They can do it at once, Felicia. I asked the girl to put a call in to them. You could be back across the water by Monday – you could be back a free spirit, Felicia, the whole thing lifted from you. It's what's right, Felicia.'

She takes the mug he offers her. She sips the Ovaltine, leaning against the dresser. He asks her if she'd like a biscuit, and she says no.

'It's right to erase an error,' he says. 'It's what's meant, Felicia.'

15

Magazines are on a square central table. The fitted carpeting is flecked, grey and brown. There are pale clean walls.

Two different nurses keep passing through; and once a specialist, white jacket and trousers, short sleeves. Behind a glass window that slides open a staid receptionist is occupied at a desk. Classical music plays.

Two girls wait also, one with a youth, the other alone. The one on her own leafs through *Woman* and *Hello!*, a tough-looking creature in Mr Hilditch's opinion, with aluminium hair. The couple whisper.

Mr Hilditch is certain that conclusions have already been reached in the waiting-room. Twice he has approached the staid receptionist, apologizing for doing so, seeking assurances that there are no complications. On both occasions she suggested he should go for a walk, or simply go home and return later, which is the more usual thing. 'If you don't mind, Nurse,' he replied, the same words each time, 'I'd prefer to be near my girlfriend.'

He could feel the youth thinking about both of them before they called her in: a man of fifty-four or -five, the youth was speculating, the kid no more than seventeen. When he called her darling, telling her not to worry, the youth heard every word.

'Now then,' a nurse with a mole says. 'Miss Dikes?'

'It's Mrs, actually,' the youth sharply corrects her. The girl with him doesn't move. 'Go on, Nella,' he urges in the same sharp voice. 'You'll be all right.'

'Just the prelim, Mrs Dikes,' the nurse says. 'Nothing to worry about.'

'I'll come back in a while.' The youth is on his feet also, halfway to the door.

'I'd be grateful if you'd remain until the prelim's complete, Mr Dikes,' the nurse requests.

The girl with the coloured hair reaches for another magazine, *Out and Away*. The youth raps on the glass of the receptionist's window and when she slides it back he asks if there's a coffee to be had. She closes her eyes briefly, snappishly. Coffee isn't available.

'Bloody marvellous.' The youth addresses Mr Hilditch. 'You pay through the bloody nose, you think they'd supply a coffee.'

'I imagine the young ladies get something. I imagine they're well looked after, it being private.'

'We had the dosh put aside for Torremolinos, but there you go. Nella wouldn't touch the other. Gets around, she says, if you go on the public, and she don't want that. The wife's far on, is she? Don't look it to me.'

'No, she's not far on.' Mr Hilditch pauses. 'Actually, she's not my wife.'

The girl with the coloured hair looks up from her magazine, interested now.

'Girlfriend,' Mr Hilditch says, and when a second specialist, smaller and bald, enters the waiting-room and raps on the receptionist's glass, Mr Hilditch hopes the youth will ask another question so that the specialist and the receptionist can be drawn in. But the youth says nothing further and the bald specialist requests that when the eleven-fifteen appointment arrives he is to be informed immediately. 'Cut it a bit fine, the eleven-fifteen has,' he comments, hurrying away again, and Mr Hilditch smiles and catches his eye.

It is then that the excitement begins, creeping through him, like something in his blood. He is the father of an unborn child, no doubt in any of their minds. The girl they have all seen, who was here not ten minutes ago, whey-faced and anxious, is at this very moment being separated from their indiscretion. A relationship has occurred, no way can you gainsay it.

That he is an older man is just fact. Girls can take to an older man, they can take to a stout man: it's a natural thing; it isn't peculiar, it isn't wrong. 'You're never that big boy's mother!' people used to say, the other way round then; strangers would say it when they were out somewhere, down town or at the Spa they went to. Funny if she were here now, Mr Hilditch reflects; funny if she came back from the dead.

Mr Hilditch closes his eyes and the indiscretion that occurred is there, an episode in his car. It's dark; they can't see one another; nothing could be nicer, the Irish girl is whispering to him; she wants to be with him for ever.

In the waiting-room a tremor afflicts him, a slight thing, nothing serious: he has experienced this before. It's in his legs and then his arms; he steadies the quivering it causes in his hands by pressing the tips of his fingers into his knees. He would like to rest for a moment, to close his eyes again, but he does not do so. He smiles in order to control the quivering when it affects his lips, hoping it will not be taken as untoward that he should smile at this time.

16

The watch is her father's. She sits among the daisies, waiting for him while he looks for it. She arranges the pink flowers on a dock leaf and they are strawberries on a plate and it is a party except that no one comes to it but herself. The dandelions are another fruit, maybe pears, she doesn't know. 'Crickets talk with their legs,' her father says when he comes back.

The watch always dangles into his top pocket, only it wasn't there when he looked. He took it off to keep it by him, so that he'd know the time when his jacket was off. He drooped the watch-chain over a fallen branch and then walked away without it. 'We'll go and look,' he said in the kitchen. Her mother was there too. A Sunday because they'd all been to Mass.

It's too hot where she is so he says go under the tree. His grandfather's the watch was, brought back from Dublin the time his grandfather was killed by the soldiers. 'It won't take long,' someone else says. 'Try and relax now.' It's when he worked for the Mandevilles, before he worked for the nuns. 'There it is,' he says. 'Right as rain.'

There is music a long way off, a man singing and the music. 'That's Felicia, ma'am,' her father says, and a tall woman bends down and holds her hand out. 'Shake hands with Mrs Mandeville, Felicia.' But she doesn't want to, and the woman laughs. She has smooth hair drawn back from her face, and trousers. 'Felicia's a nice name,' she says.

A white dog sniffs her foot and she cries. The tall woman puts a finger into the dog's mouth to show it won't bite.

The music is still playing, and the voice is singing. 'Look, Felicia,' her father says, and she sees people sitting on chairs in front of a house, a man and another woman and a boy. The music is coming from there. 'John Count,' her father says.

The house is green, a big square house. The bottom of a curtain has blown out of an open window and trails on the windowsill, white net on green. The hall door is open as wide as it will go, darkness inside. Tall Mrs Mandeville walks with the dog behind her, going slowly towards the chairs, her footsteps sounding on the gravel, silent on the grass. There is a rattle of plates and cups when the music ceases.

In a shed in the garden her father shows her the garden tools he uses. He tells her what each is called: rake, fork, shears, spade, hoe. This is where he spends his days. He shows her a bird's nest in the roof of the shed, and lifts her up to see speckled green eggs. 'Isn't that a queer thing?' he says.

They pick bluebells to bring back. She can hear the music again, but it's different now. Jazz, her father says, the music of the southern American negro. 'A black man that is, Felicia. Black all over.'

It's hot when they come out of the wood where the bluebells are, she can feel it on her head. Her father takes one hand and she holds the bluebells in the other. The hinge on the watch is faulty, he says, he must get it fixed in MacSweeney's. 'Aren't you the big girl now,' he says, 'able to be a companion on a Sunday?'

On the road they stop while he opens a packet of cigarettes. Sweet Afton he likes, but sometimes he'll try another brand. He doesn't smoke much, just now and then during the day. 'Keep the midges off us,' he says, lighting a match.

He tells her about when he was small, as small as she is, and about how his own father had bare feet going to school. His own father and his mother are dead, but he still has his grandmother. They go into Lafferty's shop and he has some of her lemonade because he is thirsty, too. He carries her on his shoulders and she can smell the tang of tobacco on him. 'All done,' someone says and it isn't him, and there are lights and a smell that isn't cigarettes, clean like Jeyes' Fluid or the stuff when the sink's blocked. The sheets are cool, a soreness is just beginning. 'All done,' someone says again; the fingers on her wrist have black hairs on them. 'She can take herself off now,' another voice says.

She's there in the waiting-room, standing in front of him, white as a sheet. The youth who saved up to go to Torremolinos doesn't pay any attention. There's no one else in the waiting-room now except the receptionist behind her glass window.

'Sit down a minute, dear,' he says, and as he approaches the receptionist's window it is drawn back. He pays in cash. 'Thank you,' he says to the woman. 'We're greatly obliged.'

'See she keeps warm.'

'We have a little journey and then I'll tuck her up.'

The woman nods, glancing at him once. He can feel her wanting to ask if he's the father, even though she must have clearly heard it when he said girlfriend. He says the word again, mumbling through the rest of the sentence because in the time he can't think of anything coherent to say. He smiles at the receptionist. It could happen to a bishop, he wants to say, that expression of his Uncle Wilf's. But already the glass has slid back into place.

It's sunny, crossing the street to the little green car. 'You rest yourself now,' he says, settling her in the back, and she closes her eyes, trying not to think about it. The most terrible sin of all, her mother would have said, God's gift thrown back at Him.

'OK?' he asks and she says yes, but in all sorts of ways she doesn't feel OK. She wants to ask him to lend her the money now. She wants to ask him to drop her off at a railway station, even though her belongings are still in his house. It doesn't matter about her belongings; all that matters is going home.

But when she tries to find the words to put to him she can't.

Burger with egg, he orders, and a portion of chips. He feels tired:

the experience has left him drained. 'Thanks,' he says when he receives his change at the pay-out, picking up his tray again and looking round for an unoccupied table.

It is while doing so that he notices the man and woman sitting in the corner window. There's something familiar about the man, something about the sharpness of his face and the grey frill of his moustache. That moustache used to be jet-black, Mr Hilditch comments to himself, still not recognizing the man.

He is sitting like a ramrod and the woman is bent, suggesting arthritis. Again, there's something familiar about the cocky way the man holds his head, and it dawns on Mr Hilditch then that this is almost certainly the recruiting sergeant who deprived him, thirty-six years ago, of his chosen way of life. The food in front of him cools, remaining untouched while he continues to observe the couple.

When they rise he rises also, and follows them to the car park. But they walk in the opposite direction from where the Irish girl is waiting, and his hope of being able to get her out of the car – to let the couple see her hanging on to his arm – is dashed. He returns to the table he has been sitting at, but the contents of his tray have been cleared away, even though anyone could have guessed he was returning. He orders another burger and chips to take away.

There's a picture of something, a kind of bird. *Welcome Break* is on the container from which steam rises, a smell of meat. 'Fancy a Bakewell brought out?' he says when he has finished.

Her shoulders are too wide for the seat; her feet have to be on the floor because there isn't room for them anywhere else. When she closes her eyes again Effie Holahan is swinging her legs on the play-yard wall. The wall is rounded at the top, newly cemented because the stones were always falling out, nice to sit on now, nice for Effie Holahan and Carmel and Rose and Connie Jo, and another girl. 'We're on the off,' he says when he returns from depositing the empty carton in a bin.

The engine starts up. There's sun on the rug, a bright patch on the tartan. 'You're feeling good, eh?' he says. 'All the old troubles over.'

She dozes, and then her own voice rouses her, crying out that she shouldn't have done it.

In the driving-mirror he catches a glimpse of her: peaky, hair requiring attention, her round white face.

'God forgive me,' she whispers, quieter now, after her noisy outburst caused him to jump.

'Fancy a fruit jelly?' he offers, passing the bag over his shoulder, wondering if that man had really been the recruiting sergeant or if he'd suffered a delusion, the way anyone might after an emotional experience.

She doesn't take a fruit jelly, but says again that she shouldn't have done it.

'I'll make you a Bovril, dear, when we get home.'

She is warm beneath the bedclothes, safe in the bed with the wide mahogany bedstead and carved headboard that almost fills the room, one of its sides pressed against pink flowered wallpaper. A single window is a yard from its foot, and there's a mat to step out on to, the only covering on the stained floorboards. There are plain blue curtains, which she has never drawn back, through which light filters in the daytime. Three heavily framed pictures are murky on the other walls, scenes of military action. The room contains neither a wardrobe nor a chest of drawers.

She is aware of the pain that lingers, worse than it was, and the bleeding that lingers also, and of tiredness. Again her eyelids droop and she drifts away, her body seeming strangely elongated as she lies there, her feet so far away they might not be there at all, a numbness somewhere else. On the Creagh road a car going by sounds its horn; Johnny waves because it's someone he knows, and then they turn off into the Mandeville woods. People are made for one another, he murmurs, his lips kissing her hair and her neck. His grey-green eyes are lit up because they're together again, because all the looking for him is over. 'Will I put the potato stack on the top of it?' Miss Furey's brother asks, and points at the hole he has dug in the corner of the field, beyond the yard. 'Would we do it at night?' he asks. 'Only someone might come into the yard.

If it was daytime we'd have to think of that.' The corpse is under the hay in the barn. She carries it to the field, following him in the darkness and laying it down in the pit, the small amount of skin and blood that remains already disintegrating. 'It's the only way,' someone says, and clay is shovelled in, the sods put back.

She begs for forgiveness, clutching at the robes of the Virgin. But the eyes of the Virgin are blind, without whites or pupils, and then the statue falls down from the dresser and is gone for ever also. 'Oh, aren't you terrible, Felicia!' The Reverend Mother is cross, sweeping the pieces into a dustpan. And her own mother is shelling peas in the doorway, the door open to the yard, and tears fall on to the peas in the colander. 'Supposing I'd done that to you, Felicia,' is what her mother tries to say, speaking made difficult because of her sobbing. But Felicia knows anyway. She knows what the words are even though they aren't spoken.

18

*No orders to attack the enemy were, however, given to the flotillas, and they
therefore steamed passively along their course without instructions or information. Jellicoe's signal to his flotillas was picked up by the German listening
station at Neumünster, which reported to Scheer at 10.50 p.m. 'Destroyers
have taken up a position five sea miles astern of enemy's main fleet.'*

Abstractedly dwelling upon these facts, with the volume that
contains them propped up in front of him, Mr Hilditch eats alone
in his dining-room: a Fray Bentos steak-and-kidney pie with all
the trimmings, a couple of slices of Mother's Pride, pineapple
chunks, condensed milk heated up, tea. His attention wanders
from the sentences he peruses: the face of the youth in the
waiting-room, and the faces of the staid receptionist and of the
specialists and the aluminium-haired girl, crowd out the words.
He sees, as clearly, the people in several Happy Eaters, in Little
Chefs and Restful Trays, in the Dog and Grape and the other
roadside public houses, the Blue Light fish bar, and Buddy's Café.
It is as it always is when an end has come: remembering is the
best part in a way. He loads his fork with kidney, potato, and
cauliflower in a white sauce. A couple of passers-by noticed them
on the street, walking across the pavement to the car, passers-by
who would naturally know what business was conducted at the
Gishford.

*Thus the German Admiral, if the Neumünster message reached him, had
from this time forward a fairly clear idea of the relative positions of the two
fleets . . .*

Again Mr Hilditch's concentration falters. When the second
outburst occurred there'd been a wildness in the eyes that were
reflected in the driving-mirror, and her fingers were groping at her
forehead in agitation. At the time he'd again been endeavouring to

establish if it had really been the recruiting sergeant, reflecting on the irony of the man being in the company of a bent-up elderly woman, while only yards away his own companion was a spry young Irish girl, the point he'd wanted to make to them in the car park.

At about 10.30 p.m. the 4th German Scouting Group came in contact with the British 2nd Light Cruiser Squadron which was following our battlefleet. There was a violent explosion of firing . . .

Once more the words are obscured by the remembered image in the driving-mirror. She took no notice when he pointed out that sitting up wasn't good for her. She began about a living soul destroyed, then something to do with a slop bucket. He had to turn off at the Rywell Services, thinking it would be easier to reason with her if the car was stationary. By the time he'd parked and managed to get a look at her, the tears were flowing like a fountain, hysterical you'd have to call it. He got out and left her for a while, considering it better to let her get it out of her system on her own, but as soon as he returned to the car with some nourishment she started up again immediately.

Mr Hilditch reaches out and closes the volume, then pushes it aside. There's a pattern of faded orange flowers on her pale-blue nightdress, the material so flimsy you could hardly call it decent, her flesh showing through in places, white as her face. She shook her head over the sausages and bread he brought her an hour ago. But at least she is quieter now, sleep being a healer.

Nylon the nightdress material is, Mr Hilditch supposes. When she pushed herself up in the bed a strap of the nightdress slipped from her shoulder. The outline of two slight breasts, like little sandcastles, showed beneath the flimsy covering. Mr Hilditch doesn't wish to dwell upon what is coming into his mind now, but the recollection of the inadequate nightdress persists. In an effort to distract himself he pours condensed milk over the pineapple cubes, but the ploy doesn't work.

'Going out, dear?' his mother said, turning from the looking-glass on her dressing-table, her hair already pinned up beneath the turban she wore at night. 'Just for a while,' he said, and she said surprising, at this hour. He could tell she knew, something in her eyes. He could tell she was pretending, the casual way she asked the question.

In his dining-room Mr Hilditch pours tea into a cup he bought in a junk shop in Leighton Buzzard. It is cream-coloured, with a green band on the rim, matching two others on the kitchen dresser and the one that's upstairs now, on the tray. He stirs in sugar and adds milk, then crosses to the door and listens. He moves from the room and stands for a moment at the bottom of the stairs, listening also. There is no sound. In the dining-room he sips his tea.

'Quick time, lover?' the professional offered and he said yes. She tucked her arm into his as they made their way to where he had left the car. Cathy her name was and he gave his as Colin. 'Drive out a bit,' she instructed, mentioning the money before he turned on the ignition, stating the sum. Her face had a sick tinge in the night light, a mouthful of bad teeth, drink on her breath. She shifted in the car seat, doing something to her clothing, and it was then that he wanted to be on the street with her again, noticed by the passers-by, as they'd been a moment ago. 'Just talk, could we?' he mumbled. 'Fancy a tea?' Another quid, she said, and brought him to an all-night transport place, where the lorry drivers addressed her by name. She said she was hungry; he went to get her something, and when he returned a lorry man rose from the chair that had been his. 'See you, duck,' the lorry man muttered to her.

Mr Hilditch gathers up the dishes he has eaten from and carries them to the kitchen. 'What's with you?' the professional asked, and he said nothing. 'That it, is it?' she asked. 'That all, Colin?' He didn't say he hadn't known when he approached her that that was all; he didn't say anything, not feeling up to making a comment. 'Any time, sunshine,' she said.

He drops the Fray Bentos tin into his garbage bucket and washes the dishes in the sink. He rinses the teapot and puts it to drain. He scours the potato saucepan and brushes away the faint scummy ring left by the cauliflower. He places what remains of the pineapple chunks and the condensed milk in the refrigerator. The professional had something wrong with her jaw, misshapen in some way.

In his big front room he puts on 'Besame Mucho' and leaves the door open so that the melody can spread through the house. In the kitchen he stacks away the saucepans and wipes the draining-boards and the stove. He hangs the cup up on the dresser and notices that there isn't a chip on any of the three, and none that he can remember on the one that's upstairs by the bedside. On all of them the green of the rim is worn away in places, as naturally it would be after time.

In the recruiting shed the recruiting sergeant had run a finger over his thin moustache, hiding a smirk. He hadn't attempted to disguise the fact that he considered it amusing that a would-be recruit should suggest a quartermaster's duties when two small disabilities, to do with sight and feet, ruled out the career that all through childhood had been taken for granted. 'You'll never remember me,' he might have said in the car park, catching up with the couple.

Mr Hilditch pours milk for Ovaltine into a saucepan, enough for two cups, which they can drink together in the little bedroom now that she has calmed. He pads across the hall to change the record to 'Five Foot Two, Eyes of Blue'.

'I'll go in the morning.' For the second time that day she causes him to jump. She is there at the bottom of the stairs when he emerges from the big front room, her red coat on top of her nightdress, her feet bare. She is carrying the tray, the sausages still untouched.

'I'm heating milk for Ovaltine.' He can think of nothing better to say, and she follows him into the kitchen, clearly more tranquil now. When he has made the drink he suggests they might like to have it in the big front room. 'Make a change for you, eh?'

They sit on either side of the electric fire. When 'Five Foot Two, Eyes of Blue' comes to an end he puts on 'Charmaine'.

'Forty-two pounds,' she says. 'If I could borrow that.'

'I doubt if that's sufficient, dear. Any little mishap, it's terrible to be short. Well, you've had experience yourself of course.'

'I'll send every penny back. And every penny it cost today.'

'Today was my treat, dear, I'm happy about that. Ada would have wanted today.'

The music is soft enough to permit their conversation; they

don't have to raise their voices. She is in no fit state to travel anywhere: gently he says so.

'You said you couldn't face them, dear. You said it to me several times in the car. I'm nervous for you, dear.'

'I have to go.'

'You weren't at all well in the car. All the way back. And in the hall. I thought I'd have to send for assistance the way you were in the hall. You can't set out on a journey in that condition, dear.'

'I shouldn't have done it.'

'What's done's done, dear. No one ever got rich on regrets. What about the bright side, eh? For as long as you want it, Felicia, there's a welcome at Number Three. You have your own little room now. The sensible thing would be if we took it day by day.'

'I had dreams. All the time it was happening I had dreams. And then again afterwards, upstairs. That I was carrying the child in my arms, that we buried it under a potato stack.'

'Drink up your Ovaltine, dear.'

She repeats that she'll pay back everything and he reminds her that this doesn't matter. He paid debts for Jakki and for Beth, quite sizeable a few of them; he bought Elsie Covington a suite of furniture. All of it gave him pleasure, keeping them by him. He didn't know at the time that the furniture was sold again immediately.

'I have to go home now. No matter how I'm feeling I have to face them.'

Her coat has fallen back, revealing more of the blue and orange nightdress. She's still wearing the cross around her neck.

'I'd like you to stay on. Just for a day or two. You're calmer, Felicia. It's good to see that. You've come to terms with what was necessary.'

But she shakes her head so vehemently that he fears another outburst. She holds her tears back, twisting her fingers together, her knuckles turned white with the effort. Again she doesn't trust herself to speak, which he's grateful for. He lets the record come to an end before he speaks himself, quietly, not pressing the point.

'It's only that I'd rather see you with some nourishment in you before you set off anywhere.'

148

He crosses to where she's sitting and removes the skin from the surface of her Ovaltine, returning the teaspoon to her saucer. He changes the record to 'Chattanooga Choo Choo'.

'I'm sorry to be fatherly, Felicia. I can't help being fatherly because I've grown fond of you. The first day I saw you, you were there with your bags, woebegone and bedraggled. I'd like to be sure you were on the mend, that's all I'm saying to you.'

'I'm all right.'

'I have to say far from it, Felicia. I'll be honest with you: your Johnny wouldn't know you, the way your eyes have sunk back into your head, and the big patches of black around them, and not an ounce of flesh to spare. I couldn't let you go like that, I couldn't let you walk out on to the streets. God knows what would happen, Felicia. D'you understand me, dear?'

She still hasn't touched her Ovaltine. Her bare feet are petite on the patterned carpet – her best feature, now that he notices them.

'I want to go,' she says, and he explains that people often want to do something that isn't in their best interests, that often it takes someone else to see what's what.

'That's all I'm saying to you, dear. I wouldn't forgive myself if I didn't say it.'

'*Dinner in the diner, nothing could be finer,*' the Chattanooga Choo Choo traveller promises, '*than to have your ham 'n' eggs in Carolina . . .*'

He lets a silence grow. There's a deadness about her eyes now, all the fervour that was present earlier totally gone. She'll sink into a corner in that household where she came from, she'll dry up into a woman who waits for ever for a useless man. The Black and Tans should have sorted that island out, his Uncle Wilf said, only unfortunately they held back for humane reasons. Choosing his words, he puts all that to her, though not mentioning the Black and Tans in case it upsets her. When he has finished, as though she hasn't heard a word, she says again that she must go back now, that there is nothing else, that she has no choice. Then she stands up, and like a zombie makes her way out of the room.

It wasn't the recruiting sergeant with that woman. 'Wishful thinking, dear,' his mother used to say. Easy to get something wrong when you want to, she did it on occasion herself. 'Well, you know that, dearie,' she reminded him, in a twinkling mood, all dressed up, the fox's head of her fur upside down, the fragrance of her lavender water.

They were just some couple; a vague resemblance there had been and in an emotional state he had let his imagination run away with him. 'Wishful Wally,' she used to say, and laugh to show she was only being a tease.

The whine of the needle on the no man's land of the record has begun. Mr Hilditch listens to it, not moving from his chair, the ornate electric fire casting pink shadows on his trousers. Of all his rooms this is his favourite, the crimson wallpaper and set against it the soft green baize of the billiard table it took four men to carry in. The sofa and the well-stuffed armchairs, the cabinet of paperweights, the mantelpiece ornaments and the portraits of other people's ancestors, the two grandfather clocks: all are at peace with one another and have a meaning for him.

But for once the room's tranquillity fails to influence the torrent Mr Hilditch's emotions have become, and after some minutes he crosses to the gramophone and lifts the needle from the record. It is dangerous for the Irish girl to go. He said it and she didn't listen; he said it clearly, he even repeated it. She's going back to less than nothing. He doesn't understand why she can't see that.

Beth couldn't see it, either, when he put it to her that it was foolish to move south. Nor could Sharon when she said she had to go; nor Bobbi come to that, nor Gaye, nor Elsie Covington, nor Jakki. Mr Hilditch closes his eyes. A confusion oppresses him, blurring what he is trying to say to himself. This present one came up to him at his place of work, he didn't make an approach. She let him drive her all over the place, mile after mile; she permitted him to wait on her hand and foot, no better than a servant. She made no payment for petrol or oil, nor for food consumed away from the house, nor in the house itself, nor for the cost of heating and light, soap and toilet paper. Why had she sat like that? Why had she leaned forward and then leaned back again? Why had she come down in the first place, indecent in that nightdress? He knows the answer. He doesn't want to hear it, but it's there anyway: she doesn't care how she appears to him because she sees him in a certain light. She has guessed, as Beth guessed, the first of the others to do so. When Beth announced out of the blue that she was going south, everything she'd guessed was there in her eyes. It was there in all their eyes in the end. They were his friends and he was good to them. Then there was the other.

Tears flow from Mr Hilditch, becoming rivulets in the flesh of his cheeks and his chin, dripping on to his neck, damping his shirt and his waistcoat. His sobbing becomes a moaning in the room, a sound as from an animal suffering beyond endurance, distraught and piteous.

19

'No, write it out,' Sister Francis Xavier insists. 'Fifty times till you know it.'

The minute the bell goes all the voices begin at once, and there's the noise of the chairs scraping, and footsteps running, and Sister Francis saying running's not allowed. The voices dwindle, floating back up St Joseph's Hill, until there is silence except for the ticking of the wall clock and a door closing. The maps are still hanging on the blackboard. They should have been put away, the physical and the political they're called: mountains and rivers, the counties all different colours. Through the window, her father is in the garden, tying up Michaelmas daisies. He doesn't see her looking at him; he doesn't know she has been kept in. *Is maith liom*, she writes, and then the coffin is by the dug grave. Her mother is going into that hole, but Father Kilgallen says to heaven. Peace, Father Kilgallen says, and clay makes a clatter on the yellow wood. Father Kilgallen raises his hand for the blessing, and Carmel is the bridesmaid then. 'Who's that?' Johnny asks, and someone says a nightclub singer. The singer has long black hair and bangles and earrings, high heels that shine, black like her hair. She smiles when she sings, a white flash in her face, the sunshine of Spain she calls it. 'Where's Johnny?' Carmel asks, and Aidan says he came into McGrattan Street Cycles and Prams to buy a pram for the baby, but when she goes there she can't find him. She looks for him by the old gasworks, but he isn't there either. She calls out to him because it's dark. He doesn't come into the fish restaurant, he isn't in Mr Caunce's house. 'Johnny!' she calls out, going up in the hotel lift with the children, and the children make a singsong of his name. 'You're wanted, Johnny! You're wanted!' Connie Jo is laughing, drinking wine with Mr Logan. Rose says it's a queer thing, Johnny going ahead on the honeymoon. '*Take my hand,*' the Spanish woman sings. '*Take my whole life too . . .*'

He's not in the Spud-U-Like when she climbs in through the window. He's not in his mother's kitchen. She opens all the doors in Mr Caunce's house, where there are people lying down in the rooms, but he isn't there either. The lavatory water drips down through the ceiling and the Spanish woman is crouched shivering on a bed, her scarlet dress thrown on to the floor. It's what you'd expect, Miss Furey says, anyone called Johnny would cause you grief; terrible work, anyone called Johnny could get up to. 'My God, that's an awful sound to come out of any human being!' Sister Benedict cries when she hears the Spanish woman's weeping.

He isn't in Sheehy's or in the Mandeville woods. He isn't in the canning factory. She asks in Chawke's and the Centra foodstore and Scaddan's. She asks in the convent, but the weeping of the Spanish woman is so loud she can't hear what anyone says to her. The crying of the Spanish woman is a weight that crushes her, pressing her down. 'It's there in your eyes,' someone else says, sitting on her bed, a heaviness pulling back the bedclothes so that it's cold. There is the sound of breathing, a catching sound, as though snagged with each emission.

'What you're thinking is there, Felicia.'

She tries to wake up, to wrench herself out of her dreaming. But she can't wake up.

'Don't put the light on.' The breathing becomes deeper, an urgent throatiness only inches from her face. The voice is a whisper. 'It ruins everything, Felicia. Everything is destroyed.'

She opens her eyes. No light comes from the window, no hazy dawn filters through the curtains. His presence on her bed causes a depression that draws her own body towards him.

He talks about other girls, naming each of them, describing them. No one ever knew except those girls, he says; they knew because of the closeness of the association. All he ever wanted to do was to sit with them; he spent a fortune on them, presents, meals, driving them wherever they wanted to go. Beth, and Elsie Covington. Sharon, Gaye, Bobbi and Jakki. It is a private thing that they have been his friends.

153

'I'm telling you so's you understand, Felicia. I never told another soul. We could have continued the association, you could have stayed in my house. No other girl ever came into my house. There was never that.'

It isn't in any way like a dream now. She says she's sorry if she did anything wrong. Because he mentions staying in his house, she says she didn't mean to intrude.

'You came downstairs in your nightdress.'

'I only came down to ask you to lend me the money. Nothing only that.'

'I took chances every hour you were here, dear. Every day I thought someone would find out. You occupied a bed. You used the lavatory and the bathroom. God knows what shadows on the glass.'

'No one saw me. I did everything you said.'

'It was enough what we had, Felicia. Just sitting and talking in the places we went to, you telling me all those things. But when I looked in the driving-mirror it was in your eyes too.'

'What was? Could I put the light on? I don't follow what you mean.'

'When you know a thing like that it isn't easy for any girl to pretend.'

The nervousness she felt at the bus station when he first offered to give her a lift is there again. She was nervous when she looked around the next morning and realized his wife was not in the back of the car. She hadn't thought twice about it when he explained that unexpectedly his wife had had to go into hospital but now, suddenly, without having to think, she knows he never had a wife.

'I pushed it away when I saw your eyes in the driving-mirror. I didn't want to accept it. But then you came downstairs.'

'I'm sorry if I upset you. I didn't mean to upset you. I don't understand what you're saying to me.'

'No one's blaming you, dear. Things happen. Things take a turn.'

A hand is placed on one of hers. It's only a pity, he says, that everything is ruined. No, don't put on the light, he says; he doesn't want the light.

154

'Leave me alone, please.'

'They said they were going and I asked them why, but I didn't have to, Felicia. You understand that, dear? You appreciate what I'm saying to you?'

'I'll go away. I won't bother you. It doesn't matter about the money.'

'I was the world to them. In their time of need they counted on me.'

She knows the girls are dead. There is something that states it in the room, in the hoarse breathing, in the sweat that for a moment touches the side of her face, in the way he talks. The dark is oppressive with their deaths, cloying, threatening to turn odorous.

'I'll drive you away from my house.' His whisper comes again, and she senses the blubbery mouth close to her. 'Dress yourself and we'll drive away. I have money to give you for the journey. Just walk out of the house and get into the car.'

She knows she must not do that. As surely as she knows about the girls, she is aware that she must not be drawn into the humpbacked car. He has waited for night to come and to settle: the dark is what he chooses, and the car.

'Yes,' she agrees. 'Yes, I'll dress myself.'

The floorboards creak as he lumbers his way to the door. She hears the rattle of the door handle, but no light shows when the door is opened, no silhouette appears. She hears him on the stairs, still in darkness, his footsteps heavily descending.

Unable to move, petrified by fear of what may happen next, more frightened than she has been in his presence, she lies where he has left her, doubting that she will find the strength to leave the bed. But in time she does, and shakily feels her way across the room. Softly, she opens the door, to grope for a key on its other side. There is none. She feels a run of blood on her legs, then turns the light on and uses part of a sheet to wipe it away. Her hands and arms are trembling, which makes all movement difficult.

She sits on the edge of the bed, looking round the room, her eye finally caught by a broken piece of fire-grate. Soot and specks of masonry have dropped on to the red crêpe paper that has been bundled into the grate; the broken bar has become dislodged and lies on the hearth. It blackens her hand and is too short to be effective in her protection, but at least it's something. She dresses and drags her coat on. From far below, outside, she hears his footsteps on the gravel. She pulls back an edge of the curtain, but it's still too dark to see him. The car door bangs softly, and she knows he's waiting in it now.

Cautiously she steps out on to the landing, still gripping the bar of the grate, her two carrier bags slung from the crook of her free arm, her handbag looped about her body. She descends the unlit stairway, pausing every two or three steps to listen in case he has returned to the house. The metal bar makes a clatter on the tiles of the hall when it slips from her fingers. In a panic because she can't find the latch of the hall door, she feels for a light switch.

20

As he often does on a Sunday, Mr Hilditch visits a stately home. Arriving early, more than an hour before he will be able to gain admission, he parks his car in the empty car park, spreads his mackintosh coat on the grass beneath an oak tree and eats the sandwiches he has made: tuna and egg, with lettuce, tomato and spring onions.

The car park is a level expanse that has been cut into a hillside; from his position under the tree, he can see most of the long, tarred drive that winds through parkland, and the house itself, a sprawl of red brick and stone, with turrets and chimneys, and walled gardens. Swards of crocuses bloom close to where he picnics. The bark of the tree is jagged on his back.

He watches a blue bus turning in at the distant entrance gates, and coming closer on the drive. It disappears for a moment below the edge of the hill; the sound of its engine reaches him before it comes into sight again. Creeping into the car park, it reverses, moves forward, repeats these manoeuvres before finally positioning itself. A chatter of voices begins as its passengers step out; a girl in a blue uniform makes an announcement, saying that everyone should be outside the gift shop at half past four. The passengers disperse, descending by different paths to the house. Left alone, the driver lights a cigarette and spreads a newspaper out on a rustic table.

Cars appear on the drive, and eventually turn into the car park also. A second bus – yellow and grey – arrives, disgorging further visitors to the house. Mr Hilditch watches them stretching themselves and setting off in pairs or groups. Then, having finished his sandwiches, he unwraps a KitKat before making his way in the same direction.

He feels as he always does when a friendship has come to an end: empty, some part of him deflated. Already the Irish girl has joined the others in his Memory Lane: her round, wide-eyed face stares back at him when he thinks of her, the image as luminously alive as that of Beth or Elsie Covington. He always plans an outing as soon after a parting as is possible, in an effort to combat the lowness of his spirits. The day after Gaye went he came to this selfsame stately home.

In the gardens that are spread out around the house Mr Hilditch lingers while shrubs and flowerbeds are examined by the other Sunday visitors, the winter buds identified. He keeps with the crowd; he is not in a hurry. 'Nice, this time of year,' he remarks to two women, sisters they seem like. 'Nature lying low, eh?' The women are amused by that, and smile. At a turnstile that leads into a cobbled stable-yard the charge for adults is a pound. Mr Hilditch pays, and passes with the others into the kitchen quarters of the house, where antique cooking utensils are laid out to offer a flavour of the past. Pantries and sculleries have been scrubbed clean and are empty except for vast copper jelly moulds and domes of fly-proof mesh.

'Fascinating, eh?' Mr Hilditch remarks to a couple who are admiring a device that turns butter back into cream. His enthusiasm is genuine, since professionally he finds much to interest him.

Upstairs, in a high square hall with pillars, and in a dining-room and other reception rooms, life-size models of footmen stand in stately idleness. Petrified housemaids dust volumes in a library, or polish the surfaces of ornate tables. A family that occupied the house is recalled from another age also, in conversation or performing on musical instruments, or dancing; a girl brushing another girl's hair; a solitary figure reading on a window-seat. Tasselled red ropes separate each display from the living observers who now file whispering by. In the scented bedrooms there are scenes of discreet undressing, hipbaths ready.

As the hours pass, the tranquillity of the house and its landscape continues to please Mr Hilditch. In the café next to the gift shop he is served by girls wearing flowery dresses that reach down to their shoes, but it is too soon yet even to wonder if any one of them would appreciate the warmth of friendship: today there is no need for that.

'Makes an outing,' he remarks in an easy way to the people he shares a table with. 'Fills a Sunday, eh?'

The people politely agree that it does, then continue with the conversation his comment has interrupted. When they rise to go, Mr Hilditch smiles and says goodbye.

The last to leave the café, he purchases, as he pays, some of the cakes and scones that are left over. The two buses and most of the cars have driven off by the time he reaches the car park.

As he eases himself behind the steering wheel, he sees again the girl he last befriended and with that image drives slowly through the dwindling twilight. When he arrives in Duke of Wellington Road, darkness has long ago preceded him and for a few moments he sits in his car after he has drawn it up on the gravel, not wishing to open the front door and step into the hall until he has gathered a little strength that may be of assistance in the silence of the house. In time he finds it, and mounts the four steps to his hall door.

Later that same evening, depositing garbage in his dustbin, Mr Hilditch is aware of a faint aroma of burning cloth when he lifts the dustbin lid. He passes no private comment upon this, nor is his curiosity stirred: not even remaining as a smudge in his recollection is his burning, the night before, of various women's garments and accessories, having started the blaze in his dustbin with the day's newspaper and half a cupful of paraffin. Nor does he in any way recall that he returned his mother's shoes to the outside shed where they had gathered mildew before recently he found a use for them. Nor that he picked up a bar of a fire-grate from the tiles in his hall and threw it into the shrubberies.

It is usual, when a friendship finishes, for Mr Hilditch to suffer in this manner. He is mistily aware that something may be missing and attributes the aberration in his memory to the intensity of his loss – the moment of each departure having been so painful that an unconscious part of him has erased the surrounding details. At first, when Beth went, this concerned him, and he endeavoured to find his way back to the moment and all that accompanied it. He was not successful, and has since accepted the lapses he has experienced as offerings of mercy, private even from himself, best not questioned.

This evening, after he has eaten, he sits in his big front room, indulging in the day he has spent: the crocuses in bloom, the passengers stepping out of the blue bus, the copper jelly moulds, the girl brushing her friend's hair. He derives consolation from these unexacting recollections, one succeeding another, then fading away before returning, the images stark and soundless. He does not, this Sunday evening, play music on his gramophone; his mood is not for music, as it never is when a friendship has ended. It will be a day or two before music is heard again in 3 Duke of Wellington Road, Tuesday probably, or Wednesday.

At half past nine Mr Hilditch ensures that his front door is locked and the back door bolted. He is in bed, and asleep, by five past ten.

During the following several weeks Mr Hilditch goes about his professional tasks with the care and attention for which he is well known at his place of work. At weekends he cleans his house – the hall and the stairs, his dining-room and big front room. He sweeps his backyard and rakes the gravel at the front. He shops in Tesco's for supplies. He relaxes with his records and the *Daily Telegraph*.

In idle moments, or in bed at night, he is drawn into the surroundings he so often heard about during the friendship that has ended: the bedroom shared with a woman in her hundredth year, the square with the statue of a soldier, the diamond-patterned table-tops of the café. The father and the twin bachelor brothers are there, the convent friends, the mother of the seducer. In Mr Hilditch's private life there is nothing new about this excursion into someone else's background. When Beth went, he found it hard to rid his thoughts of the pimps she had told him about, who had once pursued her; when Gaye went there were the house-breakers she had assisted. There was Sharon's impetigo when she was a kid, Bobbi's blind eye. The Irish girl's name was found by her father, honouring some woman who took part in a revolution: it was in the car he heard that, or in Buddy's Café, hard to be exact.

'Very tasty, them faggots,' an employee remarks, as well he might in Mr Hilditch's view, since under his precise instructions the faggots have been skilfully prepared and cooked.

'Glad you enjoyed them.' He smiles his gratitude. Compliments are welcome when a finished association is still raw in his thoughts.

Another employee comments on the marmalade pudding and he gives away a secret: that the suet must be finely chopped, that the marmalade and the beaten eggs must be added to the dry ingredients, not the other way round. He points out that the process and the measurements vary according to whether the pudding is steamed or baked. Since childhood he has preferred it steamed himself.

The women among the employees often request a recipe and invariably choose to approach him rather than a member of the kitchen staff. He likes to oblige them in this way. It pleases him to think of the canteen dishes being served to the employees' families. 'Mr Hilditch's pudding' or 'Mr Hilditch's way of doing it' might be expressions used. Although he never mentions it, he believes that this may be so.

'See, we live in a miracle. Look here at this garden. See the fruits of the trees and the peoples of all nations.'

A black woman, bejewelled and painted, proffers a lurid illustration on the cover of a brochure. A young white girl, tidily attired, stands at her side with a sheaf of similar illustrations.

Mr Hilditch, who has been interrupted in the polishing of his shoes at the kitchen table, greets the pair genially, but indicates his lack of enthusiasm for the conversation that threatens by shaking his head.

'Today we bring you the Word of our Father Lord,' the black woman continues, ignoring his response. 'I myself am from Jamaica. This here is Miss Marcia Tibbitts. If my friend and myself could just step inside we wouldn't take up no more than ten minutes of your day. May I inquire, sir, if you are familiar with the writings of the Bible?'

161

Mr Hilditch is not particularly familiar with the writings of the Bible. As a child, he was packed off by his mother every Sunday morning to Sunday school. Vaguely he remembers outlandish stories about lambs sacrificed and sons sacrificed, and walking on water. It is all a long time ago and he has never felt the need to reflect on any of it. *What Would Jesus Do?* an inscription in coloured wools speculated, shown to the Sunday-school class by its teacher. She had turned it into a decoration for her walls, framing the glass that protected it with passe-partout.

'I'm afraid I'm not interested.'

'If we could step inside your home my friend would offer you her own experience, how she was gathered in.'

Again Mr Hilditch shakes his head, but does not succeed in halting a tale about being rescued from a video shop, and the promise of the paradise earth in which serpents lie harmlessly coiled and the cobra is a plaything for children.

'I was lost and have been found,' the white girl states in a singsong tone. 'As it is written.' Then she begins again, about the video shop and the better world of the cobra as a plaything.

'Look here,' Mr Hilditch interrupts at last. 'I'm busy.'

'We would return,' the black woman offers. 'We would come at any hour.'

'No, no.'

'Ten minutes of any day is not much sacrifice to make. The Father Lord gives us time eternal.' The black woman displays a mouthful of healthy teeth and pushes at Mr Hilditch the brochures she carries. 'There is a future for the one who dies, sir,' she adds, her tone intimating that the literature on offer reveals further details of this claim.

It is then, while she is still speaking about the one who dies, that Mr Hilditch notices, and is bewildered by, a sudden curiosity breaking in her dark features. Being professionally familiar with the practices of salesmanship and assuming that the toting about of religion can fairly be placed in such a category, he wonders if this is some kind of selling ploy. But to his consternation and alarm, the explanation is not a commercial one.

'An Irish girl mentioned you, sir. I remember that now as we

162

stand here. A good man, the girl said, a helpmeet to her. Duke of Wellington Road, she said. Big and big-hearted was maybe the description.'

'I know no Irish people at all.'

'You helped that girl on her way, not passing by on the other side. Sir, you are at one with our Church.'

'No, no. I'm sorry. I have to get on. This isn't my kind of thing.'

'That girl was chattering, it came up like that.' Miss Calligary pauses. 'A confidence trickster, as it turned out after.'

'I must ask you to go now.'

'That girl tried to get money from us. Is this the same story for yourself, sir?'

Mr Hilditch closes his hall door with a bang, and leans against it with his eyes closed, remembering how the girl said she'd spent a few days in these people's house. He goes over the encounter that has just occurred, from the moment when the black woman suddenly realized she was talking to someone she had heard about. Mentioned? 'An Irish girl mentioned you': what exactly did that imply? Chattering, the woman said, and then something about a confidence trickster, whatever that meant.

For a moment Mr Hilditch wonders if the whole thing isn't some kind of error or misunderstanding: by no stretch of the imagination could the Irish girl he has associated with be called a confidence trickster. Others he has known could be described in that way, but it's the last expression you would use where this recent girl is concerned. And yet clearly it is the same girl: a girl he helped, going out of his way to do so. She said so herself; apparently, she'd repeated it to others.

Slowly, he eases his bulk from where it rests against the hall door and moves across the hall to the kitchen. It's nothing much, he assures himself, no more than an untidiness, a trailing end; if it seems out of the ordinary it's only because it has never happened before. A girl he has been good to has never afterwards been mentioned to him by anyone.

'Right as rain that man was at first,' Miss Calligary remarks as she

163

and her companion make their way along Duke of Wellington Road. 'Right as rain and then he goes peculiar.'

It worries Miss Calligary that this has happened. This big, stout man was there for the gathering; she would have sworn it. A solitary man, a lonely man: anyone could tell. He could have got the wrong end of the stick, thinking that the Irish girl was a Gatherer herself and backing off now for that very reason – once bitten, twice shy. Miss Calligary ear-marks a day for their return, requesting Marcia Tibbitts to note the number of the house.

21

For several days, whenever his thoughts are disturbed by the fact that his befriending of the Irish girl is known to a third party, Mr Hilditch continues to assure himself that this is of no possible significance. By now the West Indian woman has probably forgotten all about it, being more concerned with her paradise. A woman like that, with her brochures and her talk, has enough to fill her day without poking into a privacy.

But, even so, as a little more time goes by, unease begins to agitate Mr Hilditch. He recalls how he sensed, when the Irish girl first accosted him, that the promise of an association was different from the others there had been. In the end it hadn't been, because the Irish girl had parted from him also; but now it seems as if his intuition might have been right in some other, as yet unrevealed, way.

During a wakeful night he hears the black woman's voice, informing people that he didn't pass by on the other side, that the girl sought assistance and he gave it. It's not impossible that the woman would talk in that way, he reflects, his eyes unfocused in the dark; it's even likely, since she brought the matter up with him. As that night advances, as the West Indian lilt and all it conveys become more insistent, Mr Hilditch makes an effort to distract his thoughts by directing them elsewhere: to the catering department, to his kitchens, to the bustle of the lunchtime canteen. He wrenches his concentration back to the days when he was still an invoice clerk, to the surprise of being summoned and told to sit down while it was confided that his name had been put forward for the position of catering manager. But although he pleasurably recalls the occasion – the details of training and remuneration pressed upon him before he had even properly said he was interested – he finds himself led by this same stream of thought into an earlier period of his life, when he still had hopes of a military career. 'Oh, khaki'd suit you!' His mother's voice is joky at the Spa where she drank the water and bathed, while he sat waiting or strolled about the town. At the Spa there was a carved frieze: soldiers lying wounded with their shirts off, officers offering succour. *The brotherhood that binds the Grave*, were the words that formed the accompanying inscription, cut in the stone. At the baths his mother got talking to a woman who suffered from Garrad's disease and his mother said what's that? Related to Dupuytren's Contracture, the woman maintained, though some denied it. The woman's face was painted, magenta lips, smudges of mascara, powder on a pimpled skin. 'Listen to this, dear,' his mother urged. 'Very interesting, this lady is!' But he didn't listen while the woman talked about her ailment, while his mother said fancy that and dearie me. 'Wouldn't khaki suit him?' his mother said in the bar of the Clarence. 'Going for a soldier, this little man is!' On the train, returning from the Spa, a man with a beard gave him a threepenny piece. 'Well, what a surprise!' his mother said, her neck and face flushed crimson when they'd passed through the Longridge tunnel. 'Well, I never!'

In spite of this evocation of his private past, when Mr Hilditch's eyes droop he is again possessed by his speculations about the black woman's doorstep talk. Then, when he tries to envisage the Irish girl among the pretty portraits that are his memory of the others, for the first time he fails to do so. The day he visited the stately home she was meekly there: now there is nothing, as if the black woman's talk has robbed him of her.

When the light of morning dawns Mr Hilditch rises, hours before he normally does. He makes tea in his kitchen, and walks slowly about his house, entering one room and then another. When the time comes to cook his breakfast, he finds he isn't hungry. Later he drives away without food in his stomach.

As more time passes, people notice; Mr Hilditch sees them noticing. In the canteen he picks at fricassee of lamb and Pineapple Surprise; he hardly touches the silverside, and is seen to help himself to a

166

modest portion of his Wednesday favourite. Interviewing applicants for washing-up duties, he has several times to be reminded of names that have already been given to him. His teatime biscuit tin does not require replenishing for more than a fortnight.

Driving home one evening, he runs out of petrol, a misfortune he later relates to his state of mind. He has to walk almost a mile, borrow a tin from a surly pump attendant, and put on a show of being amused at his own folly. Policemen from two squad cars have surrounded his small vehicle when he reaches it again, and retaining this mood of genial self-mockery he apologizes for any inconvenience he may have caused. The policemen are petulant and censorious. When he smiles at them they don't respond. Useless men, importantly roaring about in their Fords and Vauxhalls, thick as walls. He smiles at them, and watches them driving off.

From the moment she appeared on the forecourt in her red coat and her headscarf, he was generous to her. He listened, he did not once display fatigue. He assisted her with advice; he guided her and protected her, warning her against street criminals and the dangers of hitch-hiking. He gave her as much as he ever gave the others, begrudging her nothing. Did she pass all that on to the black woman? Is all that being said? And what besides? What elaborations added, what curiosity aroused? What titbits of gossip are there by now?

Unsettled as he continues his interrupted journey, he goes over, yet again, all that was said on his doorstep. Later, in his big front room, he reflects how slight, how unimportant, it seemed when the Irish girl said she had been taken in by the people who are calling her a confidence trickster now. He turns the volume of his music up in an effort to stifle his worries and the black woman's voice, and the whisper of inquisitiveness it feeds. That night he again sleeps fitfully, and has nightmares he can't remember when he wakes up.

'Oh yes, there's been changes,' the woman using the cash dispenser agrees, arranging four five-pound notes in the wallet of her purse. 'Can't say there hasn't been changes.'

'No more than eight years of age,' Mr Hilditch volunteers. 'Used to come down on the train.'

'Out of all recognition in that case. No argument on that.'

She is a woman with spectacles, older than Mr Hilditch, with a basket on wheels, grey lisle stockings and a fuzzy grey coat. Her hair is grey and fuzzy also.

'Thought I'd come back,' Mr Hilditch continues, not yet inserting his plastic card in the cash dispenser. 'Lift the spirits, I said to myself, to visit the Spa.'

'Nothing much of a spa about it these days. They packed that in donkeys ago.'

'The springs dried up, eh?'

'Never was no springs, some geezer fixed it. People'd believe anything in them days.'

'Mother did.'

'Well, there you go then. No more'n a con.'

'Mother said it did her good.'

'There's a lot that's in the mind when it comes to a sickness.'

'There probably is.'

'It was Len was a great believer in that. All in the mind was the expression he had for it.'

'Your husband would this be?'

'Late. 1970.'

Mr Hilditch presses his plastic into the slot and registers his personal identification number, 9165. The woman draws on grey gloves and seizes the handle of her mobile shopping basket. Notes to the value of forty pounds emerge from the wall.

'A great convenience,' Mr Hilditch remarks, agreeable to prolonging the encounter. 'Our flexible friend.'

'You spend too much's the only thing. If it wasn't there you'd be better off.'

'Fancy a coffee?'

The woman hesitates. She doesn't reply, but she raises no objection when Mr Hilditch falls into step with her. He couldn't agree with her more, he declares; cash dispensers induce you to spend too much by making your money so readily available. The banks know what they're doing, he suggests, and outside a store

168

which he imagines will have a refreshment floor he repeats his invitation.

'I'm not fussy,' the woman says, preceding him through swing doors.

It came to him in the early morning that he'd drive over to the Spa, the day being a Saturday. A change was what he needed, an outing to somewhere that belonged to some other time of his life. Two hours it took in the car; longer, with a change and a wait, it used to be by train.

'Well, this is nice,' he remarks with genuine enthusiasm when they are seated. 'I enjoy a mid-morning cup.'

'It warms you, this weather.'

This woman is flattered: he can tell that by the way she looks about her to see if they have been noticed by anyone she knows. It was the same on the street. She would enjoy people speculating as to who the stranger is, a good ten years he could give her. He says:

'I should have commiserated about your husband. Sorry about that.'

'It's twenty-two years. You get over it.'

'Even so I should have said something.'

'No call for it really.'

'Even so I'm sorry.' And since the subject is there, he states that he never married himself.

'No more'n Vera did. Wouldn't touch it, according to herself.'

'A daughter, is this?'

'A sister as was. We never got on, never saw eye to eye.'

Their coffee arrives. Mr Hilditch feels the first stirrings of appetite for several weeks and asks if there are cheese scones available. 'I was up at all hours,' he explains, apologetically, to his companion.

'She wanted Len is my own belief, and when she couldn't get him that was that. Wouldn't touch it once she couldn't get Len.'

In the course of further conversation Mr Hilditch voluntarily supplies his name, and the information that he is a catering manager. He gives the name of the town where he lives and works, adding that he was born there, population well over a quarter of a million these days and growing all the time. He butters three cheese scones while he is relaying this information, pleasurably watching the butter melt on the warm surface. Not once since he dropped into conversation with the greyly clad woman has he been harassed by the annoyance that keeps him awake at night and confuses him in the daytime.

'It was always his ambition,' she is saying now, 'to see the Hanging Gardens of Babylon.'

'This is your husband, is it?'

'His great ambition and of course she played on it. Brazen in that respect. Read up on the subject – the names of the hanging plants or whatever it is they have.'

He nods understandingly.

'I have to employ a lot for the kitchens. Any forward type of woman wouldn't stand a chance. It's one of the little rules I have.'

'The last words she spoke. "I'll have him now," she said. Brazen to the end.'

Soon after this the woman announces that she has to be getting on and, since the encounter cannot be further prolonged, Mr Hilditch smiles agreeably and says their meeting has been a pleasure. He remains at the table, buttering the last scone when the woman has passed out of sight. Almost immediately, the annoyance that her company has kept at bay returns.

It accompanies Mr Hilditch as this day wears on, and the appetite that came back so briefly does not do so again. He distracts himself as best he can: it isn't difficult to believe that some enterprising businessman once upon a time created a myth about a local water source, deluding the afflicted for generations. He thinks about that for a while, then slips into his private past. 'That's a public toilet,' his mother pointed out the first time they came here, indicating a brick building near the railings of a park. 'Remember where it is, dearie.' She had a cameo brooch pinned to her lapel and a double necklace of pearls. She carried her bathing costume in a little blue suitcase, with the sandwiches she always brought, and a flask of tea. At the station buffet she had a gin and pep while they waited for the train, and another when they changed and had to wait again.

Mr Hilditch attends the two o'clock showing of *Basic Instinct* and finds it unpleasant, but remains to the end since he has paid his money. Then he walks about the streets, admiring the terraces of pale, pretty houses with fanlights, the pillars that distinguish crescents and parades, the lofty statue of Queen Victoria in front of the town hall. But neither all that nor what remains with him of *Basic Instinct* is as efficacious as his companion of the morning in combating the intrusion that distresses him. As the shops begin to close, he judges the day a failure.

Driving home again, he remembers Beth saying goodbye, the last moment before memory became too painful. She broke it to him suddenly: that tomorrow she planned to go south. Jakki said it first thing when he met her one evening, outside the home-decorating shop where they always met. Sharon didn't tell him at all, and intended not to, but he guessed. Bobbi was the most casual. Elsie Covington said she'd miss him. Gaye cried, putting it on because she wanted money before she went.

They are there, standing by his hall door, their backs to him at first, then turning to face him when they hear the car on the gravel. Their two faces are caught in the headlights, the one black and gleaming, thick lips drawn back, the other timidly peering at the glare. He has a few times wondered about their threatened return, resolving not to answer the doorbell without first ascertaining who was there. Slowly, tiredly, he switches off the engine of the car and extinguishes the lights.

'Sir, we are happy to see you.' The black woman speaks as soon as he steps on to the gravel.

He locks the car door, then turns to shake his head at her smiling face. He doesn't smile himself. He's not in the mood for this: he lets that be seen.

'Ten minutes out of your day, sir —'

'My day has been a long one. I must wish you good-night. I must request you not to come bothering me again.'

'Have you taken the opportunity to meditate on the story of Miss Marcia Tibbitts? As we agreed, sir?'

'I didn't agree to anything.'

'A while back we called to see you, sir —'

'Yes, I know, I know.'

'We have been anxious to hear how my young friend's tale has affected your troubled heart, sir.'

Mr Hilditch is startled by this. His small eyes stare at Miss Calligary until he blinks in an effort to shake out of them the consternation he is unable to disguise.

'Troubled?' The word escapes from him without his wishing it to, his lips unconsciously giving voice to his alarm.

'Sir, the girl you were a helpmeet to was not of our Church. A lodger only in our house, sir. Just passing by.'

'You've got all this wrong –'

'That girl makes a song and dance that she is stolen from, expecting a whip-round in the Gathering House.'

'I'm telling you you've got your wires crossed.'

'If she said different from just passing by it isn't true. Better to consider my young friend here tonight, sir. Better to consider her joy as she stands before you.'

The girl isn't much to look at. Her nondescript hair grows in a widow's peak and is pulled straight back and held with hair-clips. She is a small, rabbity girl.

'Consider her daily trade, sir, before she came to know the promise of the Father Lord. Consider the grisly acts she sold across the counter, sir. Decapitation and viciousness, harems of animals. Unnatural practices, sir, the excitements of pain.'

Mr Hilditch, hardly hearing what is said, continues to observe the small girl. He wonders if she'll pass on from the people she has fallen in with and end up roaming. She has the look of that, an empty look that is familiar to him.

'Soon the folk will come from all over for our Prayer Jubilee. May I ask you, sir, if you have rooms going spare in your house?'

'Rooms? What're you talking about?'

'Sir, the folk come to rejoice.'

Mr Hilditch wants to push past them and unlock his hall door and then to bang it in their faces. He wants to say that he will summon the police unless they go away, that they have no right to harass a person on his doorstep, that they are trespassing on private property. But no words come and he does not move forward.

'For the future is written, sir, in the writing of certainty. There is fruit for all, heavy on the trees. And the green hills stretch to the horizon, and the corn is lifted from the land. See the foxes, sir, tamed in their holes, and the geese happy in the farmyard barn. Hear the cries of the children at play, and the voices raised in song for the Father Lord. That is the promise, sir. That is the future for the one who dies.'

'Why are you talking to me like this?' Hoarsely, and again involuntarily, the question escapes from him, asked before he realizes it. His voice sounds as though it is someone else's, some angry person shouting. He does not mean to shout. 'Why do you keep coming here? What do you want with me?'

He pushes past them then, roughly elbowing between them. He drops his car keys and the girl picks them up and hands them to him, her fingers touching his but he doesn't notice.

'Do not come back here,' he brusquely orders. 'I don't want to see you here again.'

Unperturbed and undismayed, Miss Calligary advises him to consider what has been said. None of us can flee the one who dies, she asserts, for the one who dies awaits us when we, too, have been cleansed and are ready for the paradise earth. And then, as though there has been no objection to the visit, no turbulence or crossness, Miss Calligary adds:

'There is solace for the troubled, sir.'

A black hand is laid on Mr Hilditch's arm. Miss Calligary's even teeth are again on display. Marcia Tibbitts is writing in a jotter.

'What's she doing? What's she writing down? This is a private house, you know.'

'What is written is the address, sir — 3 Duke of Wellington, and the number of folk you have room for when the Jubilee is at hand. Sir, with the folk around you, you would soon discover a heart-ease. Until that time come we will not desert you.'

Mr Hilditch's hands are shaking, so much so that he cannot fit the keys into the locks of his door. He is obliged to turn his back in order to hide his agitation, and to steady one hand with the other. He does not respond to the request that he should lodge people in his house.

In the Gathering House Miss Calligary reflects upon the irrational behaviour of the man who occupies 3 Duke of Wellington Road. Her efforts to rectify any misunderstanding there might have been inspired a response that causes her now to believe there was no such misunderstanding in the first place. Something else is the matter. When first they called on the man he refrained from interrupting Marcia Tibbitts' personal saga, and while it is true that he made some small protestation when it came to an end, the nature of this was not out of the ordinary. Indeed, in Miss Calligary's experience the more opposition there initially is the greater the conviction later. The intimation she experienced after their first encounter − that the man would sooner or later enter what the Priscatts call 'a relationship' with the Church that is her life's work − is something she now finds herself questioning: clearly, more work needs to be done. For not only has the fellowship she offered been peremptorily rejected, it appears to have become a cause of alarm. Miss Calligary has more than once explained to the young companions who bear the Message with her that you can't hope to get anywhere unless you persevere, that a lack of interest, even abuse, should not be permitted to upset or dishearten. But alarm is quite another matter; as a reaction, she has not experienced it before.

'Irrational, certainly,' Mr Priscatt agrees when she tells him, and Mrs Priscatt recalls a couple who behaved queerly in the early days of her gathering, inviting her and her husband on to their premises and then playing jokes on them: mechanical spiders crawled up Mrs Priscatt's legs; every time she and Mr Priscatt moved on their chairs an unpleasant sound erupted; and the bottoms fell out of the cups they were given tea in, drenching their clothes with warm liquid.

'No, it is not like that,' Miss Calligary explains.

The edginess of the occupant of 3 Duke of Wellington Road is retailed among the other Gatherers also, Miss Calligary still seeking advice. The old Ethiopian hears about it, as Bob and Ruthie do, and Mr Hikuku, and all the others. And when it reaches Agnes she recalls that it was she to whom the Irish girl first spoke of this man, and mentioned Duke of Wellington Road.

Responsible for the Irish girl's presence in the Gathering House, Miss Calligary does not shirk blaming herself, and there is certainty in her tone when she offers her final opinion. 'That girl brought pain to the Gathering House, and what I am thinking now is she brought pain to this man also, for at the mention of her he turns his back.'

This could be so, Mr Priscatt agrees, and the old Ethiopian, who has seen a thing or two on the streets and on the doorsteps, sagely nods his head. Bob and Ruthie murmur together, saying to one another that all this makes them sad.

'He has been diddled and is distrustful,' Miss Calligary states. 'He is jumpy to an extent.'

The others do not argue with this. Since they have been offended themselves by the pregnant girl they gave shelter to, it seems likely that a good-hearted man would suffer also.

'We have a duty in this matter.' Confident that guidance has been offered, Miss Calligary is more cheerful.

22

He recognizes him at once: the tidy dark hair, the greenish eyes, the high cheekbones. Other features have not been included in the description Mr Hilditch has heard so often: a shiftiness in those eyes, a knowing smile that slants the mouth, a freshly grown moustache.

Mr Hilditch waits until he is certain – until he hears the youth's name used – before drawing back into the shadows of the corner he has chosen to occupy in the Goose and Gander. This is the first public house near the Old Hinley barracks he has tried, twenty minutes from Duke of Wellington Road. He was in his corner only long enough to sip half of the glass of mineral water he ordered before the five soldiers noisily arrived. Although they're not in uniform, you can tell they're soldiers from their haircuts and their gait.

Fragments of their talk flutter across the bar to where he sits: it appears to be about motor-racing, a loose wheel spinning off into the crowd. 'Bloody killed a bloke,' one of the soldiers says.

Mr Hilditch doesn't know why he has come here. Some compulsion has drawn him to the place, and further presses him to eavesdrop on this conversation. As he listens to subsequent exchanges about car-racing tracks, he does not remember what his thoughts were before he left his house, and senses that there were no thoughts: he simply drove off, knowing where he was going.

'Your bloody round, mate,' one of the soldiers roughly reminds another, and there's a general noise of agreement. Glasses are drained. As an encouragement to the soldier whose round it is, the surface of the table is repeatedly struck.

Extraordinary to think of what she went through, deceived by this lout who cleared off without leaving her any means of contacting him, cunningly aware that he would be protected by an embittered mother. Mr Hilditch remembers the tears that so often flowed when they sat together watching the door of some café, the distress there was when another blank was drawn at a factory, the guilt induced by the aborting of the unborn child. A Wednesday it was when she appeared on the forecourt. Without making an effort, he has always been able to establish the day of the week on which events occur: a Friday when the recruiting sergeant said he'd better try something else; a Monday when he got the transfers and stencil set for his birthday – the smell of washing, the small red candles, Uncle Wilf there specially. It was a Saturday, always, when they went by train down to the Spa.

'Bloody poofter,' one of the soldiers says. 'Corner of Brunswick Way every evening on the dot. Forty quid he's offering.'

'Bloody never,' is a disdainful comment, and: 'Pull the one that chimes, boy.'

'Pull bloody nothing. Fancies a uniform, that poofter does.'

Mr Hilditch doesn't know why he can't see her as he still sees all the others, and can offer himself only the explanation that it is because she went from him in some different way, which is the feeling he has had since the black woman stirred everything up by mentioning her. His presence here has to do with how they parted: he recognizes that now, he knows it. He is here because there's no place for her in his Memory Lane, because any moment she may walk in. He leans back in the shadows, the conversation of the soldiers lost to him. With his single glass of mineral water he remains in this corner until the landlord calls last orders and then inquires if his customers have a home to go to. The glasses are collected by a barmaid whom the five soldiers flatter with attentions before rowdily making off.

Outside, Mr Hilditch watches them from his car and then drives about the streets, searching as desperately as his quarry once searched herself.

One day, a Thursday, a week after his visit to the Goose and Gander, Mr Hilditch does not go to work. He walks to the telephone-box at the end of Duke of Wellington Road and puts a call in to the kitchens, stating that he is unwell. He returns to his house and sits all day, not eating, listening to a selection of his records in his big front room. When one comes to an end he does not immediately rise to place another on the turntable, but listens for a while to the whine of the needle. After that Bing Crosby and Frank Sinatra, Perry Como, Alma Cogan, Nelson Eddy and Jeanette MacDonald, Eve Boswell, Doris Day and Howard Keel congregate to fill his day, a background to the worries that have multiplied and persist. When darkness falls he does not move from the room. The *Daily Telegraph* remains unread in the hall, where he placed it on the hall-stand on his way out to telephone the kitchens.

At nine o'clock he makes a pot of tea, and toasts a single slice of bread.

There is no reply when Miss Calligary rings the bell. This surprises her because the little green car is parked on the gravel in front of the house.

'No, we wait a little, child.' She restrains the presumption of her companion, who has already begun to move on. The occupant of this house is maybe out for a stroll, or gone down on foot to the off-licence. Miss Calligary rings the bell again in case the summons hasn't been heard.

'Hullo, hullo,' she calls through the letter-box.

Three further weeks pass. The days lengthen. Were Mr Hilditch to visit the same stately home again he would find daffodils in bloom on the hillside above the car park where earlier there were crocuses, and green shoots everywhere in the gardens.

But Mr Hilditch does not do so. He has not returned to his catering department since the day he telephoned with an excuse; he has only once been shopping, and then half-heartedly. *I am undergoing treatment for boils,* he has written in a letter of apology to his superiors, adding that this is treatment that necessitates a strict regime of rest and diet. Since he has never before, in all his years of employment, been absent through illness, a lenient view is taken, and there are get-well cards from the canteen staff and the kitchen staff.

At night he continues to sleep poorly. He has lost some weight; there is a haggard look about his features now, the surplus flesh loose and drooping. If she meets up with the black woman again, God knows what she'll come out with. God knows how it'll be spread around then, how many people will know she was in his house. Already it could be known to the kitchen staff and the canteen workers, to all kinds of people, everywhere. Any day now the tea woman could be embarrassed to pour out his tea.

One morning, having fallen into an exhausted doze soon after dawn, he awakes with the eccentric notion that the Irish girl has invaded him, as territory is invaded. There is a faint impression – so fleeting it's hardly there – that on some forgotten occasion the gravel in front of his house was brightly lit from the hall, that in his car he had to turn his head away from the glare.

I regret to say the treatment is taking time, he writes to his superiors a few days later, having again scoured the streets late the night before. *This is unfortunate and unforeseen, but I trust it won't be much longer now.* First ascertaining that the black woman is nowhere in sight, he hurries to the pillar-box at the end of Duke of Wellington Road to post this letter, the first time he has been out of his house in the daytime for a fortnight.

'Hullo, hullo,' Miss Calligary calls through the letter-box.

The car is still there, exactly as it was. The curtained windows of the house seem the same also.

'Hullo, hullo,' Miss Calligary loudly repeats.

Still there is no response.

He roams the streets on foot in case his car is recognized by an employee, doing so at an hour when he trusts he won't be recognized himself. He goes to places he hasn't visited for years, to the neighbourhoods the Indians or Pakistanis have taken over. The Boroda Express offers the variety stars of India: Bhangra Garta, Miss Bhavana, Deepa the Voice of Lata. The Koh-I-Noor Restaurant is under new management. The Wool Shop he remembers, stockists of Sirdar Wools and Bairnswear, is the Rupali Boutique now.

He hurries by where shops and cafés have been abandoned and are empty of furniture and fittings, with only a scattering of junk mail left where it has fallen, beneath the low-slung letter-boxes of business premises. He walks through the Foundries, which was a thriving area in his childhood, the only reminder now of its one-time prosperity being the black brick and stone of its purposeless yards and gaunt façades. He walks through suburbs, already leafy, cars parked in car ports, houses sleeping, their windows dark. He passes close to the leisure centre he considers unnecessary, and the cream-tiled Bingo hall that was once an ABC cinema. Without noticing them, he passes churches and a synagogue and a mosque, and one of the two schools he attended, and the old town hospital, Victorian and grand, given over to offices now. In the early morning he watches the Salvation Army hostel from across the road, observing each face as the night's lodgers emerge.

It is after one of these outings, as he is wearily making his way back to Duke of Wellington Road, that Mr Hilditch finally concludes the girl he has been seeking must have moved on. He nods to himself, cosseting the thought, eager to accept whatever comfort he can pluck out of his gloom. The girl is again in her home town, the back of beyond by the sound of it. Only there will people know, and what interest would they have in a person who is strange to them, several hundred miles away?

In his kitchen that morning he opens a tin of beans and has them with bacon and fresh bread, the *Daily Telegraph* spread out in front of him while he eats. His euphoria is modest, no more than a change from what there's been, but he is determined to hold on to it, convincing himself that if the girl were still in the neighbourhood it would surely have dawned on her by now that her father was right about Lysaght being a soldier. She would have found her way to him, which clearly she hasn't. And if it hadn't dawned on her, she'd be visible on the streets. Which means that, strictly speaking, the only continuing concern is about what she passed on when she was in the God-botherers' house.

Mr Hilditch carefully goes over the ground: she stayed in the

God-botherers' house at a time when all there'd been between them was the lift he'd given her the morning they made the journey to that factory and the hospital. Nothing much was said then. And the state of play was similar when she associated with the two derelicts she'd mentioned; not that there is any reason to suppose she'd given the address of Number Three to those people, or said what he looked like. What it amounts to is that less damage has possibly been done than he has persuaded himself to believe.

Washing the dishes he has eaten from, Mr Hilditch considers that he is owed some luck, having lately been deprived of it, and feels that it may have come at last. But as the day advances he loses heart again, and when two or three further days have passed he finds himself back in the slough of uncertainty that has claimed him for so long now. His appetite is not sustained; increasingly, his single desire is to keep himself entirely to his house.

One evening when the bell rings he rises from his armchair after a moment's hesitation to lift the needle off a record. The only way to set himself at rest is to know what was said. Impelled by the confusions that torment him — the hope that is there one minute and isn't the next, the reaching out from his despondency in search of some crumb of consolation — he slowly crosses his hall. Releasing one lock and then the other, he tells himself that inquiries can be made without giving anything away. No need for many words on his part. Let the black woman talk, let her trip herself up. Ask a casual question when the moment is ripe.

'Sir, you have been in our hearts these many weeks,' the woman at once, and gravely, asserts when he opens his front door, and he sees reflected in her features the thought that here is a man who is greatly changed, whose clothes are not as they have been before. He observes it registering with her that the collar of his shirt does not seem clean, that the dressing-gown he is wearing at seven o'clock in the evening is ragged in places, that at this hour also he is unshaven. The expression of the girl accompanying her, the same girl as on the two previous occasions, remains blank.

'I have been doing jobs about the house,' he explains. He essays a smile, wishing to go about his business with these people in what may be taken as a cheerful manner. 'Fires and that. I like to have a fire.'

His fires are electric now, with a single gas one, but they are not to know that. Once upon a time he laid coal fires, with kindling and newspaper dried in the hot cupboard to get them going. He used to put on old clothes for the task and wear old gloves. Nothing peculiar about any of it, any more than there should be now.

'Sir, if it don't bother you, we might step inside?'

Odd the way her grammar occasionally lapses while at other times her speech is fancy, as if she's preaching at a corner. In his mother's day when some salesman came to the door she would call out from wherever she was that nothing was required. 'Tell the lady she'll save a bundle, sonny,' a brush salesman said once. 'For black-lead, for shoes, something for the dustpan. Sweepers, brooms. You name it, sonny. You tell the madam that.'

He holds the door open and the black woman and the white girl step into the hall. He is aware of the difficulties that lie ahead, but the compulsion that possesses him is greater than his natural caution. In his big front room he invites his visitors to sit down.

'My, my,' the black woman remarks, looking around her at the billiard table and the gramophone, the two grandfather clocks, the cabinet crammed with paperweights, the knick-knacks on the mantelpiece. 'My, my,' the black woman says again.

Mr Hilditch is patient. The Prayer Jubilee has taken place, he hears: the folk who arrived from all over have returned to their homes. It is not the Prayer Jubilee she has come about, the black woman divulges, but to say she can offer an assistance in a time of jumpiness and alarm. She speaks of the paradise earth and outlines in detail the vocation of the Gatherers, their Dedication and their Task. While she does so, Mr Hilditch's mind races, endeavouring to find some way of making his queries in a well-disguised manner. The girl sits silent, not called upon to comment.

'*Is not the life more than meat, and the body than raiment?* Would you carry from door to door, sir, the Message we bring you now, that you may know a heart-ease? For it is there in spreading the word of joy for the one who dies.'

Momentarily distracted from his purpose in admitting his visitors, Mr Hilditch retorts sharply:

'Why do you keep saying that to me?'

'It is the Message of today and of every day. Strong in faith, and giving glory.'

'I have done nothing wrong,' Mr Hilditch hears himself saying, not meaning to say it. He doesn't know why he says it, or where the protestation has come from. He is frustrated in his thoughts, for when he searches his brain for a neat way to extract the information he needs, no solution occurs. There is no response to an inward pleading that becomes frenzied when the black woman presses more suggestions on him and quotes again from the Scriptures. The girl who accompanies her is still quiet, and while he struggles unsuccessfully Mr Hilditch finds himself distracted by the consideration that he could, at this very moment, be sitting in a Happy Eater with this girl, listening to her tale of woe. He knows she has one; all of them have a tale of woe.

'*The good shepherd giveth his life for his sheep,*' the black woman is saying now, and what feels like panic spreads in Mr Hilditch. He has made a mistake. He is guilty of an error of judgement. He should not have brought these two into his house: there is no way he can deviously interrogate them. He dare not mention the name of the Irish girl, nor refer to her in some other manner. He should have opened the door and told these people once and for all to clear off.

'In the future, another Prayer Jubilee will be upon us and you have rooms unoccupied, sir. With the folk who come then, you may go forth in the joy of the Message.'

Mr Hilditch, who did not sit down when his visitors did, says there is no question of lodgers in his house. His voice has lost some power; beneath his clothes the skin of his back has become damp and warm. Beads of sweat form on his cheeks and his forehead; his spectacles have misted. He stumbles over the words he attempts to utter, slurring them.

'There can be nothing like that.' His voice comes hoarsely from him now, a whisper he hardly recognizes as his own. He shakes his head. The black woman wants him to pray with her.

'I'm not interested in this,' he tries to say and can feel his lower lip shaking. It's that that makes speech so difficult: every time he tries to get a word out it becomes lost in the shaking of his lip. If he attempts to rouse his anger, he knows he won't be able to.

'Parthians and Medes and Elamites,' the black woman enumerates in a crazy manner, on her knees already. The girl kneels also. 'And the dwellers in Mesopotamia, and in Judaea . . .'

The black woman's hands are pressed hard together, raised above her bent head. The girl has arranged herself similarly, one of the exposed soles of her shoes in need of repair, her short skirt riding up a bit.

'We hear them speak in tongues. We hear them, some from their gardens, some from deserts. O, Father Lord, we offer thanks.'

The only girl he took under his roof passed from this selfsame room in her nightdress: of their parting, that is what remains. Then the first of the two buses appears on the drive to the house, and there's the taste of tuna in the sandwich, the lettuce crunching between his teeth. Listening to the black woman's prayers, he sees the blue bus again, the passengers stepping out of it, the driver with his newspaper.

'I'm not interested in this,' he protests, successfully uttering the words now.

But the black woman continues to speak gibberish, and the girl's lips move as if she is making a contribution of her own. What life is it, Mr Hilditch wonders, for this child, with her face like a rabbit's? She's not a religious, as the black woman is; you can tell that without thinking. All she has done in joining up with these people is to find somewhere to go, a niche to cling on to. She's running from something; you can tell that too, the giveaway in the eyes. What life will it be for her, to spend the rest of it with nutters, trailing about with brochures and gibberish?

The girl unclasps her hands and rises. The black woman does so too. He leads the way into the hall and opens the front door, anxious now to be rid of these people. He clears his voice with a cough. When he speaks it's still weak, but the panic that possessed him has subsided a little.

'Good-night to you.'

'We understand your trouble, sir. When first we called by I said it to my young friend. We have put two and two together, sir.'

'What two and two? What d'you mean?'

'The Irish girl brought pain to our people, sir, as she has to you. I myself am responsible.'

'What did she say to you?' The words rush out from Mr Hilditch, careless and unchecked. He meant to shake his head, to say he doesn't follow. He manages to smile, and to add:

'I only ask in passing. I don't know the girl in any way whatsoever. I only met her on the street.'

'As I did myself, sir.'

'She asked me the way.'

'We would have shown her the Way, sir, as tonight we have shown you. You knelt down with us, sir —'

'I did not kneel down. Please go away from me. That girl was just a girl on the street.'

'Sir, in your goodness you gave her the money she tried to trick out of the folk in the Gathering House. Put two and two together, you come up with that. Mr Priscatt says it, Agnes too. It's natural to be jumpy with a stranger that rings your bell. It's natural when you're taken on a ride.'

'I didn't give her any money. Money doesn't come into it. She asked me for directions.'

Mr Hilditch is aware that he's dealing in contradiction, that each denial is more flawed than the last. He is aware that he isn't making sense. And again he is unable to control what he says.

'Any girl's welfare would concern you if she came up to you on the street.'

'It's best she has gone, sir. Put that girl out of your mind, sir. The pain will wash away.'

'I'm not in pain. I don't know what you mean by pain.'

'The healing will commence. For that reason we are sent out to gather.'

There is a sickness in Mr Hilditch's stomach now. Already descending the four steps to the gravel expanse, the black woman turns to ascend them again. Sent by the Father Lord, she says, and suggests that there should be further prayer. She is smiling at him, her black lips drawn back from her crowded, sturdy teeth. For a moment he wants to reach out, to push her away, to watch her lose her balance on the steps and fall to the gravel. But the temptation is resisted, and his tone is calm when he speaks.

'Do not ever come back here. Keep away from my house.'

He bangs and double-locks the door, and when the bell rings almost at once he ignores it. The letter-box is rattled and the black woman's voice speaks through it, but he pays no attention. His will has left him, he says to himself in his hall: he admitted them to his house, he invited them in, when all the time they are a mockery of his suffering.

How could she be back in her home town when she has no money? That is the thought he is left with. It has come, as so much else has recently, from nowhere. The Irish girl is roaming the streets, which is why he cannot see her as he sees the others, among his happy memories.

23

In time Mr Hilditch returns to work. It is the best chance he has, he considers, of feeling himself again. He is welcomed in the kitchens and in the canteen and conscientiously devotes himself to the backlog in his small office. But his appetite has not returned, which continues to be something of an embarrassment for a catering manager. He explains it away as best he can, and it is generally remarked that he has not yet fully recovered from the ailment that laid him low for so long.

Then, one afternoon, without warning, an adjustment occurs in his memory. Between the Irish girl's going upstairs in her nightdress and the blue bus appearing on the drive of the stately home there emerges something else: there is the sound of footsteps on the stairs, of a door closing at the top of the house. In his recall there is his awareness that she knows, that there have been moments, that day and in the evening, when he saw the knowledge in her eyes.

It is on a Tuesday that the remembrance occurs. The last day of March, twenty-five to four. Interrupted in his perusal of last month's overheads, Mr Hilditch gazes at a calendar that hangs on his office wall and fails to register its familiar details: two children in Victorian dress blowing bubbles, the compliments of Trafalgar Soup Powders plc. The fragment of recall he experiences is more vividly projected than the scene that has been chosen by Trafalgar Soup Powders. He wept when she went upstairs again in her nightdress, already on her way to the beck and call of a father and two brothers, to a stifled life, to guilt on her conscience for ever more. The gramophone needle rasped on the record. The glow of the electric fire was pink on his shoes and the bottoms of his trousers.

'A tea, Mr Hilditch,' the tea woman offers. 'I've brought it to you first.'

It is what the tea woman always says. He always gets his tea first, suitable treatment for a catering manager.

'Thanks very much.' He tries to smile and wonders if he succeeds.

'Nice again,' the tea woman comments, but he does not hear and so does not reply, which causes the tea woman later to remark that the malady that laid Mr Hilditch low has left him on the deaf side.

His eyes drop from their sightless survey of the bubble-blowers on the wall. Print-outs cover the surface of his desk, the cup of tea on its saucer among them. He reaches out and mechanically stirs two lumps of sugar into the warm, milky liquid. On her way back to nothing, he repeated to himself in his big front room, on her way to a bleakness that would wither her innocence: what good was that to anyone? He called to her but she didn't hear, and then he went upstairs to put it to her that they should go for a drive. All that comes back now.

He plays 'Blue Hawaii' again. He makes himself read the *Daily Telegraph*, cover to cover – foreign news, financial, a column about television programmes he has not seen, the gossip pages. He roasts a four-pound turkey breast, an effort to coax his appetite back.

But what began in his office as a trickle of memory on a Tuesday afternoon becomes a torrent as more days go by. The night the Irish girl was in her nightdress his last task was to burn in his dustbin the garments he'd dotted about the place. The night Elsie Covington said she'd miss him he watched her eating a peach melba and then drove to the car park by the Canal Wharf, deserted on a Monday. 'You're planning to take off,' he said to Sharon and she laughed.

His memory flows destructively, the debris of recall seeming more like splinters from forgotten nightmares than any part of reality. For surely the moment of Gaye's knowing, too, comes from some nightmare pushed away – her look, the way she glanced at him when she asked if he could spare a twenty just till she got on her feet again? The only one he'd endeavoured to explain to was the Irish girl. Her innocence drew it out of him: how they had called him by different names – Colin, Bill, Terry, Bob, Ken, Peter, Ray, any name that came to hand, they being the kind of girls who liked to use a name. No harm in a different name, any more than there was harm in a man in his position not taking a girl out locally. 'I'm going south, Bill,' Beth said, and neither of them spoke for a while, and he went on driving. 'Where're we headed?' Beth asked, and out in the country he turned on to the refuse-tip road and drove on past the closed iron gates. 'Where are we going, Bill?' she asked again, her cigarette glowing in the dark. He said a surprise, drawing in to the lay-by where he'd once stopped to have a sandwich and a drink of tea from his Thermos. He had to watch the cigarette. He had to be careful; anything could happen with a lighted cigarette in a car. Afterwards he drove straight back to Number Three, taking her with him because that was best.

Malign, unwelcome, the content of what has crept into his recollection causes Mr Hilditch to believe he is suffering from a mental aberration: that he is moving into madness is the only explanation he can offer himself. Every morning he parks his car in the factory car park and crosses the forecourt, greeting the employees who are about, and they return his salutation, unaware. Once in a while there is a dispute in the kitchens, two of the dish-washing women at loggerheads, and he reasons with them as he has always done. He tastes the food, he chats to afternoon callers. A team from Moulinex demonstrates its wares. And beneath the semblance of normality he achieves, scenes lightly flicker, and voices speak.

His days become an ordeal, and on returning each evening to 3 Duke of Wellington Road he faces in private his suspicion that he is being deprived of sanity. He searches through the time that has passed from the moment when his unease began, reliving the first of his worried nights, recalling his effort to shake away the gathering obsession by his visit to the Spa, recalling his presence in the Goose and Gander. Why has he been picked out for attention by a black woman? Why cannot he eat? Why has he written false letters to his employers? Why do delusions now occupy his mind? Mr Hilditch has heard of such developments in other people's lives, he has read of them in the *Daily Telegraph*: the normal balance of the mind upset for no good reason. He visits a library, a thing he has never in his life done before. He consults a number of medical books, eventually finding the information he seeks:

Delusional insanity is not preceded by either maniacal or melancholic symptoms, and is not necessarily accompanied by any failure of the reasoning capacity. In the early stage the patient is introspective and uncommunicative, rarely telling his thoughts but brooding and worrying over them in secret. After this stage has lasted for a longer or shorter time the delusions become fixed and are generally of a disagreeable kind.

It isn't easy to know what to make of that. He sits in his car in the library precinct and while people pass close by, while other cars start and drive away, he tells himself that the fragments of nightmare are nothing more than that. None of this has happened. There was no girl, ever, in his house. There was no tale of a father and two twin brothers, and a bitter woman with a scar on her face. There was never Beth; wishful thinking, the others too. He is Hilditch, a catering manager, liked by the employees.

Safe again in 3 Duke of Wellington Road, a house he has known all his life, where he cried as an infant and played on the stairs with Dinky cars, he attempts to dispel the fantasies that torment him, by whispering the words of 'You Belong to Me', accompanying Jo Stafford. But the fantasies nevertheless persist and when the record ends, when his big front room is quiet again, he stands in the middle of it, drained of the energy to assert his will. His lips don't move, no sound comes from him, yet a voice is speaking, an echo in the room, his own voice telling him that this is real.

One night, when too much has happened in a single day, Mr Hilditch resolves more firmly than before never to leave his house again, to barricade himself within it if need be, for how can he go about his cheery life, with this ugly mockery constantly there? How can he, who has furnished his gaunt rooms to his taste, who is respected and troubles no one, be the protagonist in this darkness that is suddenly lit up, like a film projected in a cinema? From his bathroom looking-glass his face looks back at him, the same face he has always had, but he takes no heart from that. He turns the pages of a photograph album and there is a plump child, with a seaside bucket and spade in a garden, and racing with other children at a school sports. His mother laughs with him, his Uncle Wilf lights a cigarette. Pigeons perch on his outstretched arms, one on his shoulder. *First long trousers*, his mother's handwriting records.

In a cupboard there are his Dinky cars, and other toys too: a Meccano set, a Happy Families pack of cards, a gyroscope he could spin on the point of a pin. He throws dice out on a Snakes and Ladders board. 'The little chap always wins,' his mother says, and there's a school report that calls him attentive and neat. The badges that once were sewn into his Wolf Cub jersey are among these small mementoes, one with a brush on it, symbol of house-keeping assistance, another with a rake, for gardening.

'I'm sorry you're going,' he said outside the home-decorating shop when Jakki told him, and later he drove out to the refuse-tip road and past the closed iron gates. A car went by when they were stationary in the lay-by, and he remembered being there before and having to go somewhere else because a car drew in beside them, a couple cuddling. With Bobbi that had been. 'Well, thanks for everything,' she had said ten minutes before.

Often, at night or in the daytime, his doorbell rings. The voice calls through the letter-box, offering him assistance through prayer. He listens for the reference to the Irish girl or to the one who dies. That doesn't come but he knows that such references are cunningly withheld, that they would be there immediately if he opened his door. In the mornings he takes in his milk, checking first from a window that there is no one on his doorstep. After dark he shops from time to time for a few necessities, always careful to ascertain that nobody is waiting at his house when he returns. He answers a letter that comes from his superiors, inquiring if there has been a relapse. He affirms that there has been, but gives no more information. Nothing like that matters now.

One early morning he stands in his shrubbery of laurels and looks down at his feet, at the layers of old leaves that cover the several patches of turned earth. He pokes with a finger: the used-up clay is dusty beneath the obscuring leaves. In the hell that possesses him he sees the laurel roots already creeping among bones half-stripped of their insects' nourishment, the misshapen roots twisting in the clay. He sees himself: his face, afterwards, in the car, each time crying as uncontrollably as he did the day he caught his leg in the railings, when he was six. 'Oh naughty, *naughty*!' she exclaimed, cross because they were going to be late. Leave him for a moment and he does a thing like that! Two seconds she was gone and now she has to beg assistance of a policeman! 'Easy does it, son. What goes in must come out, eh?' And the policeman listened while he told him he'd only done it to see if his knee would fit between the two upright bars. 'Ever so kind!' she cried when the policeman was successful, and the policeman said all in the day's work. 'Call in for a drink when you're passing near,' she invited. '3 Duke of Wellington.'

Opening a tin of pilchards, thinking he might fancy them, he cuts his finger. He watches the blood run over the metal, not attending to the small wound at once, only drawing his hand away from the contents of the tin. Drips fall on the edge of the sink and the draining-board. What would analysis reveal about this liquid in which his own bones swim, which fuels his heart and gives him life? Is it different in some essence from the blood of other people? Is the torn flesh different also? He chatted to the young father in the waiting-room of that clinic, as any man might. He walked with others through the stately home; in his friendly way he remarked that it made an outing. He listened while the woman spoke of the Hanging Gardens of Babylon and of her sister, who'd been untrustworthy. No one moved away from him when he spoke. That woman liked his cheerful face.

He draws his great weight about his house, restless all day long. A stroke of bad luck, and then another and another. If the girl hadn't stayed in the nutters' house he would be going back and forth to his catering department as he has always done, content and occupied with his work. Instead, by chance she went there, allowing a black woman to threaten his privacy, poking and grubbing, flashing her teeth and her jewels, trapping him with her gibberish. A religious has a sixth sense, there have been cases. A religious can disturb you and play on your confusions until you can't find the subtlety to ask the questions you want to ask and then say too much, your own worst enemy. 'The little man's his own worst enemy!' He remembers that being said, the smile that emphasized the humour of it.

And remembering, he is able for the first time to say it had to be the way it was: there was no option, no choice. Think of the Irish girl roaming the streets and you can see it at once. Think of her carrying, wherever she goes, what does not belong to her, spreading it about: you know immediately the other had to happen. And if he could find her there would be, once more, merciful oblivion: that's how things are, he can tell that now. He breaks his resolution not to leave the house and again goes out to look for her. Again, she is not there.

He stares into his mother's face, blurred and misty in the photograph he decorated with black crêpe because he had to say this was his deceased wife. The eyes stare back at him, the features crinkled because his mother simpers lightly, a way she had. 'Oh, wasn't it lovely!' she enthused when they stood in the bus queue after *The Wizard of Oz*. A Wednesday it was, cold for October. Egg in a cup as soon as they got home; egg in a cup and nice hot chocolate.

'And how's that knee?' the policeman inquired when he called in for the drink she'd pressed on him. 'All bright and beautiful again?' And her voice came from upstairs, asking who that was, and he said, calling up to her, the policeman from the other day. 'Well, isn't this nice!' was the comment she made in the dining-room, pouring out drinks, the helmet on the table. She'd put on her high heels before coming downstairs. 'Cheers!' the policeman said, and: 'See you again,' when he was leaving. And she said yes, why not?

She found the name Ambrose in a novel. 'Oh, years ago there was a Joseph,' she said when he asked where that came from. 'Just a beau.' *Joseph Ambrose Hilditch*: he wrote it when they were asked in class to write their names in full one day. 'Ambrose?' a boy said afterwards. 'Sissy, that.' Ambrose Lafitte, a man who used to read the News, she said. As well as which, he was a cat burglar. The novel was a romance; she delighted in romances. People all over the nation would listen to the six o'clock News, not knowing that within a couple of hours the man reading it would be making his way over the rooftops, all in black. 'Really caught my fancy,' she said. 'Ambrose.'

J. A. Hilditch: that became his signature, practised when he was fourteen, the J looped with the A, the middle of the surname unrecognizable. When he asked who Hilditch was she clammed up. No one much, she said.

The brush salesman spread out his brushes for her, even though she'd called out nothing today when she heard him at the door. 'He certainly can make you laugh!' she said about the policeman when he'd been back a few times. And on another occasion: 'Stop for the night, Uncle Wilf? Blustery outside, it is.'

In the Longridge tunnel it was with a man she'd never laid eyes on until a few minutes before. When the light began to flicker again she was tidying her hair, and the man bent down to pick up his mackintosh from the floor. Afterwards he spoke to her on the platform and she laughed when he'd gone, saying a person wasn't safe in a railway carriage these days.

Major Hilditch he once wrote down, privately, when no one was around. He never had to think about it if people asked what he intended to do with himself when he grew up. In films there were ATS girls and, still privately, he said to himself that that's how one day it'll be: walking with one of them beneath an arch of swords. Manoeuvres on Salisbury Plain; a house in Wiltshire that had been a rectory once, a garden, and a family growing up.

He winds the clocks in his big front room. All the years he has lived with them he has liked to hear them tick, soothing after a tiring day. He cleans the room with his Electrolux, and the hall and stairs, and his bedroom. He mops the vinyl of the bathroom and the lavatory, and scents the air with a herbal fragrance. Such activities momentarily keep his thoughts at bay, but when he rests they are there again.

Had she always foreseen, when he was six and eight and ten, when he sat beside her watching *Dumbo*, and *Bambi*, when first he practised his signature, when he wrote down *Major Hilditch*: had she always known that she would turn to him when there was no one else? When the insurance-man winked and said no time for anything today, did she foresee – already – what would happen in this house? The barman at the Spa said the wife had put her foot down, no more hanky-panky. After a few months the policeman didn't drop in any more. 'No, I'd best get back,' Uncle Wilf whispered on the landing.

Had she foreseen it when he played with his Dinky cars or, before that, when the steps of the stairs were too steep for him, when she took his hand to help him? Had she foreseen it when first she said, 'Just you and Mamma in their own little nest'? Or was it all different, the spur of the moment when she woke him up to show him the rings on her fingers? His blue-striped pyjamas, a shred of tobacco on her teeth when she smiled down at him, her ginny breath: in his private life, the occasion has always been there, never lost – not for a moment – in the oblivion that kindly claimed the other. Like a tattoo, she said, the lipstick on his shoulder. Her face was different then.

He scours his saucepans. He removes the enamel surround of the electric stove and cleans the metal plates beneath the rings. He defrosts his refrigerator and washes its shelves and containers.

Her powder was scented; it clogged the pores on the two sides of her nose, a shade of apricot. She said she liked the best in the way of powder, and she sat there, afterwards, at the looking-glass, passing the puff over her skin. Lovely skin in its day, she said, and she slipped her eyelashes off, and he could see that in the looking-glass too. 'Have to dress up for a chap!' she said. A Saturday it was.

Again there is the ringing of the doorbell, again the attempt to communicate through the letter-box. Protected already by the

Yale and the double lock, he has bolted the door as well, at the top and bottom, and has bolted his back door also. He keeps the curtains drawn across his downstairs windows, but not to disguise the fact that he is in the house: his car on the gravel indicates his presence, and after dark there are chinks of light. It's just that he likes the curtains drawn now. 'Hullo, hullo,' the voice of the black woman booms in the hall until it's drowned by the voice of Rosemary Clooney.

You could see Beth thinking it; you could see her searching her thoughts and finding it. And Elsie Covington, then the others: they broke in somehow. They trespassed on his privacy even though he took them places and lavished a bit on them in their time of need, the Irish girl too. You could tell, from the way she stood there in her nightdress, that she respected neither his house nor himself because she knew. Beth would have passed it on when she had a drink in; Elsie would have, to some man who picked her up. When the Irish girl went he said he didn't want the light. But the hall was illuminated behind her, and if she came close to him it would be there again in her eyes. It was because he looked away that she ran off, her footsteps on the gravel, not stopping at the car even though he'd made the car ready for her. It had to be the car; he couldn't do it in his house, no man could. All he'd asked of her was to get in beside him, no need to say anything, not even that she was sorry.

From the photograph that not long ago he draped with mourning crêpe the faded eyes still twinkle at him, the plump mouth crimped into its winsome pout. 'Brush Mamma's hair, dearie,' a murmur faintly begs. The hair is thick and grey on the pale powdered back, and the blue ribbon is laid out ready on the dressing-table.

'Hullo, hullo,' cries the voice in his hall, and then there is the peering through the letter-box.

'Sir, are you all right?' Miss Calligary solicitously inquires, and Mr Hilditch stands silent in his hall until the flap of his letter-box clatters back into place and footsteps move away.

'Come back,' he whispers then, one hand raised to the Yale latch of the hall door, the other on the key of the double lock. Weeks ago he sought to discover information from this woman that has since shrunk in importance, there now being the more urgent consideration that the girl is still about the place. This woman can lead him to the girl because she knows what the girl looks like and could have seen her around, being always on the streets herself. The girl walked out into that Saturday-night fog, preferring to take chances than to associate with a man whose childhood she knows about through intuition.

'Come back,' Mr Hilditch calls out from the steps of his house.

His ponderous form is lit in the open doorway as Miss Calligary and Marcia Tibbitts turn to retrace their steps. The Irish girl, he says: the Irish girl is alive.

'That girl's a bit of no good, sir.' And Miss Calligary adds that such a girl can work a trick with both eyes closed.

He doesn't appear to hear. On his chin and his forehead there is a glistening of sweat. It was they who disturbed the calm, he says, by referring to the Irish girl in the first place. It was they who caused a muddle where there was peace of mind before. Where is the Irish girl now?

'Sir,' Miss Calligary interrupts, but he shakes his head and the eyes of Marcia Tibbitts pass from one face to another, excited because something strange is happening here.

'Tell me the truth,' the man begs. 'I am a catering manager. I have lived in this house all my days. I am a respectable man. Hilditch I am called.'

'Mr Hilditch, we're concerned for you. Why not kneel down with us? Why not permit us to ask for guidance?'

'Is the Irish girl with you? Has she returned to your house?'

'No, no. She's not with us now. That girl wouldn't be welcome.'

'Where is she then? Where has she gone to? You are out and about, you know what she looks like.'

'No one has seen the girl, sir. No one knows.' Surely, Miss Calligary suggests, the girl is back in her Irish home by now.

'She has no money.'

'A girl like that can always get money.'

'Her boyfriend drinks in the Goose and Gander. Out Hinley way, a squaddies' pub. A stone's throw from the barracks.'

He visited the place, Mr Hilditch divulges. He sat drinking a mineral in the Goose and Gander.

'Because you're teetotal, sir? You drink a mineral because you have put strong drink to one side?'

Mr Hilditch says no. He sat in the Goose and Gander because of a compulsion, which afterwards he realized had to do with the possibility that the Irish girl had noticed an army lorry going by, as sometimes an army lorry does. It had to do with it dawning on her then that her father's statements concerning her boyfriend's occupation were well founded. It had to do with her making inquiries and being led into her boyfriend's company.

'Mr Hilditch –'

'You have driven me to the medical shelves with all your bothering of me.'

'You've got this wrong, Mr Hilditch. It was never my intention to drive you anywhere. I don't even know what you mean by that.'

'You brought the subject of the girl up. Day and night, you kept mentioning her.'

'Mr Hilditch, we mentioned that girl to you in order to compliment you on your charity. We have come to gather you, Mr Hilditch, as we come every day to the houses of other folk. Nothing to do with a dishonest girl.'

Mr Hilditch shakes his head. He shows his finger, where he cut it on a pilchards tin. The blood dripped on to the draining-board, he says, causing him to wonder about it and to wonder about the open flesh. He adds, to Marcia Tibbitts' greater excitement:

'You have come to convey me to my coffin.'

'No, no, sir. It is the living we gather to us, not the dead. These are morbid thoughts, without the joy that makes all things beautiful. You are not yourself. I have seen that and have said it.'

'That girl told me things about herself. She told me how her mother died and how the old woman lived on, and how her father pasted up his scrapbooks. She walked out into the Saturday-night fog in order to take another lift in my car, but for reasons of her own she walked past it.'

He continues to speak. Hilditch his name is, he says again. Joseph Ambrose, called after a newscaster, a cat burglar in his off-time. Felicia the Irish girl is, a name unfamiliar to him, the name of a woman revolutionary. Strange when you think of it, how people are given their names. Strange, how people are allocated a life. Strange, what happens to people, the Irish girl and himself for starters. All he needs is to know where she is now.

'It would definitely be a help to you, Mr Hilditch, if we showed you the way to the Gathering House so that you could call in at any time. There are kindly folk on hand to bring back to you your peace of mind.'

'I can hear her now,' is Mr Hilditch's response, delighting Marcia Tibbitts further. 'Her footsteps on the gravel.' He walked back into his house that night and the black bar of the fire-grate was on the tiles where she'd dropped it.

'Mr Hilditch, this girl —'

'I took her money to keep her by me, but even so she went away.'

Here is a mad man, Marcia Tibbitts comments to herself, the first she has ever been on a doorstep with. And Miss Calligary, experienced in such matters, recognizes a ring of truth in the last statement that has been made to her, and in less than several seconds she says to herself that this man is not as he seems. From his own mouth has come a confession to leave you gasping. He has stolen a girl's money for some heinous purpose, causing a girl to be maligned in the thoughts of others. Miss Calligary requests a repetition of the statement, to ensure beyond doubt that it has been as she heard it. Quieter now, the man says he suffers from delusions. He gets things wrong, he says, and then abruptly turns his back.

Treachery was the word he used, in private, the day he knew about his Uncle Wilf. Guide and friend, his Uncle Wilf had called himself, and who could have said it wasn't true? He'd been the source of knowledge about the regimental life, an inspiration in that respect. 'Always been an army family,' his Uncle Wilf said, but he was making it up as he went along. Everything fell to bits then: there'd been no army family, nothing like that; it wasn't to be a guide and a friend that his Uncle Wilf had been coming to the house all these years, it wasn't to encourage a vocation. Bit on the side, until he didn't fancy it any more and never came back again. 'Be nice, dear,' the ginny rasp whispers again, that special voice.

He bangs his hall door shut as soon as he sees it in the black woman's eyes. Of course it wasn't feet and short sight: God knows what talk had got around, God knows what the recruiting officer's opinion had been. All lies, what the black woman said about not running into the girl again. The black woman knows; that's why she comes to his door. In her black imagination there is the lipstick tattoo, and the blue ribbon laid out on the dressing-table, and the little-boy hands that always have remained so, clothes falling from a woman's body, the nakedness beneath. There is that odour of scent, of powder too, in the black woman's nostrils, and it's there among the employees, in the canteen and in the kitchens and the painting bays and the offices. There's the whisper, going on and on, the words there were, his own obedience. 'Be nice, dear,' in the special voice, the promise that the request will never be made again, broken every time.

It never was his fault that there was prying later on, after years and years; that there is prying still. Each time he hoped there wouldn't be. Each time he hoped that a friendship would last for ever, that two people could be of help to one another, that strangers seeing them together would say they belonged like that.

No one passing by in Duke of Wellington Road, no hurrying housewife, or child, or business person, no one who can see Number Three from the top of the buses that ply to and fro on a nearby street, has reason to wonder about this house or its single occupant. No one passing is aware that a catering manager from a factory, well liked and without enemies, is capable of suffering no more.

In the cavernous kitchen of this house Mr Hilditch's shoes are neatly laced and the laces neatly tied. His socks are chequered below the turn-ups of his trousers. The suit is his usual blue serge, its waistcoat fastened but for the button at the bottom. His shirt is clean, the cufflinks in the cuffs. The tie is the striped one he always wears. His glasses are in place. He shaved himself an hour ago.

The back door is no longer bolted, in fact is slightly open, thoughtfully left so. A light that in the darkness lit the dustbins in the small backyard and glanced over an edge of laurel and mahonia remains unextinguished. In the kitchen there is no sound.

When twilight comes again a scavenging cat, earlier attracted by the open door, returns and this time slinks through it. Black, with a collar that once had a bell attached to it, this cat has long ago strayed from a domestic life too soft to satisfy the instincts of its feline nature. Soundlessly, it tours the kitchen, leaping from time to time on to different surfaces until its survey is complete. Its green, lozenge eyes pass over the crockery of the dresser and the white enamel of the electric stove, over wall cupboards and shelves, the taps above the sink, the wooden chairs, the table on which another chair is overturned, a human body hanging. This is suspended from the single ham hook in the wooden ceiling by a length of electric flex, the head slung forward awkwardly, the mound of flesh beneath the chin wedging the sideways tilt. It isn't of interest to the scavenging cat. Nothing is of interest except a saucepan on the stove, with a little milk left in it.

24

The convent girls climb up St Joseph's Hill, hurrying while the bell still tolls. Their conversation is breathless as they turn in at the convent gates, feet running now, faces flushed. Sister Benedict awaits them by the window of a classroom, where other girls are already assembled. A distant figure digs the patch where soon the first of the maincrop potatoes will be planted. Reminded by this figure of the missing girl, Sister Benedict prays.

In Hickey's Hotel a traveller in office stationery, coughing through cigarette smoke over the remains of a late breakfast, checks his call-book for the day. Above the cycle and pram shop, Connie Jo experiences the morning nausea that her friend, then newly her sister-in-law, experienced five months ago. At Flanagan's Quarries the lorries are loaded with chippings while the drivers wait beside them, silently smoking. In the Co-op yard Shay Mulroone fork-lifts bales of sheep wire. 'God, she's a cracker,' Small Crowley confides elsewhere; and Carmel, of whom he speaks, mops a floor at the hospital and worries a little about being a cracker perhaps once too often.

The old woman dies on the day before her hundredth birthday. The stiffened body is taken from the bedroom, and the bedroom is empty now. An irony, the general opinion is, being taken at this particular time, but there it is.

One night the boots of the big twin brothers thump into Johnny Lysaght's stomach and his ribs, and he lies insensible in the dark, by the memorial statue in the Square. Blood oozes from his face, an eye is closed beneath contusions. The cigarettes have not been removed from his attackers' lips while the punishment was meted out. No word has been spoken. The unconscious youth remains where he has fallen, and the glasses that have been left waiting in Myles Brady's bar are emptied and then replenished.

The photograph of a girl in a bridesmaid's dress has long ago been circulated. In one police station or another it has been perused, and details of the disappearance noted. In time, the details and the photograph are filed away.

She will come back, her father believes, guilt assailing him. At Confession he recalls his anger at the time and is forgiven, but feels no forgiveness himself. He makes the bedroom ready for her, arranging her shells on surfaces that are now entirely hers, emptying the drawers of the old woman's possessions. He dismantles the old woman's bed and makes room for it in the backyard shed. 'Have faith,' the Reverend Mother urges in the convent garden. 'One day you'll walk in and she'll be waiting for you in the kitchen.' He knows that too, he says; he knows she'll be there. Hers is the forgiveness that matters. She'll come back to offer it, that being her simple nature.

Mrs Lysaght shops in Chawke's for thread, a shade of pale blue. She takes the spools she's offered to the door, to examine them in the daylight, but is not satisfied and returns them. More will be coming in, she is informed, and she says she'll come back. The unpleasantness is over now and there's a satisfaction to be found in that: as she leaves the shop she reminds herself of this, which is something she does many times in the course of a day. He has been taught a lesson by the circumstances that developed; in a sense, even, all that has occurred may have been for the best.

In the kitchens and on the work floor a conclusion is reached. The catering manager, so affectionately part of everyday life for so long, suffered an illness of some mysterious nature: he took his life in the belief that the bewilderment of doctors indicated a grim prognosis. A collection is made in the canteen. A wreath is sent. The funeral is well attended.

Notices outside 3 Duke of Wellington Road announce it is up for sale. 'A useful property,' a young estate agent remarks, showing prospective buyers around, adding that an auction will be held, that all the junk will go. Found parked on the gravel in front of the house, the car owned by the deceased has been disposed of already. All there is belongs to the state, there being no inheritor.

'Well, he would, wouldn't he?' a police sergeant retorts when Miss Calligary insists that this same deceased, on his own admission, suffered from delusions. 'He'd hardly have done it, miss, if he wasn't in a state.'

'That man wasn't what he seemed.'

'Happen he wasn't, miss. Happen all sorts of things. But for the record what we have is that the gentleman is no longer with us.'

Miss Calligary mentions the Bible, inquiring if the sergeant ever has cause to consult it. She offers a brochure. For the one who dies there is a paradise earth, she promises, and adds that the deceased displayed an interest when this was pointed out to him, that he invited her young friend and herself into his house so that he could hear more about it. When all the time he was stealing money. 'The Lord knows where that child is now,' Miss Calligary adds. 'We pray for her day and night.'

'You keep on at it,' the sergeant breezily advises, and points out that he's on the busy side this morning.

Other girls set out, on the run from a mess, or just wanting things to be different. Mysteries they're called when they are noticed on their journey; and in cities, or towns large enough to have a trade in girls, the doors of Rovers and Volkswagens and Toyotas open to take them in.

At Mr Caunce's house they come and go. They try out the doorways of shops. There's a first time for everything, they say, settling into this open-air accommodation. Missing persons for a while, they then acquire a new identity. Riff-raff they're called now.

25

'Have they closed the breakfast place?' a man from the cardboard settlement inquires on the street.

Yes, it's closed, Felicia tells him, and he mutters a cacophony of curses, glaring furiously in the direction of a charity hall that is similar in all respects to the one Felicia was brought to, a long time ago, by Lena and George. She has queued for breakfasts in many since.

'You have to get there early,' she tells the man, but he ignores the admonition, continuing to swear to himself. When he ceases it is to ask the time.

She doesn't know. She sold her watch a while ago, with the cross she used to wear round her neck. She tried to sell her handbag but no one wanted it. It was Tapper who showed her how to dispose of the watch and the cross, to a friend he knew well and trusted. Forty pence she got; fairly good, that, Tapper said. The city she has come to, moving on from other cities and other towns, is no longer strange to her. She knows the way to the river and, as she walks towards it now, what comes into her head is Effie Holahan saying she saw the Virgin, and Carmel saying it was only a dream. Typical Effie, Carmel said, typical not to know the difference. Poor Effie with her dull eyes and her chilblains, and her way of dropping things! 'Sure, doesn't everyone have dreams like that?' Carmel was scornful, and they all laughed, swinging their legs on the convent wall, and Effie Holahan was flustered, red as a sunset. It's a long way away, that sitting on the convent wall; it's further by ages than Lena and George; it's history, as the voice in the police station said that day, which is ages ago also.

Felicia doesn't beg as she continues on her journey. At this time of day people don't like being bothered because they're in a hurry to get to work. She's not in a hurry herself. The sun comes out, dispersing wispy clouds, warming her face and hair. With a bit of luck, it'll dry the clothes that got wet last night. Ages ago, too, her first couple of carrier bags disintegrated; after careful examination, in case possibly they were of further use, their remains were thrown away. She has other bags now, five in all because she likes to collect things as she moves about. It's surprising what people are finished with.

Walking slowly, she nods over that, and what comes into her head is the first time Mr Logan opened his cinema, when he stood on the steps in his suit with the chalk line on it, and his blue bow-tie. A masher, her father called Mr Logan, and she didn't know what it meant until he told her. Cagey, her father said another time; cagey to gauge the entertainment business the way Mr Logan had, making a success of his dancehall and his cinema, still a bachelor in his fifties. *The Woman in Red* the film was the night of the gala opening, and Rose said if Mr Logan was looking for a child bride she wouldn't say no, and the girls on the wall, even Carmel, gasped to hear a thing like that.

You have to move about. You get to know the windows of the shops, the streets in different weather, faces you're always seeing, the H. Samuel clock, post-office clocks and clock-tower clocks, the parking-meter women, the obstruction of scaffolding on the pavement, red-and-white plastic ribbons to warn you, the street lights coming on. You move about because you want to, the bits and pieces coming into your head. *Hail Mary, full of Grace*: the first time she repeated it she felt grown up, the beads cold to the touch, smooth in her fingers. *Blessed art thou amongst women* . . . The votive light on the stairwall never went out, a red speck in the dark, a tiny glow you could overlook in the daytime because you were used to it. Her father stood for the Soldier's Song whenever it was played, still as a statue while people shuffled away, particular about that he was. God's will, he called it, the day her mother died, and her brothers wore black diamonds on their sleeves, sewn in by Mrs Quigly. The sun shone, the day of the funeral; they were back in the house by twelve, before the Angelus. 'The cross we bear,' Mrs Quigly said on another day. 'Every month a reminder.'

Yeah, definitely, Carmel said. 'Every blooming month.' And Rose said calmly what's wrong with an older man if he brings home the bacon?

People collect cartons of coffee from a take-away: office-workers, girls with their make-up fresh and bright, young men in long coats, belts tied at the back. They march along the streets she dawdles in, stepping round her, one man conversing on a telephone he carries with him. A plate-glass window is being replaced, the new glass not yet taken from the clamps on the side of a van. Five workmen stand ready to lift it into place when the timber sheet that covers the damage has been removed. A passing taxi driver greets one of them, shouting a joke.

'Hullo, Felicia.' She is greeted herself, by an Indian who's arranging fruit on the stalls outside his shop. He always speaks to her when she passes if he isn't busy with a customer. He gave her some kiwi fruit when he was packing up his wares one evening, because it wouldn't last the night, he said. She doesn't know his name. Last night a woman she begged from in this street said no, then changed her mind and broke open a sliced loaf in her shopping-bag. Have that instead, she said, offering four slices, saying she knew for a fact that any money given would be spent on drink. Felicia didn't contradict the assumption; you get used to what people say to you; it doesn't matter.

She knows she is not as she was; she is not the bridesmaid at the autumn wedding, not the girl who covered herself with a rug in the back of a car. The innocence that once was hers is now, with time, a foolishness, yet it is not disowned, and that same lost person is valued for leading her to where she is. Walking through another morning, fine after a wet night, she accepts without bewilderment the serenity that possesses her, and celebrates its fresh new presence. She dropped the bar of the fire-grate because her hands were nervous; she turned the light on because she was fumbling at the hall door, unable to find where the latch was. She didn't think she'd get away; she prayed it would not be painful, that when it happened it would be swift. The novice at the convent said your mother's waiting for you in heaven, Felicia; she thought of that as she turned the Yale latch. And then the light from the open hall door illuminated the fog, only just reaching the small green car on the gravel. He was bent over the steering wheel, crouching away from the light that had come on, covering his face. When she ran, the car didn't follow her. But the strings of the carrier bags cut into her fingers because she was hurrying so, not holding them the way she'd taught herself to. The houses were shrouded, the street lights blurred; her feet made the only sound there was until she reached the wide main road where traffic thudded and headlights were dim before they burst out of the fog, white or yellow. 'Hardly saw you,' the driver of the lorry said, and later added that he had two daughters of his own, his crinkly hair grey in the light of the cab when he drew in to dissolve an Oxo cube in his flask. On the steps of some building in the town near where he dropped her she watched the sky lightening; the fog was gone then. A woman, raving, sat beside her for a while, and a street-cleansing vehicle crept by, hosing and brushing as it moved. When it was quiet again, sparrows sang. 'We was married one time,' the woman confided. 'Benny Hill it was.' Voices spoke to the woman, Benny Hill, Gary Glitter. 'Lovely, them boys. Do anything for you, dear.'

Thrown into a bin attached to a lamppost, a coffee carton miraculously remains upright, the liquid it contains unspilt. Felicia drinks it, and finds most of a muffin still stuck to the paper it was baked in. 'Young for a bag lady, ain't you?' someone going by said two days ago, and she said yes, liking to agree. 'Cheers,' an old man greeted her last night, tidy in an overcoat and hat, stepping out of the crowd to tell her she looked like Marilyn Monroe, swaying because he had a few drinks in.

'Santa Ponsa,' a girl says now. 'Fantastic!' And a man drops a section of a newspaper, the pages slipping from beneath his arm. Someone else calls out, shouting to the man that he has lost his paper, but the man says it's only the Sport and Business. Felicia picks the pages up because they may be useful later on. 'Can't stand that Lovejoy,' another girl says, and her companion argues, insisting that Lovejoy's sexy. A shop window is full of wigs and beards and false moustaches. *Theatrical Needs!* a red sign flashes. *The Big Emporium!* In the field by the old gasworks a nettle stung her leg, and it didn't matter, she hardly felt it. The only guilt is that she permitted her baby to be taken from her: she shouldn't have done that, but there you are. She looks out now from where she is, and does not brood: what's done is done. She does not brood on her one-time lover's treachery. She walked away from a man who murdered girls. She was allowed to walk away: that is what she dwells upon.

When she reaches the river she settles on a seat that is pleasant in the autumn warmth. By chance her eyes pass over her clothes and over her hands and feet, the shoes she found in a disposal bin, the skirt a woman gave her. Her appearance, or the tale it tells, doesn't interest her. The Little Sisters of Africa come into her mind, their white habits damp in unhealthy jungle heat. Pray for our Little Sisters, Sister Francis Xavier enjoined. Kneel with us in the Gathering House, Miss Calligary begged, trudging from door to door. St Ursula stood steadfast by the helm, consoling her girl-companions when the vessel was tossed about on the waves. The Little Sisters nursed infants who were misshapen, famine infants whose bones came through their skin. See those brightly coloured birds! Miss Calligary urged. Smell the fragrance of those flowers! Do the girls who died and were never missed stroll now among the fragrant flowers, and listen to the birdsong? Do they keep company with St Ursula, who travelled to escape a marriage bed, and the Little Sisters who left their towns and townlands? Do those faceless girls occupy the heaven the novice spoke of, and touch the real fingers of the Holy Virgin? Elsie Covington and Beth. Sharon and Gaye. Jakki and Bobbi. Chosen for death because no one would know when they were there no longer. What trouble made victims of them? Did they guess their fate a moment before it came? Her mourning is to wonder.

She roots in one of her bags and finds the newspaper pages she picked up. Tommy Griffiths up, Lone Ranger has won at five to four; an Olympian champion is in disgrace; a football manager has retired. She reads for a moment, then Tapper's back again. Well, there's a sight: the fountains and the four black lions, the first time she ever saw them. Frigging marvellous, Tapper said, the empire in its frigging day, Charles James Napier on a pedestal on account he had a way with soldiers. They didn't put John Reginald Christie on no pedestal, a different bag of tricks on account he had a way with women. That's where they run him in, Tapper said, pointing on the bridge. That's where he ate his last in freedom, bacon and cabbage, the Lacy Dining Rooms. That's where that woman ran a nightclub, the one that shot a racing driver. This city's full of sights. All human life.

Redland Sells Three Steetley Offshoots, the business pages say. *U.S. Currency Holds Key*. Fancy a blow by the briny? Tapper said and they went down by train, tickets he found in a handbag. Take a gander at that, he said, when two men in teddy-bear coats got out of a polished car and held the doors for two women. Excuse me, sir, Tapper said on the promenade, the sea dirty green beneath the foam, and the man said get off. No offence, another man said in a bar the time there were wrestlers on the television. No offence, but I think you picked up my fags.

Tall as a telegraph pole, Tapper. Leaning down to tap the punters' shoulders; part of the game. Alaska's the place, he said, then again Johore Bahru. But more like Tapper's gone inside. That's Tapper all over: he said it himself, and maybe Lena said it too, you can almost hear her. You lose touch with a person who's in and out; only a week it was she knew Tapper, longer than Lena and George that time, longer than Kev and the woman with one arm.

The sun is warm now, the water of the river undisturbed. Seagulls teeter on the parapet in front of her, boats go by. The line of trees that breaks the monotony of the pavement is laden with leaves in shades of russet. Within her view, figures stride purposefully on a distant bridge, figures in miniature, creatures that could be unreal. One seagull eyes her, expecting crumbs, the others fly away. Somewhere a voice is loud on a megaphone. A klaxon sounds on the river.

She isn't hungry. It will be a few hours before she begins to feel hungry and then there'll be the throwaway stuff in the bins. The sky is azure, evenly blue, hardly faded at the edges at all. She moves a hand back and forth on a slat of the seat she's sitting on, her fingers caressing the smooth timber, the texture different where the paint has worn away, streaks of wood-grain raised. *Died with others, 1938*, was carved on another seat, and George said he'd sent a card to the Bishop of Bath and Wells, and put in the rhyme he knew, greater are none beneath the sun than oak or ash or thorn. *Carmel* with a heart round it someone carved on a tree in the Square, Packy Egan or Lomasney, Rose thought it was. Rose might be Mrs Logan now, in a flashy house on the Mountrath road. Stranger things happen.

The gap left where a tooth was drawn a fortnight ago has lost its soreness. She feels it with her tongue, pressing the tip of her tongue into the cavity, recalling the aching there has been. 'There's a woman dentist'll fix you up.' It was the Welshman, Davo, who said that, and they went along together because he knew the way. Not many would bother with your toothache, Davo said; not many would think toothache would occur in a derelict's mouth. 'Always come back,' the woman dentist said. 'Don't be in pain.'

Felicia folds the Sport and Business section several times, and slides it back into one of her bags. 'OK?' the driver of a lorry carrying furnaces asked, and she said yes because it was only fair in return for a lift of two hundred miles, all the payment she could offer, and she had to go back. It took a night and part of a morning, three different lorries and a van, but she had to do it: she couldn't not go back to Duke of Wellington Road. She had to know, and then she did: the estate agent's board outside the house, and someone told her. Then a voice called out when later she was resting on a public seat. 'Child,' Miss Calligary cried, and there were tears of anguish on Miss Calligary's cheeks while forgiveness was begged and the dead man vilified.

Felicia takes off her headscarf and opens her coat to the sun. The seagull is motionless on the parapet, its beady observation of her continuing. A breeze rattles the pavement trees and the first tired leaves of another September loosen. One floats down softly, slowly descending until she reaches out and catches it on her palm. For minutes she gazes at it, not yet withered, taken before its time; and then her thoughts begin again.

Wretched, awful man, poor mockery of a human creature, with his pebble spectacles and the tiny hands that didn't match the rest of him, his executioner's compulsion. Her living brought his death, but she didn't say so, listening to him vilified that day; she didn't say he was more terrible than a man who stole a distressed girl's money; she didn't mention murder, for what use would that be, now that he had murdered himself? 'Please, child, come back to us!' Miss Calligary cried, but she shook her head, even though she remembered the generosity and the friendliness of the Gathering House when first she arrived there. She shook her head at each repeated invitation, hearing between one plea and the next about the visits made to Number 3 Duke of Wellington Road, and how its occupant's manner had seemed like madness to Miss Marcia Tibbitts, and how there'd been an occasion at a police station after the death occurred, a sergeant who'd been dismissive. In the end, reluctantly, Miss Calligary and Miss Marcia Tibbitts walked away, passing for ever out of her life.

Again her thoughts shift: to a mother collapsed on the kitchen floor, and seaside shells brought back later in kindly compensation; to speckled green bird's eggs, and John Count's singing, no sign then of her father's bitter eyes; to the inflicted wound that answered the ignominy of a husband gone away, and love for a son, as gentle as a cancer. Lost within a man who murdered, there was a soul like any other soul, purity itself it surely once had been.

Such contemplations, alien to her once, fill Felicia's day. She seeks no meaning in the thoughts that occur to her, any more than she searches for one in her purposeless journey, or finds a pattern in the muddle of time and people, but still the thoughts are there. Alone, no longer a child, no longer a girl, with the insistence of the grateful she goes from place to place, from street to street, binding her feet up, wet by rain that penetrates her clothes, frozen when there is ice on the gutter puddles. By day the clouds scutter or hardly move, or crowd away the sun in shades of grey, or blackly advance in bunched-up density, like ominous monsters of the sky. They're there again in wind-blown tails of smoke, in big white bundles soft as down, in scarlet morning streaks. Sometimes all day there is an empty blue, hazy with mist or cleanly bright, backdrop for spindly winter trees, and backdrop again for summer greenery.

At night, there is a city's afterglow. There is a happiness in her solitude at dawn.

The leaf blows from her palm in another soft breeze. The watchful seagull struts the parapet, still hungry for crumbs that are not there. Someone stopped who need not have, and called an ambulance for Dumb Hanna when she lay senseless on the street. The ladies come at night with soup, well-meaning, never forgetting, no matter what the weather. The woman dentist said don't be in pain. The woman dentist has dedicated her existence to the rotten teeth of derelicts, to derelicts' odour and filth. Her goodness is a greater mystery than the evil that distorted a man's every spoken word, his every movement made. You would say it if you could, a new thought is, but sometimes saying isn't easy.

Idiot gawking, fool tramping nowhere: shreds of half-weary pity are thrown in the direction of a wayside figure, before the hasty glance darts on to something else. There will be other cities, and the streets of other cities, and other roads, Tappers and Georges and Lenas, Kevs and Davos and Dumb Hannas. There will be charity and shelter and mercy and disdain; and always, and everywhere, the chance that separates the living from the dead. Again the same people wander through her thoughts: the saint and the Little Sisters, Elsie Covington and Beth, Sharon and Gaye and Jakki and Bobbi, her mother not aged by a day. Are they really all together among the fragrant flowers, safe and blessed? She might be with them if it had happened; but she reflects, in modest doubt, that the certainty she knows is still what she would choose. She turns her hands so that the sun may catch them differently, and slightly lifts her head to warm the other side of her face.